CRYSTAL SKIES

Suzanne Cass

S C

STORM CLOUD
PRESS

Crystal Skies

Storm Cloud Press, Perth Australia

Copyright © 2021 by Suzanne Cass

Edits by Tanya Saari

Cover by Vikncharlie

All rights reserved.

To Gary, who helps me untangle those twisty plot knots.

CHAPTER ONE

Julie Bradshaw sang loudly, revelling in the bright sun sparkling through the gum leaves as she drove the ATV down the long, dirt driveway. It was her job to pick up the mail today, a task she always relished, as it gave her a chance to get out of the office and into the heat of the northern outback. The large, intricate, wrought-iron gates appeared over the small rise and Julie smiled. Everyone at Stormcloud called them the Taj Mahal of gates, they were so ostentatious. Her stepmother, Daniella, had the monstrosity commissioned because she thought they'd impress the guests when they arrived at the entrance.

Julie slowed the all-terrain-vehicle and expertly maneuvered it so she could reach into the mailbox without having to leave her seat. A cloud of fine, red dust surrounded her as she stopped. They had roughly twenty ATVs on the property; a sort of four-wheel-drive buggy, with a canvas roof to keep out the sun and the rain, but open on all sides for a three-sixty-degree view. The ATVs were so easy to operate, even the guests got to drive them.

The mailbox was nearly as impressive as the gates. Steve had crafted a miniature version of Stormcloud lodge and erected it on a sturdy metal pole on the edge of the main road. Julie lifted the flap gingerly and peered inside, checking each corner thoroughly before reaching in to retrieve the bundle of mail. The mailbox might be miniature, but that didn't mean the spiders were miniature. Even though she'd been brought up a country girl, she never could get over her fear of spiders. Especially the big, hairy huntsmen that had a knack for jumping.

The mail bundle was a big one today. Julie toyed with the idea of quickly flicking through the pile but rejected it; she didn't want to ruin her good mood. With the stack safely sitting on the passenger seat, she took off back down the long driveway, singing her favorite song.

"Baby, you're a firework.

Come on, let your colors burst.

Make 'em' go, ah, ah, ah!"

She shouted the last line at the top of her lungs. As she picked up speed, the wind whistled past her ears, and she nearly lost her Akubra. Shoving the hat more firmly on her head, she accelerated around a corner, enjoying the last few moments of freedom before she had to go back into the office and help Daniella sort out a missing payment for the truckload of cattle feed they'd ordered last week. Although, it was hot today, and perhaps she should think herself lucky she got to spend most of her day in the air-conditioning. She'd get enough time baking in the Queensland sun when she went out on muster next week. Skylar had assigned Julie the job of camp cook, and the excitement was already curling enticingly in her stomach. It was an enormous responsibility for someone on their first real cattle muster, but Julie loved a challenge and knew she'd be up for the task.

Parking the ATV near the front door to the lodge—she'd run it back up to the shed, where all the rest of the vehicles were parked later; Daniella hated it when she left the ATV in full sight of any arriving guests, she said it ruined the aesthetics of the lodge—she leapt out of her seat and snagged the stack of mail as she went. Most of it would be invoices or bills for Daniella, but there might be some personal mail for staff members. Removing her sunglasses, she headed toward the front steps, where a group of guests was slowly ascending, chatting amongst themselves.

"Hello. You look happy today, dear," a gray-haired woman called to Julie as she joined the rear of the group. Barb was holding hands with her husband, John, as they mounted the steps. The couple were in their sixties, enjoying early retirement, and had come with two of their friends to celebrate their fortieth wedding anniversary to do *something spectacular*, in Barb's words. Julie liked Barb and her open enthusiasm for everything and everyone around her.

"I'm always happy," Julie quipped. "Why wouldn't I be? I have the perfect job and I live in the perfect location."

"Yes, you do," John agreed, stopping at the landing, where the rest of the group waited. "If only I'd found this country when I was younger. Perhaps we might've moved out here, hey, love?"

"Don't be silly, John." Barb slapped her husband playfully on the arm. "You and me are city folk, through and through. This country would kill us. But I'm really glad to experience it this way, in the lap of luxury." She waved her hand in a semi-circle, encompassing the green slope leading down to the captivating view of the billabong glinting in the sunshine.

Julie quickly perused the group standing in the doorway. Chase and Maya stood at the back, Chase towering over his diminutive wife. Newlyweds, they never seemed to leave each other's side. Next to them stood Joseph Gambino and his father, Dominic, who were here on a father-son bonding vacation, but it seemed they spent most of their time bickering between themselves. And when they weren't bickering, they were strutting around like some kind of mafia duo as if they owned the place, with their slicked-back, black hair, wearing too-tight pants and stretchy T-shirts that might look good on a muscle-bound weightlifter, but only served to make the father-son duo's sagging stomachs look all the more pronounced.

"Hey, how ya doin', pretty lady?" Joseph called to her with a seductive wink, and Julie held in a sigh.

"Great, thanks. How about you? What have you all been up to this morning?" she asked, diverting attention back to the others.

Chase spoke from the back of the small crowd. "We've been taking it easy this morning. Went exploring down by your beautiful billabong." He pushed his glasses back up his nose and stared at her. She smiled to herself. Chase was the epitome of a nerd. Clean shaven, and conservatively dressed in slacks and shirts buttoned up to the neck, he had to be boiling in this Queensland heat. His stunning young wife was also modest in her dress, wearing a plain, black skirt and blue, high-necked, silk blouse. Julie was unsure of the age gap between them, but it must be fifteen years at least, as he looked to be in his early forties, and she couldn't be more than twenty-five. But they were sweet together, and they obviously adored one another. They'd met through their church, and she'd heard Chase mention more than once how their faith had brought them together.

"We're looking forward to the trail ride this afternoon, though," Chase continued. "I hope you've got a docile horse for Maya, she's not very confident around large animals."

"I've got just the horse for you." Julie turned to smile at Maya. "George Brown is part Clydesdale, and he is so sweet-tempered, you'll fall in love with him," Julie said. "I'll take good care of you, don't worry. But you will need to wear jeans, or long pants of some kind," she warned, glancing at Maya's skirt.

"Oh, yes, I will," Maya gushed. "I can't wait. My first time on a horse. I'm so excited."

Julie made a mental note to let her father know they had a rank beginner in their midst. Which wasn't a problem, they catered for all levels of riding skills. It meant the ride would be slower than normal, that was all. She'd lead Maya herself, Julie decided.

"You're going to love the view from the top of the escarpment. It makes the ride worthwhile," Julie said, edging past the gathering; she had lots to get done before she was due to help with the trail ride this afternoon. "Anyway, enjoy the rest of your morning. Lunch will be ready in around an hour." Julie waved a hand as she pushed open the front door and let the cool air flow over her, leaving the guests out on the veranda discussing who else was going on the afternoon ride.

She flicked through the pile of letters as she strode through the main great room and into the hallway behind. Her fingers stilled and her heart gave an extra beat as she stopped on one addressed to her. She recognized the loopy handwriting.

Her happy mood fled, replaced by a much darker emotion. Fear.

Julie dropped the rest of the mail on the corner of Daniella's desk. Her stepmother was nowhere to be seen. Perhaps she'd gone out to the stables to have a word with Steve. An urge to throw the letter in the bin overtook her. But no, she should open it; there was no point in behaving like an ostrich and burying her head in the sand. She needed to know what this asshole was saying. Perhaps, after she'd read it, then she could throw it in the bin, like she'd done with the others.

Exiting Daniella's office, she made her way toward the family wing. The family lounge room would be empty at this time of the day, and she needed somewhere quiet to open the letter.

Just as she hoped, the lounge was vacant when she poked her head around the door. She dropped her Akubra and sunglasses on the solid, wooden, coffee table and stared at the envelope in her hand. Better to do it quick, like ripping off a Band-Aid.

Oh, no. Julie covered her mouth with her hand as she read the letter. It was more of the same, but much worse this time.

She sat heavily on the leather lounge; her legs no longer able to hold her weight. Her fingers shook so much, the piece of paper tumbled from her hand and landed on the rug at her feet. The letter landed face-up, and there was no escape from the words scrawled there in that untidy handwriting.

Baby killer.

Murderer.

Bride of Satan.

I prayed for you to make a better decision this time. But you went ahead and did it, anyway.

Get ready to pay for your sins.

And tell your family to get ready to pay for their sins, as well.

I will not be cheated on a second time.

He was escalating. His words were becoming more violent and deranged.

Julie stifled a sob. Why was this man persecuting her? Why had he singled her out for his sick obsession? Not that she knew who he was. He was a stranger stalking her, hiding behind his vicious words and online persona. But why did he mention being cheated on a second time? It made no sense. Had this madman mistaken her for someone else?

This was the third letter in as many weeks.

Julie thought she'd given him the slip after she left Brisbane. The call from her father asking her to return to Stormcloud eighteen months ago to help him out of a tight spot had seemed to come at the exact right time, and she'd jumped at the chance. And up until three weeks ago, she thought she was safe. She'd arranged for the sale of her two-bedroom flat a few weeks after she left Brisbane. Deleted all her social media accounts, even closed her email, and was careful not to leave a digital trail that anyone might be able to follow. Her last name was different to her father's—she'd taken her mother's maiden name after her parents divorced when she was five—so there should be nothing to link her back to Steve or Stormcloud. How had he found her?

The exterior door to the family living area opened and her father entered, a gust of wind following him in. Noticing Julie sitting on the lounge, he said, "It's a hot one today." He removed his battered Akubra and ran a hand through his sweat-soaked hair. His plaid shirt was covered in streaks of dust, and he carried a bridle in one hand. Julie abstractly decided he must've come straight from the stables.

The breeze lifted the letter and swirled it across the floor, where it came to rest against the leg of one of the armchairs.

Steve strode into the room and picked it up just as Julie realized what he was doing and jumped to her feet. "Wait, Dad, don't…" But it was too late.

His eyes scanned the paper.

"What the hell is this?" Her father's normally placid face was a mask of shock and alarm.

Shit. She couldn't meet her father's gaze. No one knew. About the abortion. Or the stalker. She'd kept it all to herself. Because… Well, because she didn't want to see the disdain and disappointment on any of her family's faces when they found out. Because a tiny part of her agreed with her stalker. She'd made a decision to end her unborn baby's life. She had every legal right to do so. But that legal right wasn't enough to banish the flashes of doubt over whether she'd done the right thing.

"Julie." The sharp edge in Steve's voice forced her head up.

"Answer me."

"It's exactly what it looks like," she answered tiredly, lowering herself back onto the sofa. "A threatening letter from a crazy stalker guy." She tried to raise a smile, to pretend that none of this mattered, but her customary grin had abandoned her.

"Jesus Christ, Julie. Why didn't you...? What have you...? This can't be true," he finished lamely.

Julie didn't answer. She couldn't answer. An unexpected swelling of fear and sorrow closed her throat. Covering her face with her hands, she tried to hold back the sob building in her chest.

She felt the cushion sink beneath her as her father sat on the couch next to her and he placed a comforting arm around her shoulder.

"I'm sorry, honey, I didn't realize..."

She sobbed even harder.

Why was she breaking down like this? She was twenty-nine years old. A grown woman. She should be able to handle this better. But all of a sudden, the weight of her seemingly insurmountable problems felt too much to handle. Like she had when she was a toddler, Julie buried her face in her father's broad chest and wept. The familiar aroma of hay and dust and sweat only made her cry harder. It was the first time she'd let go of her feelings since the stalker began sending her threatening letters. Since the abortion. Until now, she'd kept it all bottled up inside.

"Oh, honey." Her father's soft words only made her weep harder.

Julie wasn't sure how long it took for her eyes to stop streaming and her chest to stop heaving, but when Steve took her by the shoulders and gently handed her a handkerchief, she looked up and realized she felt...better. No, that wasn't the right word. Perhaps released from a heavy burden was closer. In some ways, it was a relief to have everything out in the open. Not to have to keep it a secret, at least not from her closest family.

"You should have told me," her father admonished gently.

"I know," she replied, still sniffling.

Blue eyes the same color as her own held her gaze until he was sure she was okay, then he stood and began pacing across the room. Julie blew her nose again and stared out the large, floor-to-ceiling windows at the picture-perfect North Queensland day. The sun beat down out of a sky as blue as a cobalt ocean, the view down the grassy embankment to the large billabong surrounded by clumps of eucalyptus trees so classically Australian. Even though she couldn't hear them from inside, Julie knew the small birds would be twittering in the branches without a care in the world. If only she could be one of those birds right now.

What must her father think of her? Not only had he just found out that she was being stalked by some crazy stranger, but he now knew she'd had a termination. Julie wasn't sure which was worse in her father's eyes. She glanced at him from beneath her long eyelashes. Would he think less of her? Steve was a fair-minded man who'd always treated her with unconditional love and supported all her decisions. But he also had high standards, and she knew he'd be battling his own internal morals with this sudden slap in the face. Now he knew his daughter was less than perfect.

She opened her mouth, but had no idea what to say. Her father saved her from finding the words.

"Have there been more of these?" He waved the letter in the air.

"Yes," she admitted. "This is the third one in as many weeks. But he started sending them while I was living in Brisbane."

"We can't let this continue," he said gruffly. "This stalker…

or whatever he is, needs to be stopped." He clenched his hands tightly by his sides. Julie had always thought of her father's hands as skilful, hardworking, gentle with the animals. But at this very moment, those hands looked ready to commit violence. "If he dares to come anywhere near you, I'll—"

At that second, her stepmother, Daniella, bustled her way into the living room. She took in the mood in the room and instantly narrowed her eyes. "What's going on?" she asked.

Julie sat on the sofa, mute. This was all getting out of hand. It was one thing her father finding out, but she didn't want the rest of the family—or the staff, for that matter—knowing her dirty little secret. If need be, she'd tell them, but she wanted it to be on her own terms.

Steve answered for her, before Julie could even open her mouth. "Some bastard is sending Julie threatening letters," Steve said, his voice getting louder with each word. "And if I find out who that scumbag is, I'm going to hurt him so bad."

Julie was shocked by her father's outburst. Steve was normally the calming influence around the station. Daniella was the uptight one. She kept the luxury resort organized and running like clockwork, but she also had a steely persona that brooked no argument. Steve was the only person who could talk sense into Daniella when she got into one of her moods. But today, it seemed that Steve was the one who needed to be pacified.

"I'm not sure what you're talking about?" Daniella said in an even tone, glancing quickly in Julie's direction, then concentrating on Steve.

Steve shoved the letter in her hands and started pacing again.

The only sign that Daniella was shocked by what she saw was a slight crinkling of the lines around her eyes.

Steve let out a loud grunt of frustration.

Julie stood and shuffled from one foot to the other, not sure what to do next. She'd never seen her father this angry before. Not even when they'd found out one of their trusted staff had murdered another of their team. He was always the rock people turned to in their time of need.

"Steve," Daniella said. But instead of the sharp tone Julie was expecting, Daniella's voice was low and soothing. "You need to calm down." She went up and lay a hand on his arm. Steve flinched at her touch, like a flighty horse, but then Daniella caught his gaze. "We can handle this. But you won't do anyone any good by getting angry." Steve stared into Daniella's eyes. It was in an intimate moment, and Julie was uncomfortable, as if she were somehow intruding. It suddenly became crystal clear how strong a connection these two had. Julie sometimes wondered what her father saw in Daniella, she could be a difficult woman to be around. But right in that moment, their special connection was laid bare, and Julie could see how much they truly loved each other.

Steve let out a breath between pursed lips. "You're right," he replied. "But I can't just stand around idle, while this... asshole threatens my little girl."

Julie wanted to say that she wasn't his little girl anymore, but she bit her tongue.

"I know." Daniella stroked his arm in a soothing motion. She speared Julie with her gaze. "Have you told the police? About the stalker?" Daniella qualified. Both she and Steve were apparently avoiding the topic of the abortion for now, which suited Julie fine.

Julie merely shook her head. If she'd gone to the police, then she would've had to tell them why the guy was harassing her. At the time, she'd merely wanted to forget the whole thing. Going through the abortion had been traumatic enough, but to also air her dirty laundry was unthinkable. She had no idea how the guy had found out about the termination, or why she'd become the victim of his attacks. She'd contacted the clinic after she'd received the first few threatening letters, but they assured her all patient information was kept strictly confidential, and they were at a loss to help her figure out who this person was, or how he'd found her. Julie had wracked her brain ever since to figure out how he'd obtained information about her abortion. One option was that this guy had something to do with a group of protesters outside the clinic on the day Julie attended. But that seemed so far-fetched it was almost ridiculous. At first, Julie had decided she could handle it by herself, and then just as things had escalated, she'd been asked back to Stormcloud, and thought her problem had disappeared.

"Right." Daniella began to pace across the rug, much like Steve had been doing, but her brow was furrowed with deep thought, rather than anger. "We need to report this to the police. Nash will be able to help."

Julie cringed inwardly. She liked Nash. Her stepsister's new man was the best thing that'd ever happened to Skylar. Nash was also the Senior Constable at the police station in the nearest town of Dimbulah.

"I really didn't want everyone else to know." Julie screwed up her face in a grimace. "Especially not about…the abortion." It was a testament to the emotions that were rolling around inside her. Shame. She was ashamed of having to terminate her pregnancy. There *had* been mitigating circumstances, and she knew the decision had been the right one, but people would judge her, nonetheless. She wasn't sure she was ready for that sort of judgment.

"I can understand that," her father replied. "But it's going to be hard to keep the truth from them."

Yep, it seemed the genie was well and truly out of the bottle. Julie sat down again and ran an agitated hand through her short hair. She wasn't sure she was ready to deal with any of this.

"I also think we should look at getting a private detective," Daniella mused, almost to herself. "They can often find out things much more quickly than the police."

Julie wanted to roll her eyes. Surely that was going a little too far. But once Daniella took hold of an idea, there was usually no stopping her.

"Dean might be able to help. I'll call him." Daniella tapped a finger to her mouth.

"Do you think so?" Steve seemed to brighten at the idea.

"Of course," Daniella replied.

Dean was Daniella's brother. He lived in Montana and ran a sister resort to Stormcloud, called Stargazer Ranch. That luxury ranch had been running for over fifteen years. Dean had been the catalyst for starting Stormcloud three years later, and he was part-owner of the station. Julie had only met her step-uncle once, when he'd visited a few years back. She liked his jovial optimism and his big, open smile. Dean was also mega-rich, and Daniella would probably be hoping that he'd have connections and perhaps even help them pay for a private detective.

Daniella stopped her pacing and looked directly at Steve. "I think we need to beef up security around here." She glanced quickly at Julie and then away. "You saw that letter. He not only threatened Julie's life, but he hinted at hurting us, as well."

Steve went as still as a statue, as if the idea hadn't yet occurred to him. They might all be in danger.

Julie wanted to scoff at the idea. Surely this guy's spiel was all rhetoric? He didn't really mean it, did he? She thought about the hatred behind those words on the paper and a small shudder went through her.

"We need to look at getting some protection for Julie. And for us, as well, at least in the short term." Daniella's blue eyes went steel-gray as she formulated her plan. "I'm going to look up one of those bodyguard companies, we should—"

"I don't need a bodyguard," Julie broke through Daniella's deliberation. This was crazy talk. Almost as crazy as the idea she had a stalker. Enough was enough. She was *not* going down the path of getting a personal security guard. She wasn't that desperate.

CHAPTER TWO

Twenty-four hours later, Julie was back in the family lounge, staring out the same window. Her foot tapped restlessly on the wooden floorboards. She clenched her teeth and then worried at her bottom lip. Today was a carbon copy of yesterday; merciless sun lighting the indigo sky as the eucalyptus leaves hung limply, the heat shimmering off the branches. A fish surfaced in the billabong, sending out ever-increasing ripples toward the rushes lining the edge of the water. Most likely a big barramundi—her father kept the billabong well stocked so the guests could go fishing. The bush vista outside the window was oblivious to her internal struggle, however, and she let out a small hum of annoyance.

Her father had ordered her to stay indoors. She was allowed to help Skylar in the kitchen, and Daniella with any administrative tasks, like paperwork, or returning phone calls. But she wasn't allowed to take part in any outdoor activities. Which meant she'd been banned from the horse trek up to the top of the escarpment yesterday afternoon, and wouldn't be allowed to go on the ride out to the abandoned gold mine today, either. Instead, Dale, her stepbrother, would be taking her place, with Wazza, the lead station hand, helping him out.

She ardently wished that Steve had never seen that damned letter. Now it was as if he and Daniella had taken charge of her every movement; her every thought. She didn't want to seem ungrateful; they only had her safety—as well as their own—in mind. But this was taking it all a little too far. Julie liked to stay positive, it was the best way to be. There were too many negative people in the world already. Skylar often teased her by saying they were exact opposites; while Skylar was an introvert who loved nothing better than to be left alone in her chef's kitchen for hours on end, Julie was an extrovert who loved to chat to anyone who'd listen and who always had a funny story or a silly dance to make people laugh. Her father had often called her the light in a dark room, always quick with a smile and a warm touch. But she didn't mind being called a joker, if that's what it took to brighten the mood.

But over the past few days, she hadn't been able to find much to smile about. And when she had smiled, it'd felt forced.

Steve had called Nash in to talk to her last night. He'd turned up in his police uniform, the blond surfer curls and easy-going smile hidden behind his serious, professional façade. Nash's solemn face and his myriad of penetrating questions had made her stomach flutter with concern.

But that was last night. In the cold light of day, all this anxiety seemed a tad ridiculous.

Now three people knew her secret. At least they'd agreed not to let anyone else know. Yet. Julie had had to plead hard to persuade them to keep her problems private, saying she just wasn't ready for everyone to know. It was her confidential business, and she had a right to keep it to herself. Nash consented, saying he could wait until he did a bit more digging first, to see if he could find out any more details. But Nash had also qualified his statement, by saying that if he felt the threat posed by this guy became imminent—which Julie took to mean that Skylar in particular, or any of the rest of the family were put in danger—then he'd be honor-bound to inform them. It was a daunting thought, having to tell everyone; reveal to them all not only did she have a stalker, but guess what, he was obsessed with her because she'd had an abortion. How would they react? Nash hadn't seemed disapproving in any way as he'd taken her statement, even as she'd studied his eyes to check for any flash of cynicism. But there'd been none. How would he keep the details away from Skylar, she wondered? But then perhaps it was part of the job, and perhaps Skylar had learned not to ask of Nash what he wasn't willing to divulge. And neither Steve nor Daniella had brought up the subject again.

Nash had agreed with Steve that added security around the station wouldn't be a bad idea. Told Steve he could use the excuse that he'd been meaning to do an upgrade for ages, and no one need be any the wiser. It was really Julie's safety they were worried about. Daniella had jumped on the idea, saying she was going to make some calls straightaway, while Julie had sat, quietly fuming. There'd been no more mention of a personal bodyguard, which calmed her fears a little. This stalker guy hadn't given them any reason to think he'd follow through on any of his sick threats. He was back in Brisbane, close to two-thousand kilometers away. So, there was no reason for protection. She was perfectly safe enough here on the station, surrounded by her family and all the staff—most of whom Julie considered to be family as well—and Daniella was taking this way too seriously.

Julie's attention returned to the view outside the window. Steve's orders chafed at her soul. She didn't want to spend the rest of her life cooped up inside the lodge. Her booted foot again tapped agitatedly on the floorboards as she stared out at the billabong. A kingfisher swooped from a branch and skimmed across the water, catching an unsuspecting insect on the wing. It looked so inviting, and she longed to get outside, just for a while. Holy jeezes, she wasn't going to let this stalker guy rule her life.

Ramming her Akubra on her head, she slipped on her sunglasses and put her hand on the door to the hallway, determined not to stay locked up inside on this beautiful day. If she snuck down the hallway, she could escape out the door at the other end of the building that led to the staff quarters. She would go down to the billabong and breathe in the fresh air. No one would miss her for half an hour. And she'd make sure to stay vigilant at the same time. But her stalker wasn't going to travel all the way out to the middle of far North Queensland to follow some stupid obsession. It just wasn't going to happen.

A helicopter had landed on the pad down near the long driveway a few minutes ago—probably bringing a new group of guests to stay at the lodge—and now she heard its blades getting louder as it lifted off again. The coast would be clear, as Daniella would be off making sure the new visitors were settled properly, and Steve would be up at the stables getting the horses ready for the ride this afternoon.

Pulling the door open, she swung out into the hallway.

And collided with a solid, male chest.

"Oh, God," she squeaked, nearly losing her footing. A pair of strong arms came out to steady her.

She stared up into the face of a stranger.

The man stared back at her. One blue eye. One brown eye. A memory flickered. She'd known a man once with those same eyes.

No! It couldn't be.

Aaron?

Aaron Powell?

She stepped backward as if he'd branded her with his

touch, his name frozen on her tongue.

"Sorry, ma'am, I didn't mean to scare you."

Oh, God, that voice. Even deeper than she remembered. With a hint of a rasp that also hadn't been there before. A familiar thrill ran through her, but she tamped it down and stared at him, speechless.

"Are you okay?" He stepped toward her, as if he meant to touch her again, concern etched deep into the frown lines on his forehead.

She retreated another two steps down the hallway. "Yep, I'm fine." She wheezed the words out between locked vocal cords. Normally, she would have given him a breezy grin and laughed off the encounter, but her smile was frozen on her lips. "Pull yourself together," she muttered under her breath.

"Are you sure?" That slightly bland, concerned look hadn't left his face, and he peered at her as if trying to see through the tinted lenses of her sunglasses. A pair of mirrored sunglasses sat atop his own head, and Julie couldn't help but notice how tall he'd gotten. And how his black T-shirt underneath his sports jacket stretched enticingly across very broad shoulders indeed. Big. He was definitely bigger than she remembered; she could see how muscular he'd become beneath that shirt. He towered over her. Her gaze caught for a second on a scar bisecting his left eyebrow, giving him a rather devil-may-care appearance. That hadn't been there last time she'd seen him.

She nodded, but her mind was whirling with unanswered questions. Didn't he recognize her?

"If you're sure you're not hurt, then perhaps you could point me in the direction of the meeting room, please?" His tone was formal and polite.

No, he clearly didn't recognize her. What was he doing here? Was he a guest? Perhaps she should walk on by. Leave bygones to be bygones. If she merely indicated the meeting room—which was two doors down on the left—and went on her way, would he be none the wiser?

A sudden, fathomless anger began to boil deep down in her gut. Nope. Twelve years ago, he'd walked away from her without a word. Aaron Powell wasn't getting away with it that easily this time.

She flicked off her hat and slowly drew down her sunglasses until he was looking directly into her eyes.

"Holy shit," he whispered. "Julie?"

Oh yeah, he recognized her now, all right.

CHAPTER THREE

Aaron took an involuntary step backward. Had he really just run into Julie Bradshaw? Her blue eyes stared up at him, and he was suddenly hit with images of her from his past. A past he wasn't keen on revisiting. She was the absolute last person he'd expected to see. What was she doing here?

Aaron opened his mouth, but no words would come.

He coughed, trying to regain his equilibrium. He was never lost for words. And he was never caught unawares. It was his job to stay professional and calm at all times.

But goddammit, there was Julie, standing right in front of him. Looking just as sunny and sexy as she had when she was seventeen. Well, perhaps her face showed a few more fine lines, but the high cheekbones, aquiline nose, and pouting lips were the same. And still as alluring as ever. The only real difference was her hair. The long, blonde locks were gone, replaced by a modern, short style, with chunks of warm caramel highlights throughout. It was kind of sexy, and Aaron decided it suited her. A quick flick of his gaze showed well-worn jeans hugging her hips over a pair of dusty cowboy boots, with a white T-shirt to finish off her look. Not much different from what he'd last seen her wearing. Although those hips seemed a tad more luscious. She seemed to have blossomed into one helluva good-looking woman over the past decade. And why wouldn't she? The only thing that seemed to be missing today was the ever-ready, buoyant smile Julie was so well-known for. It was missing, because she was now glowering at him.

"Julie," he said, testing that his tone was even and controlled. "Nice to see you again. I wasn't expecting to—"

"What the fuck, Aaron?"

Aaron tried to hide his shock at her vitriol. He supposed he deserved it.

"What are you doing here? Do you think you can just walk in here and pretend everything is all right? Greet me like some long-lost friend? Because that is not how this works." She was practically spitting at him like a farm cat.

"No, not at all. But you need to understand. I had no idea —"

"You stroll in here, looking exactly the same as you always did…" The way her gaze flickered up and down his body as she spoke told him that perhaps she still liked how he looked, too. "…but you sure don't act like the man I used to know. Or dress like you used to," she added. "You have a hell of a lot of explaining to do, Aaron Powell."

Goddammit, how was he supposed to explain himself when she kept cutting him off like that? "Look, Julie, I'm not the same person I was twelve years ago." He held his hands up, palm outward. What else could he say? Neither of them was the same person they used to be. But he was pretty sure he'd changed a hell of a lot more than she had.

"I can see that," she replied darkly.

If only she knew the truth behind those words. That day he'd last seen Julie—on his nineteenth birthday—had been the day his whole world had come tumbling down. Everything he thought he knew about himself had been thrown into doubt by his mother's drunken words. It was better that he left. Julie wouldn't have wanted him if she ever found out the secret that'd driven him away.

"You left without a word?" she said, accusation thick on her tongue.

He drew in a deep breath. "Are we really going to do this now?" It wasn't the place. They were standing in a dark hallway, glaring at each other like wary jackals circling their kill. He was supposed to be meeting his client, Steve, not arguing with a long-lost lover over whether he should've said goodbye or not.

She speared him with her gaze. Normally, her eyes reminded him of a watercolor painting, all pastel and pale blue, but today they were definitely arctic; as cold as ice.

"Fine. Tell me what you're doing here, then."

He should ask her the very same thing. As far as he knew, Julie should still be living in Dalgety, down in New South Wales, with her mother and stepfather. That'd always been the plan, that she'd stay on and help Connie and Tony with the sheep farm. What the hell she was doing on this cattle station up in North Queensland, he had no idea.

His boss, Jake, had told him to hop on the first flight out from Brisbane up to Cairns, and then to charter a helicopter out to this Stormcloud Station. Aaron had been momentarily distracted by the sweet ride, a Bell 505, five-seater helicopter, bright-red in color, with two seats up front and three in the back. It was different than any helicopter Aaron had ever flown before, and on the trip over, he'd quizzed the pilot about the controls, and what it was like to fly for a charter company.

But as soon as they'd landed, Aaron had forced his mind off the chopper and back onto the job, the details of which were sketchy. Jake said Aaron would learn more when he got there, but it seemed the daughter of a wealthy landowner, Steve Clements, was being harassed by a stalker and she needed protection ASAP. There was no name given for the daughter. It was unusual protocol not to have the full details on a client before he went out on a job, but when Aaron questioned Jake, all he'd say was it'd been a request from an old friend, someone Jake had known from his time in America. A wealthy gentleman named Dean Williams, the uncle of the girl in question.

"I'm here on business," he stated flatly.

"What sort of business?"

Should he elaborate? He didn't know who or what she was in the scheme of things here. But it did seem as if she belonged. She certainly had an air of authority. Was she part of the staff? She was still staring at him with those arctic eyes.

"Shield Solutions sent me. I'm a protection agent."

Her eyes widened as she processed his words. "You? You're a bodyguard?" She took another step away, putting more space between them. "I don't need a fucking bodyguard." Julie's face turned red, her lips thinning into an angry line.

Her outburst surprised him. But then, some of the puzzle pieces began to fall into place. He wasn't sure how to make the connections, but it seemed she might be the woman he'd been sent up here to guard. Oh, hell no. His day was just getting better and better. He unclenched his hands and let them fall limp by his sides.

Then he drew in a deep breath, and said, "That's good, because I'm a protection agent. Not a bodyguard."

"Since when did you become a...protection agent?" She sneered the words. "I thought they were all military dropouts, with sniper skills and such. You were never in the army. Were you?" The last part was said with a hint of confusion.

"No, I wasn't." He kept his tone even, not letting her biting words get under her skin.

"But being an agent isn't always about shooting and fighting skills. It's more about making intelligent decisions, quick thinking, and good preparation."

She put her hands on her hips and opened her mouth, probably ready to spout more venom at him, judging by the flash of anger in her eyes. Just at that moment, a man came around the corner of the end of the hallway.

"Are you Aaron Powell?" When Aaron nodded, he continued. "I'm Steve. Sorry I wasn't there to meet your chopper; I had a lame horse to tend to."

"Not a problem, sir." Aaron turned to look at the man, continuing to watch Julie out of the corner of his eye. So, *this* was Julie's dad. He'd never met the man, but he could see a likeness already.

"Well, Daniella is on her way, so come on in." Steve removed his Akubra and dusted it against his leg, slipping a key into a lock and swinging open a door, then used the hat to indicate into what Aaron assumed was the meeting room. "I see you've met Julie already." Steve beamed at Julie, but she merely scowled at him until his smile fell away. "You may as well join us," he said to his daughter with a weary sigh.

"Oh yes, I'll be joining you, all right." Julie brushed past Aaron and stomped down the hallway. He had to keep his gaze from drifting up to her rather nice ass, swaying along in those jeans that seemed to be made for her body. "But only to nip this conspiracy in the bud and make sure this… gentleman leaves on the next helicopter out of here." She cast a quick look backward at him. It seemed Julie had lost none of her fire. She'd always been a feisty woman, even when she was seventeen, not afraid to go after what she wanted. Which was one of the things that'd attracted her to him.

Steve gave her a wan smile as she swanned past him into the room.

Aaron followed and watched as Julie dumped her hat and

glasses on a large, boardroom-style table and took a seat on the opposite side, then sat and glared at him.

Aaron shifted his bag to his other hand and extended his arm. Steve shook his hand in a surprisingly warm handshake. Aaron noted a hint of relief in the other man's demeanor. It seemed he'd been more worried than he was letting on. And to his credit, Steve never gave any indication that he'd noticed Aaron's multicolored eyes. Aaron was used to various forms of scrutiny, some people even going as far as flinching away from him. He wasn't some alien being; he was merely a man with different-colored eyes.

"Thank you for coming at such short notice."

"Not a problem. Nice to meet you, sir."

"Steve. Please call me Steve," the older man replied.

Before Aaron could answer, the sound of boots on the tiled floor alerted him to more arrivals. He turned in time to see a smartly dressed woman in white moleskin pants and light-blue, cotton shirt buttoned up high, with brown, bobbed hair enter the room, followed closely by a slim blonde carrying a tray laden with what looked to be coffee and homemade cookies. His stomach rumbled; he'd had nothing to eat since six this morning, when he'd grabbed a piece of toast and an instant coffee on his way out the door.

"I'm Daniella Williams." The older lady offered her hand to shake. "And this is Skylar, my daughter and chef here at the lodge."

"Nice to meet you both." He acknowledged the blonde with a nod and noticed how firm Daniella's handshake was in his own. At the same time, his mind scrambled to keep up with meeting these people, with all these different last names. This was why protocol dictated a good dossier on clients before taking a job, so he wasn't left floundering, trying to figure out who was who.

As if Daniella read his mind, she said, "Take a seat and

we'll explain everything to you, before we get down to the real reason you're here." She waved him to the other side of the table where Julie was sitting, much to her distaste, if the curl of her lip was anything to go by. Daniella pulled out a chair for herself, and Steve sat next to her without a word. Aaron took the chair next to Julie, tucking his backpack beneath the table as he did so, and ignoring the aura of displeasure he could feel emanating from her, as if it were oozing out of her very pores.

Skylar placed the tray next to Daniella and then excused herself, pulling the door shut quietly behind her. But not before Aaron noticed a look pass between her and Julie; one of confusion—she obviously wanted to know who this stranger was—but also solidarity. Aaron remembered that Julie had once told him about a stepsister and a stepbrother, but at that time, she didn't have a lot to do with either of them. It looked like things might've changed since then.

"So," Daniella said, pouring the first coffee and handing it to him, then pushing the plate of cookies toward him. "The man who hired you, Dean Williams, is my brother. He used to work with the owner of your company, Jake Stillton, I think."

Aaron merely nodded. That much made sense. Jake had spent time in America, learning the protection trade, so he could bring his skills back to Australia and start up his own company.

He reached over and snagged one of the sweet snacks. "Oh, wow." The words were an involuntary exclamation as Aaron bit into one of the warm cookies. He was suddenly transported out of the meeting room, caught in a memory of his best friend's mother baking something similar when he'd been only eight or nine, where he and Jason had sat in the cozy kitchen, stuffing their faces. He almost smiled. Until he remembered that his mother had never baked him cookies. She'd barely even been able to raise a civil smile for him, most days.

"Yes," Daniella smiled. "Skylar is a *very* good chef."

That was an understatement. He devoured the cookie and reached for another one.

Daniella passed more coffees around, one to Steve and one to Julie—who was still scowling—and then poured her own. Aaron watched the interplay between everyone seated at the table. Steve was deferential to Daniella, but that didn't mean he was submissive. Aaron noticed a few times Daniella threw him a look as she spoke, almost as if searching for endorsement or consent. A man of few words, but not a man to be stepped on, either, it seemed.

"Dean is part-owner of this station. He helped me and Steve get Stormcloud off the ground. Steve and I are life partners." She flicked him a warm glance. "But we never married, hence our different last names."

"We were both married before, and decided once was enough for each of us," Steve added.

That seemed fair enough to Aaron. As far as he could tell, marriage seemed far too overrated. His own mother had never married and had raised him as a single parent, and he'd turned out fine. Although, once he found out who his father had been... He halted that thought in its tracks; it was best not to go down that slippery slope.

He refocused his gaze on Julie and cleared his throat. It was time to see if he could draw her into the conversation.

"I admit, I was a little confused as to how your...extended family all fitted together. So, you're Steve's biological daughter, then?" He wanted to add that if he'd known he was coming up here to guard Julie Bradshaw, he would've refused the mission.

Julie sat up straighter. "You always knew I took my mother's maiden name when my parents divorced. I certainly didn't want to take on Tony's name, after my mother married him, that was for sure."

He turned his head and speared her with his gaze. "Yes, I did," he replied. But it seemed the details of her father's last name had slipped his mind. Perhaps he could call Jake and get Marco swapped in on this job. There was now a huge conflict of interest and surely Jake would understand that he could no longer take this job. "But that was a long time ago, and your name wasn't in the brief. Besides—"

"Wait a second." Daniella held up an imperious finger.

What was with this family? Were they all intent on interrupting everything he said?

"You two know each other?" Daniella asked.

Julie was the first to answer. "You could say that." She pushed her half-drunk coffee away, and Aaron stiffened, wondering what she might be about to say. "But he was very different back then. Aaron worked as a jackaroo on Tony's farm, Roseby Downs in Dalgety. We were…friends. I have no idea who this…" she waved a hand up and down, encompassing Aaron "…person is. The last time I saw Aaron, he was wearing jeans and plaid and wanted to start a farm of his own one day. Not become a *protection agent*, that's for sure." Julie's lips curled in disdain. At least she'd left out the part about them being much more than friends. About the times he'd snuck into her bedroom. About the intimacy they'd shared.

"Oh, is that all?" Daniella dropped her shoulders and pushed the plate of cookies toward Aaron. "I don't think that'll be a problem. Will it?" She directed her question at Steve.

Steve was studying his daughter through narrowed eyes, rubbing a hand across his stubbled chin. "No. Not unless Julie says it's a problem. This gentleman looks highly capable, and he comes well recommended by the company."

Julie stuttered for a few moments before finding her

tongue. "No, I guess that's not what's worrying me." If she wasn't going to reveal their true relationship, then she had no real reason to object to him. She'd caught herself in her own trap. "My problem is that I don't want a *bodyguard*." She enunciated each word carefully, finally looking Aaron directly in the eye.

"I'm not a bodyguard," he said coolly, managing to hide the hint of a smile that wanted to break loose.

"Oh, you..." Julie stood up, grabbing her hat and sunglasses off the table.

But before she could storm out of the room, Steve said, "Sit down, Julie. Please." He held his daughter's gaze, not threatening, but firm and unwavering. "This is important. Do it for me, if not for you."

All the fight seemed to drain out of her, and she slumped back into the chair. "Fine," she grumbled.

Good, perhaps now they could finally get down to business. Aaron took the lead. "Tell me about this stalker, then." He softened his tone slightly, not wanting to antagonize her any more. She was his client. For now. At least until he could get Jake to fix this mess. "When did it start? How is he related to you?" he asked. At the same time, he took a small notebook and pen from the front pocket of his backpack. He'd fax his notes over to Shield as soon as possible, so they could start a file.

"Ah..." Julie hesitated and then raised her eyebrows in Steve's direction, the tips of her ears going red.

"You have to tell him, love," Steve said gently.

Julie looked down and bit her lip. Aaron noticed two things at once; how lusciously pink and plump her bottom lip was, and how his inner protector stood up at attention at the sudden haunted look in Julie's eyes.

"I'm pretty sure he must have latched on to me at the clinic, but I'm not sure exactly," she said in a small voice.

"What clinic was that?" Aaron asked, voice cool as he opened his notebook to take down the details.

"The Marie Stopes Family Planning Clinic," she replied, not meeting his eyes, instead staring at the closed door to the meeting room, as if it were suddenly fascinating.

"Uh-huh," he prompted. "And why do you think that?"

She hung her head. "The only thing I can think was that he was part of a group hanging around out the front, chanting and handing out pamphlets. You know, those groups that accost women, try to stop them going through with it."

Stop women going through with what? He was about to voice the question when it suddenly hit him like a brick to the head.

Julie had had an abortion.

The thought caused a riot of emotions to rise in his chest. The feeling that took precedence was an overwhelming desire to make sure that Julie was okay. Whatever reason she'd had to terminate a pregnancy, he knew it'd have to be a good one. Julie was nothing if not a woman of principals and high morals. Now that he'd met her father, he had an inkling where that strength of fortitude might come from. But to terminate a pregnancy. That must've taken some courage. He studied her face, wondering what kind of toll that might've taken on her emotionally. There'd been no mention of a boyfriend or husband. Should he assume whoever got her pregnant was now out of the picture? He suddenly wished she hadn't had to go through that. Wished he could've been there for her.

It seemed they'd both changed in the past twelve years. Had perhaps both done things they weren't proud of. Had found out what they were capable of. She wasn't the same woman he'd known back then, either.

He had a good reason for leaving her twelve years ago. And she must've had a good reason for doing what she did, as well. It looked like they both lived with hard-made choices and decisions. When he'd found out the truth about himself, everything had changed; he'd lost sight of all his goals and motivations, which suddenly seemed petty and worthless. Plans made by a young, gullible man with no idea how the real world worked.

Now he knew better. And so, it seemed, did Julie.

CHAPTER FOUR

"I'm so sorry, Julie." Aaron's words echoed in her head. She glanced up and was caught by the contrast of his multicolored eyes. Back when she'd been seventeen, those eyes had been beautiful, beguiling, almost otherworldly. She hadn't been able to stop staring into them. Now, there was compassion in their depths, flashes of old connections they'd once shared.

Right at that moment, it was almost as if no time had passed between them; as if he'd never left her. She sketched his familiar, straight nose, leading down to firm, confident lips. Lips that'd claimed every part of her body. She shuddered at the memory.

"I'm sorry you had to go through...that." His voice broke through her contemplation of his features. He didn't say the word, for which she was grateful. But even so, it still hung between them like a shadow.

Abortion. It was such a harsh word. And one that Julie had tried on so many occasions to define but failed every time. It was a word that held power. Power over minds, and power over women's bodies. Power over life and death. What did Aaron think of her choice? And did she care?

"Yes, so am I. But what's done is done, and life goes on,"

she declared, then tried to raise a smile. It was a ghost of her normal smile, and she knew it. The jokes and her flippant humor she always relied on seemed to have deserted her over the past few days.

"Yes, let's not dwell on the past," Daniella broke in, saving Julie from any more embarrassing shows of weakness. "Can we focus on this deranged individual and how we're going to deal with him, please?"

Steve shot her stepmother a grateful glance. She knew he was just as uncomfortable with the topic as she was.

"Of course." Aaron shuffled a small, black notebook in front of him.

The compassion she'd seen in his eyes was replaced by that cool demeanor from when she'd first run into him in the hallway. A man in charge. A man not to be trifled with. Aaron had always been responsible, and dependable, even at nineteen. But now he exuded an air of boldness. Of danger. If she hadn't known better, she might almost be intimidated by him.

"Tell me how this stalker has been contacting you. I need to know everything he's done and said, no matter how small or insignificant you think it might be."

"Mostly, he's just sent me threatening letters. Both the old-fashioned kind, as well as by email," Julie offered. "They started appearing in my mailbox about a week after I went to the clinic. But I hadn't received anything from him for well over a year. Not since I moved out to Stormcloud. Then out of the blue, the letters started arriving again, about three weeks ago."

"Here's a copy of the latest letter." Steve leaned over and dropped a folded piece of paper onto the tabletop. He'd obviously been carrying it around in his back pocket. Daniella shot him a strange look, a mix of sympathy and exasperation.

"Great." Aaron scooped the paper off the table and smoothed it out and began reading. "He hasn't signed a name, which isn't unusual," Aaron said quietly, almost as if he were musing to himself. "Do we have a name?" Aaron asked, suddenly looking up from the letter. "Do you have any idea who this guy might be?"

"If we did, do you think we'd be sitting here talking to you right now?" Julie quipped. Then she pursed her lips, regretting her sharp words.

"No, I guess not." Aaron went back to perusing the letter, as if her comment hadn't affected him.

Julie couldn't describe how she felt at that particular moment, as she watched Aaron read her stalker's letter. She wanted to know what was going on in his head. Wanted to know how she truly felt about this whole sordid affair.

"Have you got copies of the other letters, as well?" He looked her squarely in the eye.

"No, I threw the other two recent ones out," Julie said. Aaron's face turned incredulous. "I didn't want to be reminded about them, so I threw them in the fire," she added, trying not to sound as sheepish as she felt. In hindsight, it'd been a stupid thing to do. But she'd been so angry. So disgusted by this creepy asshole. How dare he think he could threaten her?

"Okay," Aaron replied, but before he could control the look in his eyes, Julie saw a flash of exasperation.

"And before you ask, no, I didn't keep any of the other letters he sent me while I was in Brisbane, either." There'd been ten or twelve over the space of three months. At first, Julie had dismissed them as the ravings of a nut job. He quoted verses of the Bible at her and told her she needed to repent; to find God and He would help her see the light. But his notes had become progressively longer and more threatening, and a couple of times he'd mentioned that she'd got away with it before, but she wouldn't get away with it this time, which just confused her.

"What about the emails? Did you keep them?"

She shook her head. "I deleted my whole email account when I left Brisbane." It'd seemed like the sensible thing to do. All she wanted was to move on and forget about her stalker; about everything she'd been through over those past few months. Never in her wildest dreams did she imagine he'd continue to hunt her. It'd been a year and a half since she'd last heard from him. Why would he keep following her?

"The emails didn't start up until about a month before I left Brissy. He sent me a couple of links to Facebook pages, you know the ones where pro-lifers expound on all the reasons killing unborn babies is a form of murder. Or he'd send me invitations to church services being held nearby, saying that he'd meet me there and together we could beat this scourge of humanity. I just ignored them."

Steve shifted in his seat. She hadn't revealed the full details of the deranged man's contact with her last night, and she could see her father's face become darker the longer she spoke.

Aaron didn't perceive her father's growing outrage. It was noticeable to her because she'd spent a lifetime observing and distinguishing her father's moods. To most people, it would seem as if he coasted along on one even plane, never letting anything ruffle his feathers. But Julie knew better. Steve felt things deeply, he was just of the old school, where they never showed too much emotion; simply kept soldiering on, no matter what.

"Did he contact you via phone, as well?" Aaron asked, and Julie could tell he was holding in the sigh of exasperation that wanted to leave his lips.

"Not recently," Julie admitted. "When I moved out to

Stormcloud, I got a new number, and that seemed to stop him texting me."

"So, he was texting you before?" That seemed to surprise Aaron. "Any idea how he got your old cell phone number?"

She ran a hand through her hair. "No. But back then, I had no reason to hide it. I was pretty much an open book."

"Still. It's not that easy to pluck a cell phone number out of the air. It might help us track him down if we knew where he got your number." Aaron rubbed his thumb across the corner of his mouth, deep in thought. "Were you ever on any of those dating sites? Tinder, eharmony, OKCupid?"

"No." She sat up straighter in her chair. "Why would you think I'd need to stoop to that kind of thing?"

"Settle down," he said, not condescendingly. "I don't think anything. I'm just asking, that's all. These are all things I need to know, if I'm to help you."

She should stop being so defensive. But she couldn't help it. She couldn't get it out of her head that this was Aaron Powell. The man who'd ripped her heart out when he left without explanation. And she'd never really recovered. Her mother had told her that'd it'd only been puppy-love, you could never truly feel anything that strong when you were seventeen. Her mother scoffed at the idea that Julie had found her soul mate; the idea was ridiculous. Julie tried to believe her mother's words, tried to cement them in her mind, hoping they'd help harden her heart.

But no matter how hard she tried, no one had ever truly measured up to Aaron. Not one of her relationships had lasted past a year. Most had only gone for a few months, at best.

And now here he was, sitting there larger than life, playing at being a bodyguard, of all things.

"I know, and I'm sorry," Julie replied, going for demure, but not sure she got there. She locked eyes with Aaron, wondering if he had even the smallest inkling of what was really going on in her head.

"Anything else?" he asked. "Did he try and contact you face-to-face? Have you ever seen this guy close up?"

Julie hesitated. She should tell Aaron everything. Neither her father nor Daniella knew about the break in. She'd kept it a secret yesterday because her father had been so upset. More rattled than she'd ever seen him before. That kind of information might've tipped him over the edge. But Aaron needed to know. And something told her if she withheld the information, when he found out—not if, but when—he wouldn't be happy about it.

"Ah…" She glanced up at Steve and watched his familiar face harden slightly, as if she were about to deliver a physical blow. But there was no going back. "I think he broke into my villa. It was about a week before Dad called and asked me to come and help out at Stormcloud."

Steve tensed at her words, and Daniella leaned across the table to stare at Julie.

But before either of them could speak, Aaron held up a hand. "You think he did what?"

"Well, I'm not one-hundred-percent sure." She squirmed in her seat. "The door wasn't busted in, or anything like that," she added quickly. "But when I got home from work one night, things looked…slightly different. Like stuff had been moved and not put back exactly right. Do you know what I mean?"

"Yes, I do. Often people get a feeling that they've been violated, even if there is no evidence to prove it," he replied, and she let out a sigh of relief. He understood. But he held her gaze, not letting her escape his next question. "Did he take anything? Was anything missing? Did he leave you a note? Or a sign of some sort?"

"No, I don't think so," she replied. That night she'd rushed in her door, arms laden with bags of food shopping, but it wasn't until she'd dumped the bags on her kitchen countertop that a strange feeling had clawed up her spine. As if someone was watching her. Leaving the food sitting on the counter, she'd walked slowly through her villa, trying to find the source of her unease. Everything had looked fine. Nothing was broken and there was no sign of a forced entry. It wasn't until she wandered into her bedroom that the hairs on the back of her neck really stood on end. Her room was at the back of the villa, with a window overlooking a small courtyard. She'd decorated the room herself and it always felt like she was entering a kind of haven. Not that night, however. The first thing she noticed was the smell of her perfume. It hung heavy in the air, as if someone had sprayed it throughout the room. When she went over to her set of tallboy drawers, she ran her gaze over all the familiar items on the top. Cosmetics, perfume, her collection of rings in a small wooden box, a hairbrush, and comb. Everything was still there. But had things been moved slightly? She wasn't sure. The top drawer also sat slightly open. Only half a centimeter, or so. Had she not closed it properly this morning?

She'd tried to tell herself it was an overactive imagination, but that night she'd been scared to sleep in her own bed, and had slept on the couch, with all the lights blazing, and an old softball bat by her side.

"It was more of a feeling than anything concrete I could put my finger on?" she added, hating that she sounded lame.

"Why didn't you tell us?" Daniella could no longer hold her tongue. "Or why didn't you at least report this to the police?"

"I considered it," Julie replied, sitting back in her chair. "But there was no evidence, and I didn't think anyone would believe me." She fixed her stepmother with an unwavering gaze. Daniella was the most no-nonsense person she knew, and she probably would've been the first person to scoff at her for letting her imagination carry her away if she had reported it to the police and they'd dismissed it out of hand.

Daniella understood the implied innuendo, and her eyes narrowed. "Well, perhaps that was for us to decide." Daniella's voice rose slightly.

"It's not unheard of for a stalker to enter a person's home," Aaron spoke over the top of Daniella, effectively shutting her down. "But it does show another level of sophistication. Which is worrying." He turned his troubled gaze toward Julie. "But remember, there is no blame here," Aaron said, tone stating that he'd brook no argument. "Julie is a victim in this crime, one that she had no control over."

Steve lay a hand on Daniella's arm, but said nothing. In his unassuming way, he was telling Daniella to keep her thoughts to herself, and Julie was grateful.

"So, let me get this straight." Aaron turned his chair so that he was facing Julie directly. She couldn't help but notice the way his thighs bulged beneath his black pants, and she had to drag her gaze up to meet his. "You believe this stalker attached himself to you after you attended the family planning clinic, but you're not sure how or why. He sent you letters, emails and texts over the course of around three months, with the threats slowly escalating."

Julie nodded at his clinical evaluation.

"You think he broke into your villa, but we're not really sure why, as there was no threat left and nothing was stolen. Is that correct?"

She nodded her agreement again.

"Then you moved out here and heard nothing more? Until three weeks ago, when the first letter arrived."

"Yep, you've got it all in a nutshell," Julie replied.

"He's certainly persistent, I'll give him that much. We need to understand how he found you, and why he's continuing to hound you." Aaron tapped his finger against his lips in contemplation.

"One last question," he said. "What about the father of the…unborn child?"

Julie was taken by surprise. She hadn't thought about Judd much. Certainly not since she'd been working at Stormcloud. He wasn't important in the scheme of things. He'd left her and moved on so quickly it made her head spin.

"Judd and I only had a few dates." She screwed up her face in distaste at the memory. "Then he left me for some younger, blonde bimbo. I didn't find out I was pregnant until two months after we broke up. He never even knew. At least there are some rules that help protect mothers who have to make this sort of decision. You don't need the father's permission to go through with an abortion."

Aaron reached over and covered her hand with his in a surprising show of empathy. "I don't blame you for any of this. You don't need to defend your actions to me."

She hadn't meant to sound defensive, but obviously she had, because the way he was looking at her, with compassion in his eyes, told her he understood. His large hand engulfed hers, warmth permeating her skin. That was another thing she'd forgotten about Aaron Powell. He'd always been warm, as if he had an internal fire burning bright in his chest. Perhaps it was the touch of his skin on hers, the way his palm seemed to emit an electrical spark that travelled up her arm and all the way to her soul, but she suddenly blurted, "I didn't really have a choice. The baby had Trisomy 18. Only five percent of babies live past their first year," she added softly. "I knew I couldn't look after a baby with special needs. Not on my own…"

How did she explain the abject fear that'd engulfed her on the day the test results had come back? The baby would've needed round-the-clock care. She'd never even heard of Trisomy 18, or Edwards Syndrome, as it was sometimes called, until the day of her test. Babies who were born with it suffered from a combination of birth defects, including heart abnormalities and learning difficulties, and often died in the womb before they could even be born. She couldn't do it. Did that make her a bad person? In the eyes of her stalker, it did. Before she'd gone through with the abortion, Julie had thought it was the logical thing to do; the only thing to do. But now… She didn't know anymore. One thing was for sure, she didn't think she wanted to take the chance of having any more children. The risk was too high. The toll on her heart would be too high. If there was anything wrong with another of her babies, she knew she wouldn't survive.

Her father broke through her downward-spiralling thoughts, when he said softly, "You wouldn't have had to do it alone. You know that, don't you, honey?" His blue eyes were pale, concern furrowed his brow.

"Thanks, Dad." Of course, Steve and Daniella would've rallied around her if she had gone ahead with the birth, she knew that unequivocally. What she really meant, though, was she didn't want to have to do it without a partner by her side.

"Is there any way that Judd could be the stalker?" Aaron interjected. "That he somehow found out you had the abortion and wants to make you pay?"

Julie laughed out loud. It was the first time she'd let go of a true belly laugh for at least two days, and it felt good. A release of tension and a rush of endorphins.

"Oh, God, no," she exclaimed with delight. "Judd is the most self-centered person I think I've ever met. The absolute last thing he'd want in this world would be to be told he was a father. He'd never agree to look after a child, and certainly not a sick one. He has too many *ambitions* and *dreams* to follow first." Julie was still chuckling. What'd she ever seen in that man? He was good-looking, with his brown skin and appealing brown eyes. But the very first time she'd slept with him, she'd known it wasn't going to last. It was all about him, and how she could please him. She thought about him standing next to Aaron, and there was no comparison at all.

"Besides, he doesn't have a religious bone in his body. He wouldn't recognize God if He sent down a thunderbolt from the sky to smite him." Julie collapsed into another peal of giggles. It felt good to laugh again. Aaron was staring at her as if she'd gone a tad crazy. Then something behind his eyes shifted, as if he'd been struck by a memory. They'd laughed a lot together in the six short months they spent in each other's arms. Was that what he was remembering? His lips twitched as if he wanted to join in. But then his face glazed over, and his firm lips drew into a thin line.

"As long as you're sure we can exclude him, then I'll take your word for it. I'll get Lance to start looking into this stalker. He's our information specialist," Aaron added.

Julie wondered what'd happened to that carefree young man she'd used to know. "Look how serious you've become," she said with a cheeky smile.

He didn't smile back, and she bit back the rest of her comment, the smile fading from her lips.

"We've had a few problems at Stormcloud over the past year and a half, and we'd rather not have any more trouble," Steve said, snagging Aaron's attention. "It's way past time we did something about our security systems, anyway."

Steve went on to detail how Dale and Daisy had been involved in bringing down one of the station's ex-staff members in a murder plot nearly eighteen months ago—which was the reason Julie had come to work at the station, to help out—and she watched Aaron's eyes grow concerned as Steve laid down the details. Then Daniella chimed in and told him about Skylar and Nash's narrow escape from a misogynistic lunatic, who'd put out a contract on them both, with a sniper shooting their helicopter out of the sky a mere six months ago.

Aaron's eyes widened with each new detail Daniella revealed. Hearing it all laid down like that, hearing it as a stranger, Julie could see how fantastical it might sound to an outsider. Having lived through it all, she had come to accept their family dramas as a fact of life. And now it seemed she was only adding to those dramas.

But Aaron never said a word regarding their seeming predisposition for attracting trouble. Or was it merely plain bad luck? Instead, he said, "I'd say it's definitely time you installed a security system." His gaze found Julie's. "Especially with this new threat. And it'd make sense for you to keep an eye on your guests as well, make sure they don't go wandering off and get lost in the bush."

"We've never had a guest go missing yet," Daniella huffed. "We're very careful about that sort of thing."

"Of course you are," Aaron replied, and Julie applauded his diplomacy.

"And we've got the muster coming up in a few days," Steve added. "Which means we'll have more people coming and going. I've got ringers arriving from all over the state. Some of them will gather here first, before we head out to the stock camp."

"A muster?" Aaron's lips narrowed slightly.

"Yes, why?" Steve scratched his three-day growth thoughtfully. "Will that be a problem? It's already organized. I'm not sure I could stop it now…"

"It should be fine," Aaron conceded. She could see the tiny frown lines on his face, the scar through his eyebrow drawing down slightly, and she could practically hear his brain ticking over. It meant more logistics to be worked out, more people to be checked. "I'll need all the details, of course, but we can go over that later."

One thing her father had failed to mention was that Julie was supposed to go on the muster as the camp cook. She opened her mouth to disclose the information, then snapped it shut again, as Aaron began to question Steve about what security, if any, they already had in place.

Julie tuned out as Steve and Aaron talked, Aaron detailing what sort of system they'd need, how many cameras, where they should be positioned, etcetera, etcetera. Perhaps it *was* time the station got up-to-date security, she just wished it wasn't on her behalf. But there was no going back now. People knew about her problems. Steve and Daniella were involved. Nash had taken a statement, which meant the whole Queensland police force probably knew by now. It was going to be practically impossible to stop the rest of her family from finding out, too. She probably owed it to Skylar to tell her face-to-face. Her stepsister would never forgive her if she found out through the grapevine. Which was fair enough. And if she told Skylar, then she needed to tell Dale and Daisy, as well.

Julie wanted to cover her face with her hands and pretend this all wasn't happening.

Why did it have to be Aaron Powell who was the riding in on his white charger to save the day? Right about now, she'd even agree to take on a bodyguard, if only it wasn't Aaron.

She hated him for what he'd done to her. Taken her innocent, vulnerable heart and stomped all over it. Well, okay, hate was a strong word. She'd certainly despised him for a long, long time. Only a hardhearted pig would leave without any explanation. She'd waited for days for him to turn up at the farm, not believing her stepfather when he said that Aaron had phoned and turned in his notice; said that he wouldn't be coming back. But as the days slowly turned into weeks and then months, with no sign of Aaron—he never once tried to contact her—a stone wall had gone up around her heart. Because she was determined that she'd never be hurt like that again.

Glaring at the back of Aaron's head, she made a resolution. She would *not* let him into her life again. And definitely not into her heart.

CHATPER FIVE

Julie was staring at him. Aaron could feel her gaze beating down on him. She wasn't happy. With him, or with her current situation. And he didn't blame her.

He continued talking to Steve, forcefully pulling his concentration away from the woman seated beside him and putting it squarely on the two people on the other side of the table. He'd had reluctant clients before, and he would handle Julie the same way he'd handled the others. With calm, common sense, and strict professionalism. Never get attached to a client. It was an edict everyone in his line of work should follow. Some agents he knew let that line blur, but not him. He always kept that border between agent and client solid and steadfast.

"I'd like to take a look around the lodge, if you don't mind?" Aaron directed his question to Steve.

"Unfortunately, I'm busy taking the guests out horseback riding this afternoon," Steve replied. "Julie was supposed to accompany me, but I'm making sure she stays inside, just in case. She can show you around the lodge, instead."

"What?" Julie hadn't said a word for nearly ten minutes, but Steve's comment seemed to pull her out of whatever dark thoughts she'd been mulling over. "No. I'm not taking *him* anywhere." Aaron didn't need to turn around to know those beautiful blue eyes had turned arctic again.

"Julie," her father admonished quietly.

She blew out a breath and sat back in her chair. "Do I get any say in this?" she asked. "I told you I didn't think this situation warranted a bodyguard..." She stared at Aaron, daring him to correct her. He wisely kept his mouth shut, and she continued. "Yet less than twenty-four hours later, here we are. I think you're blowing this out of proportion. This stalker has never once given me—us—any solid reason to think he's actually going to come after me. His threats are..." She seemed to struggle to find the correct word. "Well, they're childish and laughable."

Aaron knew better. This guy might look as if he posed no threat to Julie, but the seemingly harmless ones were often the worst offenders. He hadn't said too much at the time, but the fact that her stalker had potentially broken into her house was highly disturbing. It showed intelligence, not leaving any trace of a break-in, as well as subtle intent. The other extremely worrying factor was the stalker hadn't given up when she'd moved away. That showed patience and premeditation; this guy had been able to sustain his obsession for over a year and a half. Julie should be concerned. But he also knew pushing reluctant clients only made them believe their own version of the story even more. He glanced across the table, ready to intervene if they didn't say something soon.

Steve held up his hand as Daniella also drew breath to argue. "I don't agree," he said evenly. "But I know how stubborn you are when you don't get your way."

"I wonder where I get that from?" Julie quipped, but Aaron could hear the softening in her tone. Steve smiled back at her; a special smile Aaron felt he kept only for his daughter. Julie and her dad had a distinctive bond, it seemed. It was nice to see that Julie respected and liked her father. Nice to see a healthy father/daughter relationship. He'd grown up without a father in his life, with no other men he could've used as a father figure, either. Would things have turned out differently if he'd had a male role model in his life? Aaron didn't like to dwell on thoughts of his father; they always ended up with him spiraling down into a dark place. His mother had kept his father's identity a secret from him, and had chosen to parent him on her own. But when he'd finally confronted her—wanting to know who his real father was— she'd revealed the reason for her choices, and it'd shocked him to his core.

"Why don't we agree on a compromise, for now?" Steve said. "How about we let Aaron take a few days to look around and come up with a plan for a new security system for this place? Because God knows we need one."

"Mmm," she replied, noncommittally.

"At the same time, he and his team can assess the threat this stalker poses. Aaron can stay on in a consultant capacity." Steve glanced at Aaron to see if that was the correct term, and Aaron gave a solemn nod. "So, you won't have a bodyguard, as such. He won't be following you around the property, or be by your side all the time, interfering in your life. What do you think?"

Julie's face brightened considerably at his suggestion, and Aaron was hit with a memory of how her eyes used to sparkle with mischief when she'd whisper something sweet into his ear if she thought no one was looking.

"That's good. I'd feel safer if we had someone who knows what they're doing on site, just in case," Daniella added.

It was a good compromise, and it also gave Aaron some leeway, as well. Not that he'd mention it right now. It meant he could talk to Jake and hopefully get someone to come and take his place, if they decided to go down the path of a full-time personal protection agent for Julie. For both their sakes, it was better if that person wasn't him.

"Right." Steve stood, and Daniella followed suit. "Let's meet back here before dinner and compare notes."

Aaron snagged his backpack from beneath the table and he and Julie stood at the same time. Steve was already distracted, as if his mind was back on his lame horse and no longer here in the meeting room.

Daniella said, "You can leave your bag in here, for now. It'll be perfectly safe; we keep this door locked when the room isn't in use."

"Thank you." Aaron placed the bag on the chair he'd just vacated. It was his go bag. His whole life was in here. It always sat in his cupboard, packed and ready to go at a moment's notice. It contained everything from a couple of changes of clothes, to a Taser, flashlights, spare burner phones, cash, a first aid kit, extra batteries, a compass, a lighter, his laptop, various weapons, a spare coms unit, and many other useful items he might need in an emergency. He rummaged around and pulled out a black case. "Do you have a gun safe?" He held up the case for Daniella's inspection. When she frowned, he added, "Don't worry, I can always wear them, instead." There was no way he was leaving his handguns unattended, even if it was in a supposedly locked room. His weapon of choice was a SIG-Sauer 9mm, which he wore in a shoulder holster beneath his sport coat, while he kept a smaller SIG as a second weapon that could be more easily concealed, or worn in an ankle holster.

"I have a safe in the office. Will that do?" she asked. The look on her face was one of restrained horror, that he might actually wear a weapon around the station. She probably didn't want to scare the guests. But he had a job to do, and if it meant disturbing a few of her rich clients, he wasn't going to let that bother him. He was more than used to wealthy clients and their insane requests.

He nodded. "It'll do." A gun safe was probably something else he needed to put on the list for Steve to think about. In his experience, most farms and stations had at least one or two weapons hanging around, either to shoot vermin, or put down an injured animal. Too many graziers and landowners were blasé about their guns.

"I'll leave you in the ladies' capable hands, then," Steve said, extending his hand for a quick shake before he strode out of the room.

Julie hung back, twirling her sunglasses.

"Follow me," Daniella said, crooking her little finger. She led him out of the meeting room, and watched impatiently while Julie trailed after them, then true to her word, locked the door behind them. Daniella swept down the hallway and turned into another door on the right, then beckoned him around the large desk covered in piles of paperwork and pointed to a safe tucked beneath the table. "It's secured to the floor," she volunteered, as he stared at it.

"Good," was all he said. Crude, but effective, he guessed.

Daniella took the case from him, and placed it in the safe, making a big show of locking it securely.

"Okay, Julie, he's all yours." Daniella clasped her hands and looked at her stepdaughter in anticipation. Aaron got the distinct impression they were being dismissed. It seemed work came first with Daniella.

"Sure. This way." Julie gestured. She led him down the long hallway toward the main living area, still twirling her sunglasses. He'd come in this way, but there'd been no one to meet him at the reception desk in the big main foyer, so he'd decided to find the meeting room for himself.

"We'll start in the great room," she said, not bothering to turn and face him when she spoke. They emerged into a huge, open-plan room that he'd glimpsed as he'd threaded his way down the maze of hallways, looking for where he was supposed to meet Steve. It was even bigger once they were all the way in, with enormous, floor-to-ceiling, picture windows running along the whole front of the room. He could see some of the windows opened out onto an expansive, covered verandah, where there were plenty of comfy chairs and recliners scattered around for guests to take in the stunning view of the billabong farther down the slope.

"We serve dinner over there." Julie pointed to the right. "Or the guests can have their meals delivered to their cabins, if they prefer." Two long tables filled the area, with a couple of smaller ones tucked into the corner. "We like everyone to sit together. Sort of like one big, happy family. But couples can request a separate table if they want a little privacy."

"Love the fireplace," Aaron commented as his gaze snagged on the centerpiece of the room. It was as big as everything else around here, and fitted in perfectly. It looked to be made from local sandstone, the stone facing soaring all the way to the high ceiling above. Comfortable leather chairs were dotted around in small groups, and Aaron could imagine guests enjoying an apéritif and a glass of wine as they sat and chatted.

"Yes, Dad designed that. But we hardly ever need to use it. It rarely gets cold enough up here." That much was true. It'd been bloody boiling outside as he walked from the helicopter up to the lodge. But at least it was cool inside. The high ceilings and flagstone floors kept the heat at bay. Plus, there must be some kind of air-conditioning running. Julie glanced at him, her eyes flicking over his outfit with a look that said she thought he was overdressed. Maybe he was, but his black jeans, lace-up, patent-leather shoes, T-shirt and sports coat were almost a uniform for him. He needed to look neat and well-groomed, but not too formal. Modern but reserved, that was how he thought of himself. A far cry from the clothing he used to prefer. Worn, blue jeans, checked shirt and dusty boots. He almost laughed out loud at the memory.

"Where are all the guests at the moment?" he asked instead.

"Lunch is over, so most of them will be gathering up at the stables, ready for the trail ride," Julie explained. He was a good judge of people's body language; it helped in his line of work to be able to decipher people's actions as well as their words. And Julie's body language was slowly becoming less tense as she relaxed in his company.

He was surprised she hadn't launched straight into another attack as soon as they were alone. But it was as if she'd decided on an uneasy truce. For now. Instead, she kept up a semi-stilted running commentary of the lodge, never quite meeting his eye, but slowly gathering momentum as she talked about how Steve and Daniella had brought their dream of Stormcloud Station to fruition.

The more he saw, the more impressed he became. Both with the building and with Julie.

Julie was showing signs of her old self now they were out of that awkward meeting with her parents. Her speech became more animated as she explained how Steve and Daniella had designed the lodge to have the least impact on the land on which it was built. She was proud of her father and how he'd constructed this place from the ground up. When Aaron and Julie had been together, he'd often called her his little ray of sunshine. She was one of the most optimistic people he knew. At least, she had been back then. Life had obviously thrown her some curve balls, and her positiveness was now tempered by recent angst and more than a healthy dose of cynicism. But not many people stayed the same. The world had a knack of taking people down a few pegs by showing them the hard truths and adversity. He was a good case in point. After he found out the truth about his father, his self-confidence had taken a battering. His belief in who he was had been shaken to the core. And that was one of the reasons he'd had to leave. He was no longer the person Julie thought him to be. But he also had no idea who he was supposed to be going forward, either. At least finding Jake and joining Shield Solutions had given him a direction. He didn't regret joining the agency; it'd taught him to be tough and unyielding, all things he needed to be if he were to survive.

"Can I take a look at the verandah?" he asked, when she wound to a halt about how sustainable the resort was.

"Sure." She opened one of the big doors and led him outside. A wall of heat hit them as they left the sanctuary of the lodge. Even while he took in the view from the wooden deck, he was also mentally documenting angles and best vantage points. A couple of well-placed cameras out here should do the trick. And one more inside. He'd like to take a tour of the whole outside of the lodge first, before he made his final decision.

He wandered down the length of the verandah, Julie trailing behind him. It was the first time he'd really stopped to take in his surroundings. This place sure was beautiful. The sounds of birds calling drew his attention down the grassy slope toward the billabong. A sparkling swimming pool with a wooden platform on three sides stood between them and the large body of water. Deck chairs were spread around the platform, tucked in the shade of large umbrellas. Two people, a couple by the looks of them, swam lazily in the pool. Aaron studied them, but after only a few moments of watching their body language—they weren't the least bit interested in what he and Julie were doing on the veranda, they were much more interested in touching each other—he decided they weren't a threat. A swim might be nice. The water looked so inviting, a cooling dip to wash away the sweat and drive away the heat and flies. Pity he hadn't thought to bring his swimming trunks. And a pity he was on duty.

"Do you want to take a closer look?" He'd been so enthralled by the vista, he almost hadn't noticed Julie wander up and stand at his elbow.

"Yes, please." He needed to take a tour of the whole place anyway, it'd help him to map the area in his head, and he may as well start down at the billabong.

She led him to a set of stairs that went down off the veranda and onto the lush, green grass. They gave the pool a wide berth, but Julie made a point of waving and smiling at the couple swimming. It was part of her job, he supposed, but he still didn't like her easy acceptance of everyone around her. He needed to get her to understand that she should take more care, at least until they caught this guy. He made a mental note to talk to her about putting up some boundaries.

More out of habit than out of a fear that anyone was watching them, Aaron's gaze searched the surrounding area, checking for anything out of place, or anyone showing more interest than they should. Apart from the two in the pool, the front section of the lodge was deserted. Julie must be right; everyone else had chosen to go on the trail ride this afternoon.

"This is a natural billabong," Julie said, slipping easily into tour-guide mode. "It was the reason my dad and Daniella chose this location to build the lodge. They stumbled across it and just knew this was the place."

"Doesn't it flood in the wet?" While he'd never experienced it himself, Aaron had heard how much rain they got up in the north. Rivers and creeks flooded, and roads got severed; sometimes stations were cut off from civilization for weeks or months.

"No, we're really lucky, the lodge sits up slightly higher, on the rocky foothills of the Mount Mulligan Ranges." She pointed toward the large escarpment that dominated the skyline in the distance behind the billabong. "The creek that feeds the billabong often overflows and floods the lower side," she pointed toward the other side of the body of water. "And sometimes it gets so high that our driveway becomes almost impassable. Certainly without a four-wheel-drive." She gave him one of her impish grins. "But we're lucky, the road between us and Dimbulah is rarely impassable. And we usually fly a lot of our guests in by helicopter, so that solves that problem."

She turned and planted her hands on her hips, and he was caught up in the beauty of her smile. She'd put on her Akubra as they sauntered down the hill, and the shade from the brim hid most of her face, but her teeth flashed brilliant in the hot sunshine. Just as he was about to ask Julie to show him some more, there was a loud jangling noise.

"Sorry, that's my phone." She smiled as she pulled it out of her back pocket.

"Wait." His hand descended on her wrist before she could answer the cell.

"What?" She turned wide, blue eyes up to his face.

"Do you recognize the caller?" he asked brusquely.

"No, why...?" Her mouth formed a perfect O as it suddenly dawned on her. "Surely not," she replied indignantly. "You can't think that this could be him." She gave a great smile, suddenly confident. "That'd be too much of a coincidence. This phone is different from the one I had in Brisbane; he couldn't have tracked it down. This must be a wrong number, or something."

"Answer it, but put it on speaker," he requested, not letting go of her wrist.

She did as she was told, holding the phone between them so they could both hear, but the amused smile still played over her lips as she said, "Hello?"

There was a pause, and Julie flicked a quick look at him from beneath half-lowered eyelashes, as if to say, *see, I'm right.*

Then a male voice said, "Hi, Julie. Long time no see."

She sucked in a breath and held the phone at arm's length.

A flash of adrenaline surged through Aaron. It was the stalker. His gut instincts had been right. Damn, if only he'd asked Jake to put a tracer on this phone already. But they sometimes took time to arrange, there was paperwork and permissions that needed to be sorted first.

"Do you know who this is?" the man asked, voice low and conspiratorial. He had a strange accent, with an unusual English twang, but for some reason Aaron decided it was fake.

"Yes, I know. You're the sick bastard who needs to be locked up," Julie retorted. "How did you get this number? You need to leave me the hell alone." Julie sounded mad, and rightfully so. But a slight wobble in her tone gave her away. She was also scared. He didn't like to see Julie scared. It sparked off a deep, ingrained emotion within him. A caveman-like sentiment to protect her.

The man on the other end of the phone gave a curious giggle, as if this was somehow all amusing to him.

"Try and keep him talking," Aaron mouthed. Any information they could garner from this guy might help solve the riddle as to who he was. "But don't mention that I'm here," he added.

They hadn't discussed how Julie might handle this sort of situation yet. If they had, he would've warned her not to mention anything about Shield Solutions or himself. They needed to keep the element of surprise, at least for a while longer, until they understood what kind of threat they were dealing with.

"The thing is, Julie, I don't *want* to leave you alone. You need to be saved. And I'm the only one who can do that."

Julie looked up at Aaron, a small shudder running through her. It made Aaron curiously incensed that this dickhead had the nerve to try to intimidate her like that. This guy meant her harm. Aaron could hear it in the slightly insane edge to his voice. The spark of protective instinct flared in his chest to a full-on bonfire.

She's just a client, he reminded himself. He never reacted like this. He needed to stay detached, otherwise his work might be compromised. He couldn't let emotion get in the way of doing his job; of being able to react with cool vigilance. But right now, all he wanted to do was rip this guy's voice box out, for daring to utter those threatening words. This was crazy, he needed to get a hold of himself.

Julie was so shocked, she was lost for words, she glared at the screen, and her mouth opened and closed, but nothing intelligent came out. "You...you...you fucking creep," she finally uttered.

"Now, you're just being rude," the man replied, lightly. "But that's okay, I'll let your insults slide this one time. Because I know the pathway to forgiveness." He gave a heartfelt sigh down the phone line. "And I have to say that I'm feeling magnanimous today. Because I'm getting closer. This time, you won't get away from me. Soon you'll have no choice but to learn the way of the Lord. Because I'll be right there by your side to teach you."

A thrill of unease shot down Aaron's spine. What did the stalker mean by that?

"And soon you'll have no need for those blue jeans and that white T-shirt, either. You'll be wearing the robes of a sacrificial lamb."

Holy shit. Before Julie even had time to react, Aaron had picked her up and thrown her over his shoulder, the cell phone tumbling from her fingers and landing in the grass.

The bastard knew what she was wearing.

It meant he was possibly close by.

He was an idiot. He'd let his guard drop. Had been swayed by Julie's adamant comments that there was no way the guy would bother to come here. But she'd been wrong. How stupid had he been to leave his gun inside? From now on, he'd be carrying at all times.

Aaron turned and ran up the slope, Julie pounding her fists on his back and yelling at him to put her down. No way in hell was he letting her go until he had her safely back inside.

CHAPTER SIX

Aaron carried Julie bodily up the hill, slinging her over his shoulder as if she weighed nothing. Her sunglasses and Akubra joined her phone on the lawn.

"What are you doing?" she yelled, but he didn't answer, only ran faster toward the lodge. Julie caught a glimpse of the surprised faces of the two swimmers as they flashed by, and then they were up the stairs and back inside the lodge.

Once inside, he lowered her gently onto her feet, and she exploded. "What the hell?" she demanded. "Why are you manhandling me like some kind of caveman?" She slapped at his arms, which were still wrapped around her waist like bands of steel. Very firm, very brawny, bands of steel. There were definitely muscles which hadn't been there before. She would've remembered muscles like this.

Aaron had changed in so many ways. Not only was he more way more serious than she remembered, but she could also add commanding to the list. Or should that be overbearing? Dominating, even? The way he was carrying her had left her no recourse to argue. He'd just picked her up like a sack of potatoes and carried her inside.

He finally let her go, but his eyes darted everywhere, not resting on anything for long, and certainly not looking at her.

What was going on? That creep had been spouting his nonsense, and then, all of a sudden, Aaron had gone crazy.

"My cell phone is still out there," she said, pointing through the doors while readjusting her rumpled clothing.

"Leave it there for now," he growled. "We'll get it later." Then he took her by the elbow and began escorting her toward the rear of the lodge.

"What...?" She tried to pull away from him.

Aaron stopped and stared pointedly at her, his one blue eye flashing dark indigo—a sign that meant he was angry. Really angry. But why was he angry with her?

"Think Julie. That creep knew what you were wearing."

"So wha...Oh. Jeezes," she replied faintly, the implication finally sinking in. It meant the stalker guy had been watching her. Meant that he must be here on the station somewhere. Her heart stuttered in her chest, and she moved closer to Aaron. His large, solid body offered a feeling of security. She'd been wrong. Her stalker was capable of more than she imagined. This was getting out of control. She welcomed Aaron's presence; was suddenly terribly glad he was here. How had she suddenly gone from not wanting a bodyguard to feeling the need for Aaron's presence? It was more than a tad ironic.

"Exactly," Aaron replied. "We need to get you somewhere safe, away from all the doors and windows. And away from all the guests," he added darkly.

"Was it the people in the pool?" she asked dazedly, wondering if the man she'd waved at merrily only minutes before was her crazed stalker.

"No." Aaron stated matter-of-factly. "I checked, both of them were still swimming, neither of them anywhere near their phones. And they both looked as surprised as you did," he added.

"Well, if it wasn't them, then who?" Her head was

spinning, and it was only partially from being carried on Aaron's broad shoulders up the hill. The stalker had been here. On the station. It was too much for her to compute.

"I don't know. But I have a hunch he wasn't watching us while he made the phone call, otherwise he would probably have mentioned me, because I was standing right there next to you." Aaron walked over and deftly closed and locked the large French doors leading out to the veranda, squinting into the sunshine as if he expected someone to leap from the bushes at any second. "I need to get you somewhere safe," he said again.

"The family suite is down at the end of the west wing," she offered numbly. "No guests are allowed down there."

"Show me," he commanded.

She led him down the darkened hallway, jumping at every shadow. Her breathing was coming in ragged bursts, and she had to concentrate hard on getting it under control. She was in no immediate danger, she kept telling herself. Aaron was here, he'd protect her.

Aaron pulled her to a stop outside the door to Daniella's office. He knocked once, but without waiting for an answer, he opened the door and said, "I need my weapons." Holding up a hand, he forestalled her questions. "Then, can you please go and collect Julie's phone and other stuff she dropped down by the billabong and bring them to the family suit? I'll explain when you get there."

"Of course, whatever you want," Daniella replied, all efficiency, as she bent to unlock her safe. Julie wasn't half as convinced by her stepmother's show of acceptance as Aaron clearly was. It must be shock quelling Daniella's tongue right now. Or perhaps it was Julie's pale face; if she looked half as frightened as she felt, Daniella would be able to see it written all over her features. Daniella would be seething with questions. She was a self-confessed control freak, and she ran a tight ship at the luxury lodge. Which wasn't always a bad thing, and for the most part, Julie thought her stepmother did a great job. She cared deeply, but she liked to hide those emotions behind her façade of proficiency and calm leadership.

Daniella squeezed Julie's arm in an effort to show solidarity as Aaron opened the black case. Inside sat a sizable handgun that made Julie gawp in astonishment, another, smaller gun, and a holster. They both watched in fascination as he retrieved the larger weapon and holster, then handed the case back for Daniella to return to the safe. He quickly removed his sports coat, slipped on his shoulder holster, and snapped the gun in place. It was slightly surreal watching Aaron's smooth, practiced movements. It was still hard for Julie to reconcile this version of Aaron—clearly highly trained, skilful, militant, and fierce—with the softer Aaron she'd once known.

"See you in the family suite," Aaron said, already steering Julie out the door, his hand resting lightly on her elbow. Daniella pursed her lips and gave him the barest of nods.

"I shouldn't have taken you outside. It was careless of me," Aaron muttered under his breath as they stalked down the dark hallway. His fingers tightened around her elbow. He sounded angrier at himself than her, and she finally understood. He'd didn't like the fact he'd been caught by surprise. It was self-reproach that'd caused his anger. At least he wasn't mad at her. Aaron had always been his own worst critic, even back when he'd been a simple jackaroo. He hated to let anyone down and would always take any criticism to heart. Julie remembered that she'd thought his misdirected sense of duty might have come from his mother, who'd always seemed overcritical of Aaron, on the few times Julie had met her.

Julie led him into the family sitting room and stopped by

the leather couch, unsure what to do next. Aaron took charge, striding over and tugging the heavy curtains across the large windows, so the room was plunged into semi-darkness. A small table lamp sat only a few feet away, and she switched it on.

"Are there any other entry points to this room?" he asked.

"The door over there leads to the outside. It's a shortcut for us to get to the stables if we need to. But we always keep it locked," she added.

Aaron strode over and checked the door, anyway. The door handle rattled loudly as he shook it with his large hand, but it stayed locked, just like she'd said it should be.

"Who has keys to this door?" he asked, coming back to the middle of the room.

Julie racked her brain. "All the family, of course."

"Which would be?"

Jeezes, he was barking questions at her as if she was a cadet in military training. She wasn't sure she liked it. "That would include me, Steve, Daniella, Dale, Daisy, Skylar. Oh, and I think Nash has one, too," she added belatedly. "I'm not sure if any of the staff have one. Steve might've given Wazza and Alex one."

Aaron made a noise of annoyance, and mumbled something like, "That's too many people, with too easy access."

Julie sat down on the couch, suddenly feeling wobbly.

Just then, the door from the hallway burst open. Aaron reacted with lightning-fast speed, and he had his gun in his hand before Julie had time to blink. She looked over her shoulder to see Daniella standing there with Julie's Akubra, sunglasses, and phone in her hand and her mouth hanging open.

"Sorry," he apologized roughly, re-holstering his gun. "I didn't mean to scare you."

"Is that thing actually loaded?" Daniella asked faintly.

"Of course, it is." He cast his surprised gaze between Julie and her stepmother. "This is what you hired me for, remember?" he said, frowning.

"Yes, I know, but—"

Aaron broke through Daniella's questions. "I have reason to believe the stalker is somewhere on the station. Or at the very least, has been on the property recently."

"How do you know that?" Daniella asked.

"He phoned her. And rattled off some nasty threats. Then he mentioned how Julie was dressed. There's only one way he'd know the exact thing she was wearing today," Aaron said ominously, leaving Daniella to work out the rest for herself.

"He phoned you?" Daniella swapped her appalled gaze from Aaron to Julie.

"Yes," Julie said, much more calmly than she felt. "If you'll sit down, we'll explain it all."

Daniella took a seat on the couch next to Julie, absentmindedly handing over the things she'd retrieved from outside. Julie lay her cell phone carefully on the side table, handling it as if it were about to rear up and bite her. Her stepmother recovered her equilibrium quickly and began asking pertinent questions.

"How did he get your cell number?" Daniella asked, fixing Julie with her piercing stare. "I thought you said he hadn't contacted you on this new phone?"

"I did...I mean, he hasn't...I mean, this is the first time he's called me." Julie began to get flustered, unable to answer her stepmother's questions. She'd very much like the answers herself. How had the stalker got hold of her number? She hadn't given this number out to anyone but close family and friends, and it was unlisted.

"We'll get to the bottom of that soon enough," Aaron said,

stepping closer. "I'll make sure you get a new, untraceable phone, but in the meantime, can I hang on to that one?"

"Sure." Julie gladly handed the phone over, juggling it like it was a hot potato. She was more than happy for it to become Aaron's problem. It felt like the stalker had invaded her privacy all over again, and she wanted nothing more to do with that phone, especially if it was a link to the crazy man.

Daniella watched Julie hand over her cell, but her mind was clearly on more important things. "Should I recall Steve from the horse trek?" Daniella stood and began pacing across the rug. "Dale and Wazza are out with him, as well. Should I ask them all to come back to the lodge?"

Julie could almost read Daniella's mind; if the stalker was out there, the more big, brawny men they had around the lodge, the better. And Julie couldn't help but agree. Not that she didn't trust Aaron to keep her well-guarded, but there was safety in numbers. Wasn't there?

"No, you should keep everything going at the resort as per usual." Aaron replied quickly. "We don't want this stalker to know we're on to him. If he was watching while he talked to Julie, then he's already figured it out. But I have a hunch he wasn't close enough to see us, otherwise he would've possibly mentioned me. And if that's true, then the longer we can keep him in the dark, the better."

"But he's definitely been on the property today at some stage. Could very well still be on the property. That means he could be one of the guests." Daniella covered her mouth with her hand. "Oh God, he could be right here in our midst and we never even knew."

"It's a possibility," Aaron agreed. "But somehow I doubt he'd be that obvious. It'd take some serious balls for your stalker to just walk in here, especially with you surrounded by family and staff." Aaron turned around and began pacing, and his last words were almost lost on the two women. "All the profiling usually shows these kinds of crazed stalkers to be lone individuals with a chip on their shoulder. They're also often socially inept, they don't fit in well, especially in large groups. Do you have any single guests at the moment?" Aaron lifted his thoughtful gaze from the floor to stare at Daniella.

She tucked a stray strand of dark hair behind her ear as she considered his question. Julie was usually a little jealous of Daniella's hair. Unlike Julie's unruly, short hairstyle, Daniella's blunt bob was always perfectly neat and tidy, with hardly a hair out of place. That rule didn't seem to apply today, however, as flyaway strands rose up all over her head. This, more than anything else, was testament to how rattled Daniella must be.

"No. They're mainly couples." Daniella tapped a finger against her lips. "A few groups of four—that'd be two couples sharing a cabin. And one couple is here with their adult kids."

"Right. I'll get Lance to help you go through the guest list and narrow down any potential suspects."

"Good, because I'd hate to think that he's been here as a guest, and we never even suspected."

It was a concept Julie hadn't even considered. She'd always felt so safe on the station. She loved interacting with the guests, loved to get to know them, and prided herself on making their stays as enjoyable as possible. Now she wouldn't be able to look at any of them in the same light again. She hated that the stalker could so easily ruin her one safe place. Ruin her easy acceptance of the people around her. At least there was one person she could trust. She knew Aaron would have her back, no matter what.

"Julie." Aaron waited until he had her undivided attention. "I'd like to remove you from the station. Take you somewhere safe until we can thoroughly assess the threat."

It took a few seconds for Aaron's words to sink in. "Absolutely not," she declared. "I'm not going to let this asshole frighten me out of my home. I'm not leaving." Julie got to her feet. The fact that the stalker might be on the station had rattled her, but she *wasn't* going to let him run her life.

"This changes everything," Aaron said loudly, breaking through Julie's protestations. "He made his threat very obvious in that phone conversation. The danger from this man has now escalated." His multicolored eyes flashed, snaring her focus with their burning intensity. It was almost as if he cared about her welfare. But that was ridiculous.

"I agree with Julie," Daniella came to stand beside Julie, surprising her. "Steve and I both want Julie here, where we know she's safe. After what we went through with Skylar... Well, I know it wasn't Nash's fault that she was kidnapped by the hitman, but Steve and I always wondered if perhaps she would've been safer if she's stayed at Stormcloud. The gunman wouldn't have found it so easy to abduct her, then."

Julie's breath caught in her throat. She'd never realized Steve and Daniella had felt this way. Skylar had agreed to stay at Nash's house, use it as a sort of safe house, rather than come back to Stormcloud. But the gunman had tracked her and Nash down and abducted them at gunpoint. Thank God they'd both come out of it alive. It was serendipitous that Skylar's bad luck might well be her good luck, because Daniella was now on her side.

"And isn't that the whole reason we hired you?" Daniella demanded. "So you could keep her safe if there was any danger. That's your job, isn't it?"

"I thought you'd say as much," Aaron sighed. "But I had to try." Julie got the impression by the small shake of his head that he was used to having to accommodate clients doing crazy things. "Technically, my job is to keep Julie safe, yes.

But I could do my job better if I had more control over her surroundings." Aaron held up his hand to forestall any more arguments. He was conceding defeat. For now.

Aaron began to pace across the rug in front of the couch, and both Daniella and Julie sat down again, Daniella catching Julie's eyes quickly, as if to say, *we won that one*.

"If you're staying here, I'd like to organize a locksmith to come out and fit extra security to the doors and windows," Aaron said. "Today, please."

Daniella snorted. "I'll see what I can organize. But it'll be at least tomorrow before anyone can come out. We don't have a local locksmith in Dimbulah, so they'll need to come from Cairns, which, as you know, is a two-hour drive."

Aaron looked up sharply and mumbled something under his breath that sounded suspiciously like, "bloody little hick towns."

Julie raised a smile. Her first since the phone call. He sounded like a grumpy old man when he said that. She was used to city-folk saying such ignorant things, but he should know better.

"You know we live in the middle of far North Queensland, don't you?" She went up and stood in front of Aaron so that he had to stop pacing across the floor. "Have you lived in the city so long you've forgotten what it's like not to have everything at your fingertips? What it's like to live in a *hick town*?"

He glanced up, but his gaze slid right past her. He was still agitated, and she could see the self-reproach hidden in the depths of his eyes, the fear that he'd missed something important, and it was all his fault. To gain his attention, she lay a hand on his forearm. The heat of him surged into her palm through the fabric of his shirt. She almost withdrew her hand, but managed to steel herself to the riot of emotions that single touch engendered.

"It's okay, Aaron. You couldn't know."

"What?" He rubbed the back of his neck and stared at her hand on his arm and then lifted his multicolored gaze to her face, zeroing in on her eyes. At last, she had his full focus.

"It's not your fault. None of us took this stalker guy seriously. I certainly didn't. Who was to know he might actually appear on the station?" A small shudder ran through her at the thought. "So, stop beating yourself up about it." She patted his arm and shot him a grin, hoping to lighten his mood. But his body heat still burned through his shirt, and an answering heat built inside her stomach.

Aaron's face didn't clear, as she'd hoped it would. Instead, he raised a single eyebrow, the one bisected by the scar, his gaze growing speculative. Uh oh. The last thing she needed was for him to think she still had any feelings for him. Because she didn't. Not a single one. Removing her hand, she carefully walked back over to the couch and sat down. She didn't have to turn around to know that Aaron's gaze followed her every move.

Once she was seated, Aaron finally directed his focus back to Daniella. "Would you have anything I could use to secure the outer door in the meantime? Any bolts or a padlock and a latch I could use?"

"Possibly," Daniella replied. "If we wait, Steve will know where—"

"I'd like to do this as soon as possible," Aaron interrupted her. "If we have at least one room that's completely secure, I'll feel much better. And I'm pretty handy. I'm sure I can manage to fit a few bolts," he said, looking her directly in the eye and squaring his shoulders ever so slightly.

Julie was going to remind Daniella about Aaron's time spent working on the farm, but after she caught the cold look her stepmother shot at Aaron's back, she decided not to. Daniella didn't like to have her authority questioned, but she also knew Aaron was right. It'd do her stepmother good to listen to someone else for a while.

"Right, let me go and check in the machinery shed. I'm sure Steve has got all sorts of stuff out there." Daniella's tone was icy. It wouldn't do if Aaron put Daniella off-side. But he was clearly used to calling the shots when it came to his job, and wasn't about to let anyone get in his way. She liked the idea that Daniella didn't scare him.

"I'll be back soon," Daniella said.

"Perhaps we should set up a policy of knocking before entering a room," Aaron said, right before she left the room.

"Good idea." Daniella gave him a tight smile, and her gaze hovered for a spilt second on the weapon half-hidden beneath Aaron's jacket. "I'll pass that detail around."

"Can you give me a quick tour of the rest of the family suites?" Aaron asked as soon as Daniella disappeared. "I'd like to know what else I'm dealing with."

"Okay. As long as you're sure it's safe." She didn't want to admit how much that phone call had freaked her out. But she'd been beginning to feel sheltered in this familiar room. Out of sight and out of mind. A sudden tremor ran through her at the thought of leaving this protective haven.

"You'll be safe with me, Julie," Aaron assured her, his voice deep and calming.

She wasn't going to let some idiot who thought he could intimidate her frighten her out of her own home. Straightening her shoulders, she said, "Follow me."

She led him out the door and to the right. Aaron stuck so close to her side, he brushed her shoulder with his bicep. "This is Dale's room," she said, opening the door at the end of the hallway. Dale's room was isolated at the end of the wing, affording him a little more privacy. "Although he only sleeps here about half the time. And once he and Daisy get married, he'll probably move permanently out to Daisy's place at the outstation."

"Dale and Daisy are getting married?" he said, poking his head around the door and surveying the room.

Why did he sound so surprised? "Yes, at the end of the year. Once muster is over and the rainy season starts again. They're having it here on the station. It should be lovely." Julie hid a sigh of satisfaction. It'd be more than lovely if all Daisy's plans came to fruition. Julie was so proud to be involved with the preparations. Even though she'd probably never get married, it was nice to see Dale and Daisy, who were so much in love, get what they deserved.

At least Dale had made his bed this morning, Julie noted. The room was big, decorated in dark blues and wood accents, with a large picture window affording a view of the corner of the billabong with the escarpment rising behind it. Julie often envied Dale this room, as it had the best view, by far. All the rest of the bedrooms looked out toward the back of the lodge, at the stables up the hill.

Aaron closed the door and Julie turned around and led him to the door nearly opposite the family room. "This is my room." Her hand rested on the doorknob, suddenly reluctant for some reason to open the door. "Would you rather check out the other rooms first?" She went to turn away, but his hand on her waist stopped her.

"We'll get to those in a moment." He raised his chin to indicate she open her door. "Let me go first."

She followed him closely, almost tripping over his heels. But he held her back until he made sure the room was safe. His cautious vigilance was unsettling. Surely, the guy wouldn't dare enter her bedroom? How would he even know where she slept?

"All clear," he announced, almost as if he'd been expecting someone to be hiding in her room. Which perhaps he had. It was his job to be suspicious, after all.

It felt more than a little weird, watching Aaron stalk around her room, firstly making sure the windows were locked, and closing the curtains, then opening the closet door and checking under the bed. Strangely intimate.

She tried to see her room through his eyes. A large bed took pride of place in the middle of the room. Rustic, wooden headboard and matching side tables. A brightly colored bedspread with a Mexican pattern set the theme for the rest of the room, which was also full of bright colors. A comfy armchair, stacked high with blue and orange pillows, was her favorite reading nook in the corner. It certainly wasn't prissy or pink, but then she'd never really been a girly girl.

"What's this then?" Aaron had stopped beside her tallboy dresser. He was staring at a picture in a silver frame on the top.

Jeezes, she'd forgotten all about that photo. How many times had she thrown it in the bin in a fit of rage, only to retrieve it again almost straightaway. The photo was of a much younger version of herself, smiling beatifically, with her arm wrapped around the waist of nineteen-year-old Aaron, who also had a happy grin on his face.

"Why did you keep this?" he demanded, picking up the photo and holding it out for her to see.

CHAPTER SEVEN

Aaron let the frame rest in the palm of his hand. Julie had a photo of him with her arm wrapped around his waist. He was suddenly assaulted by memories. Julie smiling at him from atop her palomino horse as she galloped beside him. She loved the speed; loved the freedom of the wind through her hair.

They'd been happy together. Young and carefree. And in love. They'd both professed their undying love for each other. Aaron had thought she was the one. So bright and bubbly, confident and cheerful, she'd lit a fire inside of him.

But on the day he turned nineteen, he'd put out the flames of that fire. Squashed the burning coals down far behind all the walls he put up around his heart, so he'd never feel that special heat again. Denial was a wondrous thing. And it'd nearly worked. He'd almost been able to forget about Julie.

Until today.

Until he stared into that photo and knew that all the denial in the world couldn't wipe away the feelings they'd had for each other.

Julie stared at him, like some wild animal he caught in the corner of the room, looking for an escape.

"Yoo-hoo, where are you? I've got the tools and equipment

you wanted." Daniella's voice drifted in from the hallway, breaking the spell over the room.

"In here," Julie called, relief evident in her voice. "We'll be out in a second."

Aaron placed the photo carefully back on the dresser. Julie might've got away without an explanation this time, but he was a patient man. He'd ask her later. Although, he wasn't sure he wanted to hear her answer. Did he really want to know she'd been pining for him all this time? Because if she had, it'd make him feel doubly like the dishonorable reprobate.

He glanced up and watched Julie draw in a deep breath and paint a happy smile on her face. At the age of seventeen, her smile had been incandescent, and she'd turned it on without seemingly any effort. But now, even though the smile was still there, there was a weary heaviness dragging down the corners of her mouth. Like the weight of the world sat on her shoulders. A pang of longing flashed through him. Longing and loneliness. He suddenly knew that he wanted to help Julie. It was the least he could do.

Wasn't it ironic? A few measly hours ago, Aaron hadn't wanted anything to do with this job. He'd been going to ask Jake to reassign him at the first available option. But now his protection instincts had kicked up a notch, and he knew he'd stay until the end. Because it was Julie.

"After you," he said with a sweep of his hand. She gave him a sideways glance, but happily trotted out the door and across the hall into the family lounge.

Daniella had laid out all sorts of tools and odd bits of metal on the floor next to the rear exit. Aaron ambled over and bent down to examine the haul. "Thanks," he said, straightening up once more. "I'm going to put a call in to Shield and get Lance caught up on what we need. Can I send him your number?"

"Of course." Daniella nodded her head regally. Aaron still wasn't sure what to make of Daniella. She was prickly and controlling. She ran this station and the resort with a firm hand and a cool business head, and it showed. Stormcloud was *the* top exclusive resort in all of Queensland, or so he'd been told. She and Steve had built this resort from the ground up, and turned it into a highly profitable asset. But then, when he'd watched her interplay with her husband Steve, Aaron could see there was a softer side to Daniella, that perhaps she kept hidden from those who weren't close to her. He wondered what Julie thought of her stepmother.

Aaron put those thoughts aside as he dialled in to HQ. Jake picked up on the second ring and Aaron spent the next five minutes bringing him up to speed on recent developments. He asked Jake to fill Nash in on the details as well; they needed to keep their police counterparts up to date.

He turned from staring at the external door and pocketed his phone, just in time to hear Daniella say, "It's okay, honey. We all have your back. No one blames you for any of this." Interesting. It seemed she did care, after all. It was nice to see that Daniella seemed to treat Julie the same as she would her other two biological children.

"Lance will call back in five minutes. He'll need the names of all the guests, so he can start checking them out," Aaron said, when both women turned to look at him.

"Right, I'd better get back to the office." Daniella's businesslike persona was securely back in place. "I'll see if I can find a locksmith who can come out as well. I'm assuming you don't need me anymore?"

"We'll be fine," Aaron replied. "We're just going to chill in here, while I add some extra security to the doors and windows in the family wing, as long as that's okay with you?"

"Do what you need to do." Daniella stood and made her

way to the door.

"I'd like to call a full family and staff meeting after dinner, however," Aaron said. "If that's okay with you?"

A pained look crossed Julie's face. But Daniella replied, "Yes, of course. That's a good idea," before she left the room.

Aaron wondered why Julie was so hesitant to have everyone gathered together. He knew it wasn't because she didn't like being the center of attention, because she could often be found in the middle of a group of people, telling one of her wild jokes, or showing off a magic trick. It was probably more to do with her not wanting to feel like a burden. It seemed Julie had been carrying this secret by herself for way too long. Which was sad. She might not want other people to know, but in his experience, they always found out in the end. Secrets had a way of coming to light. And she might need their help in the future. The more people she had on her side, the less chance this stalker had of getting even remotely close to her.

Julie sat on the leather couch and absently picked up a deck of cards sitting on the coffee table, then began shuffling them. Aaron would bet she had packs stashed all over the house. He'd noticed another deck on her bedside table in her room earlier. She'd always loved to play Solitaire whenever she had a spare moment, and it seemed she'd at least kept that little quirk over time.

Kneeling, he sorted through the bits of metal Daniella had scattered on the floorboards. There was an old latch and a couple of padlocks. That'd do to help secure the door until the locksmith could get here. He'd checked the windows earlier and was glad to see they were fixed in place and couldn't be opened—as many large windows often were— which meant it was one less thing he had to worry about. If someone was determined to get in, they could always smash a window, but that sort of noise would alert everyone in the vicinity, and he doubted that was the stalker's plan. This sort of guy usually worked alone, using the element of surprise or stealth to bring down their intended victim.

He found some screws and a cordless drill and went over to measure up the door. Julie was still uncommonly quiet on the couch.

He may as well use this time to catch up with what Julie had been doing with her life in the past twelve years.

"This seems like a pretty nice place to live," he said, finding the right size drill bit and locking it into place. "I remember you talking about it, back when…back at Roseby Downs," he added quickly. "But I thought you wanted to stay with Connie and Tony. Help them out with the property."

Julie cast him an unreadable gaze. "At the time, I did want to stay on. But then things changed. I decided to go to Uni in Brisbane, and I discovered I had other talents besides mustering sheep all day. I guess you could say I broadened my horizons." She gave a small shrug.

Aaron had made a point not to seek out any information about Julie's life after he left. On the few occasions he had allowed himself to think about her, he'd imagined her happy and carefree on the farm. She'd had lots of ideas on how to improve the pastures and increase their sheep-carrying capacity. Tony didn't have any biological kids of his own, and he'd always treated Julie as if she was his, right from the start. Tony and Connie were happy for her input, and it seemed that she was destined to take the farm over one day. He wondered what'd happened to change her mind. Why had she left the country to head to Brisbane? But those questions might take him down the path of his own reasons for leaving, so he wisely decided to leave that topic alone, for now. For some reason, he'd never been able to imagine her married. At the time, he'd told himself it was because there was no one who would suit her in that little hick town. But perhaps he'd been kidding himself.

"Why didn't you go back to Dalgety when all this happened?" He would've thought that was where she might've felt most secure. As far as he knew, Julie had only spent a few weeks every year during school holidays at Stormcloud. He assumed her connection would be stronger with Roseby Downs.

"Because Mum would've freaked out. Even though I'd love nothing better than to freak Mum out." She gave a wicked little grin, and Aaron remembered how Julie had always liked to push her mother's buttons, just to get a rise out of her. It was an interesting mother-daughter relationship, and while they were close, they were also different in lots of ways. Aaron had no idea where Julie got her sassy side from. It certainly wasn't from Steve; even his short acquaintance with the man told him that. And while Connie had loved a laugh, she was more uncompromising than Julie.

"But I also knew I'd be more easily found down there," Julie continued. "Because I kept Mum's name, and all that."

"You're probably right," Aaron agreed. If she was trying to make a clean break from her old life, Stormcloud was the better choice. Her connections with the luxury lodge would be less well known. He held up a hand to let her know he was about to make some noise, then he quickly drilled two holes into the wooden door. "Go on," he encouraged, blowing the sawdust away.

"It was a sort of serendipity, actually," Julie stopped shuffling the cards long enough to smile up at Aaron. His heart shifted in his chest. Her smile still called to him. "Steve phoned me only a few days after the...the break-in, and asked if I could possibly lend a hand. They were going through a tough time. I'm not sure if you heard, but one of the staff, Karri, was found dead in a flooded creek."

Aaron nodded. Daniella had given him a quick rundown

in the meeting room earlier, but he'd also certainly heard the rumors and read the newspaper articles—it'd been a big story at the time. It turned out that another one of the staff had been embezzling money from the station, and had killed Karri to stop her from exposing the scheme.

"Dad was beside himself with worry, and he needed help, as another girl had left a month or so ago, leaving him short-handed. I jumped at the chance to get back on a horse. I missed it. All the hard yakka, and the dust and heat and flies."

Aaron made a noise of quiet disbelief.

"No, don't laugh. I know it sounds strange, but all that time cooped up in an office, it changed me. I spent five years with that marketing firm, sitting at a desk day after day. And then with this stalker... Well, it just felt so good to get out into the open air again, feel the sunshine. Get that satisfying physical exhaustion at the end of the day. You remember that, don't you?"

Of course he did. Did he miss it, though, like she seemed to be implying with her questioning gaze? Yes. And no. And even if he did miss it, his life was in the city now. Even if he moved on from Shield, he'd always want to stay in the protection game. He was surprised at how uniquely suited he'd been to becoming a bodyguard. He slipped into the role so easily. There'd been a raft of physical and mental tests he needed to pass. And even though he had no military training, he'd learned the basic skills quickly. After a few months of intensive training in hand-to-hand combat and weapon handling, he seemed to have a knack for it, an innate knowledge that it took other men years to learn.

Perhaps he had his father to thank for that. The thought brought a scowl to his face. Aaron hated to think that his father had passed on any of his genetic traits. Especially these darker characteristics. But there was no other explanation as to why he was so good at what he did. His father hadn't been a nice man, and as far as Aaron was concerned, he had no redeemable characteristics at all. He clenched his fist around the screwdriver. He'd certainly show his deadbeat father exactly how he felt about him if he ever ran into him. But that was unlikely to happen; he didn't even know the man's last name.

"The other reason I moved here was to help Daniella promote the station. She's always hinted—and you know her hints are far from subtle—that she thought the station might become more profitable if only she could get a handle on the social media aspect of it all. With my marketing degree, I knew I could help her. It was a chance to get back into doing the things I most loved about marketing, yet be away from all the hype and pressure of the corporate business world."

"It sounds like you're good at what you do."

"I was... I am," she admitted, flipping cards over on the table. "But being good at something doesn't always mean you find joy in it."

"True." It seemed like Julie had become a lot more philosophical. She used to run at things like a bull at a gate. Even though he was good at his job, and he couldn't see himself doing anything else, there were times when he wondered what it might be like to do something else. To be someone else. Without the spectre of his father hanging over his head. Not that he'd ever admit to wanting to settle down and have a family, because that was definitely not on his agenda. He was never going to have children.

"What about you?" She waved a hand at him and grinned. "I admit, I sometimes wondered what'd become of you." Aaron noticed the tips of her ears turning pink, but she waded on, pretending to ignore her reaction. "But never in a million years did I ever imagine you wanting to join a security company. It just seems so..."

So what, he wondered? So out of character? Perhaps it had been. But he was no longer the man he'd once been. All his priorities were different now.

He took his time fixing the latch to the door and positioning the screw so he could formulate his answer. "Maybe it came as a surprise to you, but I slipped into it fairly easily. I got a job as a bouncer at a nightclub almost as soon as I got to Sydney." He winced, and rolled on with his story, hoping she wouldn't ask him why he'd left to go to Sydney in the first place. "I think because of my size, it was easy to get that job. I met Jake a year after I moved to Sydney. He and his mate Timothy were just starting up Shield Solutions, and they recruited me. Took a chance on me."

"Oh. Okay." Julie wouldn't look at him. "So, what is it exactly that you do all day? I mean, you've been here less than two hours and you're fixing a bolt to a door. That's not how I would imagine a bodyguard's day to go." She raised a hint of a smile, showing her straight, white teeth for a mere instant.

Aaron drew in a deep breath. He'd been asked this question before, but still found it hard to encompass everything that went into being a protection agent. "It's different every day. One day I might be a driver. Which often means waiting in a car for hours, or carrying a client's shopping bags." Aaron grunted. How many times had he had to do that? Especially with one client, the wife of a rich diplomat, who thought Aaron was her own personal shopping assistant. "Other times I work as a sort of personal assistant, helping clients work out their schedules and routines to make sure they stay safe. Sometimes I'm required as a personal protection agent, and then I have to stick real close to a client, follow them everywhere. You can never underestimate anyone when you're on guard."

"What kind of people do you look after? Do you really rub

shoulders with the rich and famous?"

"Sometimes," he admitted. "We get all sorts. Politicians, celebrities, government big shots, wealthy families." He wanted to add that she fell into that last category, but didn't think she would appreciate it. "Our job is to save them from harm. That's why we carry a weapon."

"Aren't you ever scared? You might get hurt, or…" She didn't finish her thought, her voice small but her blue eyes big and round.

"Nah." Aaron picked up a hammer and adopted a cocky posture. "You get hurt, hurt 'em back. You get killed…walk it off."

"What?" She looked at him, flabbergasted that he could be so flippant. "Wait. I recognize that." Her hand went up in the air. "Isn't that a quote from a Captain America movie?" She laughed as he raised an eyebrow in her direction. "Sorry, but I'm a bit of a Marvel movie buff," she said by way of explanation. "And I'm sure that's something Captain Steve Rogers might say."

"Actually, yes, it is." He lay down the hammer and stood, wandering over to where she sat. "I'm a Marvel fan myself. I've seen them all. Probably watched most of them at least three or four times."

How interesting, they had something in common. She'd never professed a liking for the movies back when he'd first known her. This was a new thing.

Julie turned her watercolor-blue eyes up to him. "I think my favorite quote is by Nick Fury." She pursed her lips and studied him for a few seconds. He thought he knew what she was going to say next, and he flinched inwardly. "I still believe in heroes."

Yep, that was the one. Ducking his head, he turned away. One thing was for sure; he was no hero.

CHAPTER EIGHT

Julie sat at the end of the boardroom table, watching everyone file in. The blinds had all been drawn on Aaron's orders, and it felt crowded and claustrophobic. Even though it was after nine at night and dark outside, they rarely, if ever, drew the blinds. The lodge had been built to take in the amazing natural beauty surrounding it, and even at night all the windows remained open, to let in the moonlight vista over the billabong, backlit by the starry skies. But not anymore. Not with a crazed stalker perhaps prowling around outside. She might have to get used to feeling caged in for a while.

Dale and Daisy came in holding hands and took their seats at the other end of the table. They were so cute together; Julie couldn't help but flash them a happy grin as they sat down. Dale raised a quizzical eyebrow, but kept his questions to himself.

Bindi, Sasha, and Wazza were already seated on the far side. The two girls had their heads together, talking quietly. They'd become firm friends from the very first day Sasha had started work at the station six months ago. Bindi was Skylar's assistant cook, and Sasha attended to front reception, as well as other odd jobs, like helping with table service at mealtime, and even cleaning the cabins if the cleaning staff were run off their feet. Everyone who worked at the lodge all had various duties, often mixing and matching skills to fill a hole if other staff were busy. It came with the territory when working for a family-run property. Even Julie herself, who was primarily employed to do the marketing and help Daniella out with the admin, often found herself in the kitchen with Skylar—she'd even taken over the cooking for a few weeks when Skylar had been involved in the helicopter crash and subsequent kidnapping—as well as helping her dad with the horses. Julie was a natural with the horses; it came from long hours spent in the saddle as a kid working on Tony's sheep farm. She was always the first to put up her hand to lead a trail ride, and had even assisted Wazza a few times moving small mobs of cattle near the main lodge.

Wazza was the only one who had a clearly defined role of lead station hand, dealing with the cattle and horses, but even his duties were large and varied. One day he could be out fixing a fence, the next moving cattle, and the next he could be teaching a guest the basics of good horsemanship. Wazza finally remembered to remove his Akubra, circumspectly placing it on the table in front of him. Daniella hated it when he wore his hat inside, but that hat seemed to be permanently fixed to his head, and he was always suffering the lash of Daniella's sharp reprimands. Her stepmother didn't seem to have noticed this time, however.

Skylar and Nash trailed in, Nash still in his police uniform, which meant he must've come straight from the station in Dimbulah. Skylar inclined her head in Julie's direction, then she led Nash to the seat next to Steve, opposite Bindi and Sasha. Nash whispered something into Skylar's ear, and she giggled like a schoolgirl. Which made Julie want to giggle. Nash was so good for Skylar, his lightness and kindness a contrast to Skylar's often darker and more reserved moods.

They were a foil for each other, bringing out the best in each other. It was great news when Skylar had announced she was moving in with Nash, who'd bought a small hobby farm twenty minutes down the road. Everyone had cheered, they were so delighted. Even Daniella had looked happy, which spoke volumes.

Alek was the last to enter. Pulling the door shut behind him, he looked a little flustered. Alek was in charge of guest activities, and Julie knew he would've been corralling the last of the straggling guests down to the open-air cinema, so he could finally leave them to their own devices and join the meeting. Alek ran a hand over his hair, patting it down and making his man-bun look respectable again. He put his clipboard on the table and then looked toward her end, where she sat with Aaron on one side and Daniella on the other. The question in his gaze was unmistakable.

Julie pulled a breath deep into her lungs, held it there, and then expelled it slowly. Everyone was about to learn the truth about her, and she wasn't sure she was ready. Drawing in another deep breath, she tipped her head back, so she didn't have to look at the sea of faces now before her. Feeling a little calmer, she cast a quick glance at Aaron in the chair next to her. His hard, competent mask was back in place.

This afternoon they'd talked as he fixed the extra security on the door in the family lounge. Talked about normal things, like how she'd done a degree in marketing, discovering she was really good at it, and had found a job almost straight away, then working her way up through the company. They even realized they loved the same type of movies. She'd followed him through each bedroom as he checked for other entry points and made sure all the windows were secure, continuing to chat and get to know each other again. Apart from when he'd found that damned photo, an uneasy sort of truce had formed between them. She still wasn't going to forgive him for what he'd done, but it was also intriguing, digging deeper into his life, finding out how he'd lived over the past twelve years.

At one stage, he'd removed his sports coat, revealing the gun he carried so comfortably in a holster strapped to his shoulder. Out of everything she'd learned about him today, the sight of that weapon really drove it home to her. Aaron was no longer the warm-hearted, caring, and courageous man she'd once been in love with. And she needed to remember that. He was a ruthless killer. Well, maybe that was being a bit melodramatic. But he was certainly much harder, both on the inside and the outside.

She could personally testify to the way the outside of him had changed. Heavily beefed-up shoulders and neck, and from what she could make out through the black T-shirt, rock-hard abs and pecs, as well. Julie had watched surreptitiously as he'd flexed his arms and back, bringing out a low sheen of sweat as he worked on the door fasteners. At the thought of all those hardened muscles, a warmth pooled in her lower abdomen. Perhaps, if he got hot enough, he might take his T-shirt off, as well…then—

Daniella stood, and a hush descended over the room, and Julie pushed away all the wildly inappropriate thoughts of Aaron.

"Thanks for coming, everyone. I know you're all busy. You're probably all wondering why we've called this meeting."

Murmurs of accord rumbled around the table. And by the looks of the glances everyone was throwing in Aaron's direction, they were all wondering who the stranger in their midst was, as well. Daniella pre-empted them all, by saying, "Let me introduce you to Aaron Powell. He can tell you who he is and then we'll go into the details."

Aaron stood, his presence suddenly filling the room.

"Hello," he said, deep voice echoing around the table. "As Daniella said, I'm Aaron, and I work for a company called Shield Solutions. I've been called out to help with a security problem." He paused and drew in a breath. "I don't believe many of you know this, but Julie is being harassed by an unpleasant individual, and those threats have escalated in recent days." A rumble of dissent started, and Julie suddenly felt all eyes on her. "I'm here to provide her protection and guidance until we track down this…person." Aaron sat down again and leaned in toward Julie, almost as if offering comfort, as if shielding her from what was about to come.

There was dumbfounded silence around the table. Nash was the only one—besides Steve and Daniella—who had any idea of Julie's secret. The looks people were throwing at her made her want to disappear through a hole in the floor. But she squared her shoulders and lifted her chin.

"Do you mean you're a bodyguard?" Wazza called out, the first to recover his voice.

Julie wanted to smirk in Aaron's direction.

"Wait, are you saying that Julie has a stalker?" That was Skylar, and she threw Nash a suspicious glance. Nash grimaced but said nothing, and Skylar's look clearly said that they were going to have a conversation later.

Aaron looked at Daniella, signaling that perhaps she should take over.

"Yes, I guess you could say that," Daniella replied, slowly standing up.

Questions began to fly around the room, and Julie could hardly hear herself think for the noise.

Steve also stood up quietly next to Daniella, never saying a word. People slowly stopped speaking as they noticed him. Julie loved how her father commanded such respect. He had a quiet strength that everyone gravitated toward. "Let Daniella finish," he said. "Then if you still have questions, we'll try and answer them as best we can."

Daniella cleared her throat. "The short version is, a man took an unnatural interest in Julie while she was still living in Brisbane. He sent her menacing letters and texts, and even broke into her house one night, but thank God Julie wasn't home."

Skylar gasped and covered her mouth. Julie understood her shock. Julie would've been just as appalled if she was the one hearing all this for the first time. Looking into Skylar's frightened blue eyes, Julie suddenly wished that she'd made time to tell her stepsister personally what was going on. After what Skylar had been through lately, of course, this news would traumatize her. But after the frightening phone call today, Aaron had kept her sequestered in the family wing all afternoon. She hadn't had time or space to talk to either of her step-siblings. It was an oversight, and Julie now wished she'd pushed Aaron harder to let her talk to her family. But at least they were keeping the abortion side of the story a secret for now, which would give her time to fill Skylar and Dale in personally later. She made a mental pact with herself to talk to her step-siblings tonight. It was unfair to keep them in the dark any longer.

"But she thought she'd got rid of him when she moved to Stormcloud," Daniella continued. "It seems she was mistaken, however, as his threats have started up again. Julie only told us about this yesterday, otherwise we would've done something earlier." Daniella was obviously doing her best to keep the condemnation out of her voice, but Julie heard it. And Daniella probably had a right to be mad. Julie had possibly put everyone on the station in peril by keeping her problem to herself. "The man in question also attempted to contact Julie via her cell phone today, and now we have reason to believe he may be in the area. This is no longer an idle threat; we need to stay alert and on the lookout. If this person has in fact been on the station, we need to find out how he got here and if he's still here."

"Is there anything we can do to help?" Wazza also stood, directing his question at Steve, ignoring Aaron. Which wasn't surprising. Aaron was a stranger, and Wazza—perhaps rightly so—didn't trust him. "Because you know we all have your back." His steady gaze found Julie's. "You know this asshole won't get near you with us around." He gestured around the table and there were murmurs of agreement. "If you see him, just point me in the direction. I'll soon make him wish he'd never laid eyes on you." Wazza flicked a quick glance in Nash's direction, but the senior constable merely twitched an eyebrow and retook his seat.

Sudden tears pricked at the back of Julie's eyelids. She'd seen firsthand how loyal and protective the staff were during the trouble with the murderer, as well as Skylar's hitman. But it was something else to know that same staunch commitment she saw in all their eyes was also attributed to her.

"Thank you," she replied softly with a smile, pushing the lump in her throat back down. The last thing she was going to do today was cry in front of everyone.

Steve nodded in Wazza's direction but remained seated. "Thank you, Wazza. And thank you everyone else. But there is no need to get physically violent. That won't help anyone," Steve warned, wagging his finger in Wazza's direction. "Nash is also helping, he's already alerted the office in Mareeba, and they'll conduct their own investigation into trying to find this man."

"Of course, I'll do anything to keep Julie safe," Nash replied, standing and acknowledging Steve, then he locked gazes with Aaron. "I've also called in a few favors from friends in the force in Brisbane, as well as a few of my...other contacts to help me dig into the reputation of this security company, Shield, and this gentleman's profile." Nash's cheery smile was nowhere to be seen tonight. His blond surfer good looks trained into a frown, and mouth drawn down into a hard line.

"I wouldn't expect anything less," Aaron replied lightly. "And what did you find?"

"That Shield has an excellent standing in the field," Nash replied. "The company has been around for nearly ten years and has grown their clientele as well as their good name over that time. And the owner of the company has great respect for you."

The last comment seemed to take Aaron a little by surprise, as he drew back into his seat.

"So, I'm happy to leave Julie in your capable hands," Nash said, eliciting a smile from Aaron. "For now," he qualified, and Aaron narrowed his gaze.

"That's great, thanks, Nash," Daniella's voice broke the simmering tension in the room. "My brother, Dean, also highly recommends Shield. So, I think we can rest assured that Aaron will do a good job of guarding Julie, as well as guiding us through the next few days. Along with your help, and that of the Queensland police force, if we need it, of course," Daniella added quickly.

Just as Nash sat down, Dale stood and took his place, garnering everyone's attention. "What does it all mean, though?" He drummed his fingers on the table. "How is it going to affect Julie? And us? And the station? I want to know what your plans are to protect her." It was Dale's turn to cast a belligerent glance toward Aaron.

What was it with all the men in her life? It was nice that they all cared so much about her, and were determined to protect her. But really? Couldn't they tone down the testosterone a little? All this male posturing was getting a bit much. Aaron seemed to be taking it all in his stride, however.

"I mean, we've been through all this before, when Skylar was under threat. Even with a damn good cop by her side, he still couldn't stop her from being abducted," Dale's voice was a low growl. "What does this guy want? How much of a threat does he pose?"

Steve and Daniella exchanged glances and then indicated that Aaron should answer this one.

"Unfortunately, I can't answer you, yet. What I can say, is that Skylar's case was very different. You had an armed and dangerous ex-military criminal hunting her down. Julie's stalker is most likely a disgruntled, slightly unhinged member of the public. We don't have a reliable profile put together on this guy yet, so I can't say for sure what he will and won't do. But…" Aaron held up a hand as Dale started to mutter under his breath "…in most documented stalker cases, especially the ones I've worked, the stalker rarely, if ever, becomes physically violent. It rarely escalates to a state where the client is under immediate threat. And if that does happen, we often have plenty of warning. These sorts of guys become absolutely obsessed with their target, and will try and contact them and get close to them in any way they can. Of course, we'll take nothing for granted. We don't have a lot to go on yet. I've got a specialist looking into the last letter he sent to Julie, so he'll be able to give us a hint as to what kind of threat this guy is soon."

This surprised Julie a little. Aaron seemed to be downplaying the seriousness of this stalker to the group around the table. Perhaps it was a deliberate ploy, so they wouldn't freak out.

"I'll also remain close by Julie's side at all times, that is the role of a personal protection agent."

Julie stifled a groan. They'd talked it over this afternoon, and she'd conceded that his presence as a consultant had been thrown out the window when the stalker called. He was determined to be her bodyguard, after all. Just what she needed, Aaron Powell invading her personal space, twenty-four-seven.

"And as to how this will affect the rest of you, Steve and I are working on getting a raft of security measures up and running. That'll entail things such as an upgrade to make the front gate work via remote control, so you can lock and unlock it from a car, or even from the lodge. It'll mean more cameras around the outside of the lodge, the stables, and other outbuildings, as well as the perimeter fencing. But nothing intrusive or personal," Aaron added, when he noticed a look of dismay pass between Bindi and Sasha. "This will all be legal and above board. These security measures are designed to help keep an eye on the sections of the station that are usually out of sight. They're not intended to spy on the staff in any way."

Julie heard his unspoken message loud and clear, as long as everyone was doing what they were supposed to be doing, there wouldn't be a problem. She hoped the others understood that, too.

"But other than that, we've decided the station will keep operating as per normal. Everyone should continue on with their daily routine like nothing has changed, but of course you should keep your eyes and ears open for anything out of the ordinary, and report it to me at once. There is no need to put this whole place into lockdown. At least, not yet."

Skylar gave a horrified gasp. "Is that something that might happen?" Her gaze flew to her mother, and Nash lay a soothing hand on her shoulder. Julie clearly remembered that when Skylar had been under threat, Daniella had wanted her to come back and shelter at Stormcloud. But Nash and Skylar had decided she'd be safer staying with Nash, that way the resort could continue to run as usual. Should Julie do the same thing? Offer to leave the station, to remove the threat from everyone around her? Like Aaron had just said, this was a completely different scenario than that of Skylar's, but still…perhaps she could keep it in mind. She didn't want to leave the security of Stormcloud, but if it came down to it, she would, if it meant keeping everyone else safe.

Sasha, Bindi, and Alek all looked alarmed at the idea. They wouldn't want to lose their jobs if the station shut down.

"Not if we can help it," Daniella replied. "I'm sure that between Aaron and Nash, they'll find this guy in a day or two, and we can all go back to our normal lives. And jobs." Julie knew that last words had been meant to soothe the team's fears. But even if they did shut down Stormcloud, they'd always look after their staff. They were the backbone of the resort, and without them, this would all be nothing.

"What about the muster?" Dale said into the silence. "We've got a crew coming in three days." He cast a worried frown in Steve's direction. "Do we go ahead with that?"

"Yes, that will continue as planned," Steve replied calmly.

Julie had almost forgotten about that in all the happenings today. Was now the right time to bring up the fact she'd be going on the muster as well? Because she wasn't going to miss this for anything. She'd been delighted when Skylar had asked if she'd like to take the job. Usually they hired in a cook; it would've been too much for Skylar to prepare all the guest's gourmet meals and cook for up to twenty hungry ringers as well. The cook needed to be out at the muster site, as they could often be a half-day drive away from the main lodge. It'd be too late to hire a cook now, on such short notice. They hadn't discussed it, but if Aaron said they should all just go about their daily business, as if nothing had changed, then surely mustering fell into that category.

"Well, it looks like you're going on the muster then, too." Julie smiled brightly at Aaron. "Because I'm the camp cook this year." Aaron would fit in just fine out on muster. All his years as a jackaroo would stand him in good stead. A memory of him in worn jeans, hugging his impressive thighs, wormed its way into Julie's mind.

Aaron's head shot up. "Not a good idea. You need to stay here, where I can control things." His handsome face remained impassive, but she saw the telltale lines around his eyes that meant he wasn't giving in on this one.

Now hold on just a minute. Julie's smile turned into a frown. She might've just agreed to take Aaron on as a bodyguard, but that didn't mean he could dictate the whole of her life.

CHAPTER NINE

Aaron glanced up from his computer screen. Where was Julie? If she wasn't here in the next five minutes, he was going to look for her. It was mid-morning, but the family lounge area was dim, as the curtains remained drawn. Daniella had impatiently flicked on a couple of table lamps when she'd come in earlier and found Aaron working in the near-dark. Aaron had turned this room into a version of his own operations center. He'd asked Daniella to set a printer with scanner and modem features up on a table in the corner, next to his laptop and other paraphernalia. He'd also slept in here, on a mattress on the floor. It was directly across the hall from Julie's room, close enough for him to be there in a split second, if she needed him.

Last night had been uneventful. Julie said she'd slept soundly, although judging by the dark smudges beneath her blue eyes, that might be a lie. Aaron was naturally a light sleeper, and he was also used to running on a few hours' sleep while working a job. It'd taken him a while to reacquaint himself with country night noises. Living in the city, he'd become used to the hum of traffic and the wail of a police siren at night. It was never truly silent in the city. But then, it wasn't silent here, either. Even through the closed windows, he could hear the silken hoot of an owl in the trees down by the billabong. The soft thumping as a herd of kangaroos jumped past the window. A symphony of croaking from the frogs who inhabited the high rushes around the water's edge. Then the high-pitched screech of a hunting fox, that sounded eerily like a human baby crying, had woken him around three am and he'd found himself reaching for his gun before he figured out what the sound was. He hadn't really been able to get back to sleep after that.

For a second, he'd imagined what it'd be like to be lying out in his swag bed beneath the branches down by the billabong, staring up at the stars. It was one part of living on a farm he'd always enjoyed. Tony's sheep property hadn't been nearly as big as this cattle station, so there wasn't often a need to spend a night away from the main house during a muster. But he'd taken part in many a campout when he was younger, usually at his best friend Jason's place. Or after attending a local Bachelor and Spinsters ball, or a country music festival, he'd unroll his sleeping bag beside his ute and sleep nestled between the blankets, enjoying the open space all around. Then there were the times he and Julie had camped down by the riverbank, just to spend the night alone. Cooking sausages over the campfire and eating them between bread, smothered with tomato sauce. Those had been great nights. Memorable nights. With Julie snuggled into his single swag, it was a tight fit, but worth it, just so he could feel every inch of her pressed against him.

Aaron shook his head and refocussed his thoughts on the computer in front of him. It'd do him no good to start wandering down memory lane. Long ago, he'd dreamed of one day owning his own piece of land. Unlike Julie, he had no family ties to the land, and he couldn't just inherit it from his parents. But nevertheless, he'd felt a connection. A calling. And he'd loved the time he'd spent working for Tony. But that'd turned out to be a pipe dream, after he found out who he truly was. There was no secret ancestral farmer's blood running through his veins. No, all he was, was a gun for hire, pure and simple.

A noise alerted him, right before Julie entered the room, closely followed by her stepbrother, Dale, pushing aside all thoughts of his past.

"Here she is. Safe and sound. She's your problem now." Dale smirked at Julie. She tried to paint on a fake frown, but it didn't last long, and soon she was smiling up at her stepbrother.

"Thanks, squirt," she answered playfully.

"Hey," he said, rounding on her. "No fair, I haven't been smaller than you for years." Then a mischievous look stole over his face. "Perhaps you'd do well to remember what nickname we had for you back when you were eight."

The smile slipped from Julie's face. "You wouldn't dare." She put her hands on hips.

"I won't tell, if you don't use that one again."

"Deal." They shook hands, and the smile returned to Julie's face.

But Aaron wasn't going to forget that one. He *had* to know what her nickname had been. He filed that nugget of information away for a later conversation.

It was heartening to see Dale and Julie throwing happy banter back and forth between them again. Aaron had sat in the shadows at the back of the family room last night after the staff meeting when Julie had finally told her step-siblings the complete truth about her stalker; how he'd found her through her visit to the abortion clinic. The shocked silence and confused looks on Dale and Skylar's faces had been hard to watch, and Aaron had wanted to leap up and place a protective arm around Julie's shoulders. But this was their family business, and he had no place interfering. Steve and

Daniella had been there as moral support for Julie, but in the end they weren't needed, as Skylar was the first to break through her shock, embracing her stepsister as both women began to cry. Dale awkwardly joined in the group hug and by the time everyone had left the room, there'd been a sense of relief and peace hanging over Julie.

After Aaron had done a tour of the house early this morning and given Julie the all-clear to leave her room and attend breakfast—even though she'd sighed and moaned about how nit-picky he was being—she'd wanted to stay on in the kitchen with Skylar and help her clean up after the breakfast rush. That'd been an eye-opener for Aaron. Julie had told him that the guests here expected the best, and Skylar had built her reputation on producing amazing meals, but Aaron still wasn't prepared. There was smoked trout omelette with spinach and feta, oven-baked tomatoes stuffed with some kind of herby delight—which Julie testified as being homegrown—freshly baked, sourdough bread cut into thick slices with butter and locally made marmalade, and the best honey-cured bacon Aaron had ever tasted. His guts were still aching, he was so full.

Julie wanted to stay in the kitchen, but there were urgent things Aaron needed to get done—calls he needed to make, Web searches to be completed, clues to the stalker's identity that needed to be followed up—and the locksmith was supposed to be coming at eleven to add extra locks to all the doors and windows. He'd been about to drag Julie back to the lounge with him, when Dale had said he'd watch her and bring her back when she'd finished. The guests were all eating in their cabins this morning—at Daniella's suggestion, because Aaron still hadn't had time to go over the guest list properly and he hadn't discounted that the stalker could be one of patrons—so it was only family and staff in the lodge this morning. Which made Aaron slightly more at ease. So, he'd agreed. Not many people would get past Dale. If the other man hadn't been so in love with his fiancée and so obviously tied to the station, Aaron might've even asked him if he'd ever thought about joining a security detail.

But he was also yet to go over the details of all the staff, and, unlike Julie, he wasn't sure he trusted them all implicitly. Both Daniella and Julie had vouched for their staff, all of whom had worked at the station for at least two years. All of them except Sasha, that was. According to Daniella, Sasha had started working for them around six months ago. It'd taken them a while to replace their last receptionist, the murderer, Sally Tsun. This time, they'd been exceptionally choosy with their hire, and had gone through Sasha's résumé with a fine-toothed comb, phoning all her references and asking the hard questions. Daniella assured Aaron they'd left no stone unturned when it came to Sasha, they were determined not to make the same mistake with a staff member ever again. But she was the newbie here, and she'd started after Julie's stalker had first made contact. And while he didn't think that she was the actual stalker, it made her a suspect as a possible associate, at least in his eyes. This stalker was intelligent and ingenious, and Aaron wouldn't put it past him to plant a mole in their midst. Another valuable thing he'd learned on the job was that no one was beyond reproach. He'd seen cases where the most trusted personnel had turned on their employers, for love, or money, or, even in one case, a well-hidden but deep-seated spite. Human beings were complicated and often selfish. You could never be one-hundred percent sure what was going on in someone else's mind.

There were other people who also needed to be considered on the list of suspects they were compiling. The chopper pilot who'd flown him to the station yesterday had used the excuse that he'd needed to stretch his legs and had wandered up to the lodge with Aaron and then let himself in a rear door, as if he were more than familiar with the place. A couple of delivery drivers had arrived during the day, and they also had an unescorted run of the place. And then there was the cleaning staff: Aaron had found out the station had two supplementary cleaners who drove in from the small town of Dimbulah whenever they had a rush on and needed extra help. This resort would be pretty much impossible to lock down completely. The list of potential suspects and leaks was growing by the hour.

"Thanks," Aaron said, standing up and stretching his arms above his head, then readjusted his gun holster as it slid up. He wasn't going to be caught out again like he'd been yesterday. He was going to make sure he was always carrying, to be on the safe side.

Dale glanced between Aaron and his stepsister, something unreadable in his eyes. Then he patted Julie on the shoulder and said, "Hang in there, sis. This will all be over soon."

Julie grimaced and rolled her eyes, then took a seat on the leather couch as Dale left the room. This morning, Julie had surprised him by emerging from her room wearing a pair of capris, flip-flops and a light blue sleeveless shirt that set off her eyes. What'd happened to the jeans and T-shirt? Not that he minded, if anything, this outfit made her look sexier than ever. The cream capris hugged her slender legs, and skimmed up over slim hips, showing off her tiny waist.

At his questioning glance, she said, "What? I'm assuming I won't be allowed outside today. Or probably ever again," she'd added in a low grumble. "And if I'm going to be locked in this cage, I may as well dress for cool and comfort for the duration."

"Fine by me," Aaron had replied. And he didn't disagree with her. The heat up here was something else, especially if you weren't used to it. Today, he'd decided to dispense with the sport jacket, and was wearing his black jeans and clean black T-shirt, the gun holster over the top, on show for everyone to see. People might be intimidated by it, but he didn't give a shit. He was here to do a job, and if that job required him to use force, then he wasn't afraid to do it.

Aaron glanced at his watch, then rubbed the back of his neck. The locksmith would be here in half an hour. And he needed to call in another sit-rep to Jake, too.

Which reminded him.

"I have something for you," Aaron said, reaching into his backpack beneath the desk and pulling out a burner phone. "I want you to use this from now on. It's an unlisted number, and only me, my buddy Lance at Shield, your father, and Daniella have it."

"Okay." Julie stood and walked over to take the phone. She turned it over in her hand. "What about my old cell?"

"We'll keep that, but we won't use it. We need to know if he calls again." Aaron put Julie's old phone on the side table next to the sofa and she looked at it as if it were a dangerous snake ready to strike.

"Do you always carry a spare phone with you?" she asked.

"Yep," he nodded distractedly. "Two, actually."

"Right."

He lifted his head from his inspection of his backpack. "It always pays to be prepared. Why?"

She was looking at him funny, a small smile playing over her lips. "I guess it does," she answered slowly. "I keep finding out new and interesting things about you, Aaron, and it surprises me, that's all."

Were they good surprises, or bad surprises? He decided to leave that alone. Instead, he picked up a slim folder Daniella had brought to him this morning.

"Your stepmother gave me a list of the guests staying at the lodge." He waved the documents in the air. "I want you to look at the list, and we'll go over it together, just to see if anything sparks a memory, or a reaction. And then we're going to take another look at your staff, as well. Their backgrounds, their families, that kind of thing."

"Jeez, are we going over this *again*?" She stared up at him, running an impatient hand through her hair. Her fingers left a trail of disorderly caramel strands, making her look a little like a pixie. A very cute, if somewhat irritated pixie.

He had to resist the sudden urge to follow her fingers with his own, as he wondered if her hair would still be as soft and silken as it'd once been now that it was short. Aaron had loved Julie's long, blonde locks, back when they were dating. She usually kept it tied up in a messy bun on the top of her head out of the way while she worked. But when they were alone together, she'd undo it and shake it out, to fall over her slim shoulders. He'd rake his fingers through it, then pull her in and kiss her until they were both breathless.

"I already told you last night, we trust our staff implicitly," she huffed. "And the guests, well…they're all much too nice to be the stalker."

"Don't be so easily fooled," he countered. "And stop sounding like a rebellious teenager," he said, keeping his tone light. "I need to get up to speed on everyone staying here, and I need you to start thinking more prudently about who you let get close to you. I know you're not even sure if you've ever seen this stalker, but keep an eye open for anyone that perhaps sets off alarm bells in your head. You might have detected more than you realized."

Julie had told him, more than once, that she didn't remember anyone specifically from the day she went to the clinic. There was a group of protesters chanting slogans and handing out pamphlets out the front, and they all blended together in a blur in her mind. They'd been there when she went in and were still there when she came out, nearly four hours later. That was some sort of commitment. But she couldn't figure out how the stalker had followed her home. It was the only way he could've found out about her abortion, however, unless someone at the clinic had recognized her, but Julie was sure she'd seen no one familiar there. Julie had told no one else about her termination, except her friend Peggy, who had picked her up afterwards. It was a rule of the clinic that no one be allowed to go home alone, which Aaron applauded, because he knew that stubborn Julie would probably have done just that. His heart ached for what she must've been through. It was so practical and pragmatic, and everything that Julie stood for. But it was also so very, very sad. Julie said that when she emerged from the clinic, her memories of getting into Peggy's car were slightly vague, but she was pretty sure no one followed them. This stalker seemed to be a very intelligent and highly resourceful man, and so far, he was eluding all their attempts at finding him. And how had he somehow finagled her mobile number? Lance was checking all the leads, including looking into Julie's friend Peggy, who Julie told him was an old friend from uni who'd kept in touch over the years.

Julie glared at him, but at least her eyes weren't that arctic blue from yesterday. They were softer, almost the pastel azure he remembered. Carefully turning around, she chose a seat at one end of the sofa. And just as carefully, Aaron chose the seat next to her and sat, handing her the folder; he couldn't very well confer over the list if he took the other end. He leaned back into the soft leather and their knees touched briefly. It wasn't intentional, but an unexpected shot of heat travelled up his leg, scalding him from the inside out, the heat settling in his groin so that his trousers tightened uncomfortably. The shock was so startling, all the words dried up on his tongue.

Julie stiffened beside him, her fingertips going white where she clung to the folder. She didn't say a word, but slowly inched away from him, making it clear she didn't appreciate his sudden proximity. Something twisted painfully in his gut. Shit. Of course, she didn't want him touching her. She'd made that abundantly clear last night. Then why did he suddenly care that she'd rejected him? And why did the urge to lay his leg against hers, just to feel that heat again, nearly override his common sense?

"Let's start with the couple in the swimming pool yesterday. Who were they?" he said gruffly, pointing at the folder. Casually, he lay a hand along the back of the sofa, as if none of the few previous awkward seconds had affected him in the slightest. She'd moved on. He'd moved on. Julie was nothing but a job to him now. He had to keep reminding himself of that.

"They're Dieter and Maria Fischer. Newlyweds arrived from Melbourne three days ago, on their honeymoon." Julie kept her eyes on the paper in front of her. "A delightful couple. This is their second marriage, but they're both so in love." Julie's eyes went misty.

Aaron thought back to yesterday afternoon. The couple had been completely engrossed in each other in the pool. Barely even flicking a glance at him and Julie as they walked by. Daniella had written their home address next to their names. These two seemed to check out, especially because they were from Melbourne, so they could probably be discounted.

"Do you get a lot of honeymooners here?" he asked. It was a surprise when she said that, but the more he thought about it, the more he decided this was exactly who the resort had been targeted toward. It was an adult-only retreat, centered on couples. They could either throw themselves into the everyday activities available on the station, or stay hunkered down in their luxury cabins the whole time; the choice was theirs.

"More than you'd think. I'd say at least one third of guests fall into that category," Julie replied. "We've even held a few weddings at the station. Dale and Daisy will be the next to get hitched here." She turned to face him, eyes alight with interest once more. This was obviously a topic close to her heart. He liked the animated glow on her face. And when she smiled, tiny dimples showed in the corner of her mouth. "I'm helping them plan the whole thing. I can't wait." She clapped her hands in front of her, almost childlike in her anticipation. He didn't want to ruin her happy mood by reminding her that if this stalker was still out there, then her attending a wedding might well be off the agenda. But that was many months into the future, and they'd have this guy collared by then. Most definitely. He hoped.

"Sounds wonderful." He tried to keep the cynicism out of his tone. Then, changing the topic, he said, "How about those mafia look-alike blokes? I believe they're a father and son duo?" Aaron had taken an instant dislike to the puffed-up guys strutting around the lodge. They looked out of place, and had his guts all twisted in a knot.

"You mean Dominic and Joseph?" Julie giggled quietly. "They're harmless. They're here to try and reconnect as father and son. Although, Joseph thinks he's God's gift to women," she added quietly. "He's been flirting a lot with me." She turned blue eyes up, her worried gaze hitting him in the solar plexus. "Don't tell me I need to be worried about a man simply flirting with me now?"

"You can't take anything for granted," Aaron replied, although he tried to soften his tone. He didn't want to frighten her, but she needed to stop walking around with blinkers on. "Let's just say, those two are at the top of the list of guests I've got Lance checking on," he added. "But they put Sydney as their home address, so unless one of them is lying about where they live, they're probably not our man."

"Wow." Julie stared thoughtfully at the closed curtains. "It seems I really can't trust anyone."

At last, she seemed to be getting the message.

"How about we concentrate on anyone showing a home address in Brisbane, for now?" he suggested. That narrowed the list down to three couples. Another newlywed pair and a group of four friends.

"Sure." Her gaze returned to the document on her lap. "Chase and Maya Graymann are also here on their honeymoon. They arrived four days ago, and Maya is just so sweet. She's younger than him, but the way they look at each other, they're just so in love."

Aaron watched her face as she spoke. She didn't seem to realize, but when she talked about people in love, the lines around her mouth softened, her eyes taking on a faraway look.

"Chase works in IT for some big finance company." Julie tapped a finger against her top lip. "I talked to them quite a bit the other night at dinner. They moved into his top-floor apartment in the city straight after they got married. They deferred their honeymoon until now, because they wanted to make it extra special."

Aaron nodded along with her remarks. "It doesn't seem like this guy is lacking money," he added thoughtfully.

"Most people who come here are...how do I put this?" Julie screwed up her face. "We're an exclusive luxury resort, and we offer top-notch accommodation and experiences. None of this comes cheap." Why did she seem a little uncomfortable?

"And there's nothing wrong with that. Just because some people can't afford to come here, you shouldn't feel guilty."

"I know that," she replied a little too abruptly. "Anyway, I don't think this couple is the stalker type. I mean, look at him. He's clean cut, with the glasses and the comb-over. I don't remember anyone like that at the clinic or in the protest group. If anything, the men were a little on the scruffy side. Some even had beards."

"What about the women?" Aaron asked quietly.

"What? I thought we were looking for a man." She seemed genuinely shocked.

"Yes. And no. We can't completely discount women from the equation. It also wouldn't be the first time a stalker had an accomplice. It could be a woman in the crowd, relaying information back to her partner."

"Oh, God." Julie covered her mouth with her hand. It was shaking. He resisted the urge to take it in his own.

"Obviously, we heard the guy on the mobile yesterday. It's clearly a man." He balled his hand into a fist beside his thigh, to stop himself from reaching out to her. "But don't think that we're only looking for a single, white male. That would be an oversight."

"Okay. Thanks for the heads-up." Julie's gaze drifted to the door in the far wall, and he got the feeling it was suddenly becoming even more real for her.

Wanting to keep them on track, he said gently, "What about the four friends staying in cabin nine? What do you know about them?"

Just as Julie opened her mouth, her cell phone made a loud, jangling noise that had Aaron immediately on edge.

She jumped up and turned to face him. "No," she whispered.

He stood and put a steadying hand on her arm. "It could be nothing," he said soothingly. Then he went over and retrieved the cell from the table, glancing at the screen. No caller ID. Not good.

"If this is him, Julie, I want you to try and keep him talking. I'm going to let Lance know that we need to trace this call. Okay?"

She just nodded, staring at the phone as if hypnotized.

Aaron took his phone out of his pocket and dialled Lance's number, never taking his eyes from Julie's face. When Lance answered on the second ring, he spoke quickly and then hung up. His call had only taken a few seconds.

He nodded and said quietly, "Remember not to mention me. Let's see what he knows first."

Holding the phone between them, resting flat on his hand, Aaron pressed the answer button and held his breath.

After a second's hesitation, Julie said, "Hello?" in a shaky voice.

"Hello, Julie." It was the same voice from yesterday. With an English accent, like the guy was speaking with a plum in his mouth. God, he hoped Lance was all over this call. If they could trace this phone, they might have this fucker in custody by lunchtime.

"What do you want? Why do you keep calling me?" Julie practically spat the words at her phone.

"I want to show you the light. But a little birdie told me you're hiding away inside. You can't see the light from inside, Julie."

The guy was being a lot more guarded with his comments today. It was hard to tell from what he was saying if he was nearby somewhere, or if he had someone doing his spying for him. Julie dragged in a ragged breath and Aaron put his hand on her shoulder, bracing her against the shudder that ran through her body.

"Has that big gorilla got you running scared? I never took you for a coward, Julie."

Aaron assumed he was the gorilla the stalker was referring to. How did he know about Aaron? Had he seen him arrive in the chopper? Or seen him with Julie yesterday down at the billabong? Where the hell was this guy? Aaron's gut was telling him the stalker had to be one of the guests to have this much information. But not one of them seemed to fit the profile. Could the guy be camped out on the property somewhere, watching Julie from afar? It seemed unlikely, but hell, anything was possible. Was there indeed a mole in their midst? Was someone on the inside slipping the stalker information? The new girl, Sasha? The chopper pilot? Everyone was a suspect.

Julie lifted her gaze to meet Aaron's. Her beautiful face was cloaked with unease. But there was another emotion flitting through the depths of her eyes. Anger. Which was good. Anger made people stand up and fight. The Julie he'd used to know always fought for what was fair; for what she wanted. He could see the heated words forming on her tongue. She was going to tell this guy to go to hell, and rightfully so. Except, they needed to keep him talking; needed to know what he knew. Aaron lifted a finger to her lips and then mouthed, "Keep him talking."

Julie shook her head. He didn't blame her for wanting to let fly. But then she swallowed and pursed her pretty lips into a pout. "What do you mean by *big gorilla*?" Julie asked from between clenched teeth.

"That big guy who showed up yesterday, all puffed up and full of himself. I bet he's there with you right now. Is he your boyfriend?" The emphasis the man on the phone put on the word boyfriend made Aaron bristle. His tone dripped with derision. And animosity. "Whoever he is, let me tell you, he doesn't scare me."

CHAPTER TEN

"Well, you should be scared," Julie yelled at the phone. "Because when Aaron finds you, he's going to…shoot you in the head, you…bastard!"

"All right, that's it." Aaron pushed the End button and slammed the phone down on the table. "What the hell?" He rounded on her.

"Sorry," she apologized. The adrenaline was already draining from her body. What had she been thinking? "I was just so mad. I wanted to… Well, I wanted him dead." The admission shocked her. Up until now, she'd thought that with enough time and patience, this guy would just give up and go away. That he wasn't really a problem. But he was a problem, and her whole life was now in limbo because of him. This had gone on long enough. This was all so unfair. She'd give anything if she could just be happy again. Her knees began to tremble.

"I don't really want him dead," she said in a small voice. An incomparable weight seemed to settle in her chest. It made it hard to breathe.

"I know you don't." Aaron's tone was surprisingly gentle. Why was he suddenly being so kind? She looked up to study his beautiful eyes, to see if she could fathom his change of mood, and a tear ran down her cheek. Where had that come from? She dashed it away, but another one took its place.

Big arms came up to enfold her. His chest was so broad and warm...and solid. Her tears ran faster. This was the second time in nearly as many days that she'd cried. What was wrong with her? A hand came up to cradle the back of her head, and she dropped her forehead into the crook of his shoulder and gave in to the tears. Inside his arms, she felt shielded from the cruel man and the troubled world waiting right outside for her. As if she was in a bubble. *My wings are like a shield of steel.* It was a stupid catchphrase from some dumb kids' cartoon Julie remembered from her childhood. But those words suddenly rang true. Being held in Aaron's arms made her feel as if she were almost invincible.

She shouldn't feel this way.

He was her sworn enemy. Okay, enemy was a strong word, but he was definitely an untrustworthy pig when it came to her heart.

Her tears began to slow, but he continued to cradle her, not saying anything, just letting her cry. But as her weeping subsided, she became aware of the bands of muscle wrapped around her back. Then she noticed that her breasts were pushed up against the solid wall of his chest. Her nipples tingled at the idea. She became acutely aware of every single place on her body that was touching his. The top of her thighs, the way his hands nestled in the small of her back, his thumb rubbing tiny circles on her spine, his biceps wrapped around her shoulders. A thrill of desire ran through her. The old chemistry was still there. If anything, it'd increased, not faded. She couldn't help it, she breathed in deeply, inhaling the scent of his masculinity. He smelled clean and pure, like soap, overlaid with a much deeper musky scent. Then she caught the faint hint of something metallic. His gun. It was that thought which finally lifted the spell. She raised her head and tried to push away from him, but he resisted, strong arms like a vise around her.

She tensed, but he didn't seem to notice, his gaze was fixed on her face. It took her a moment to understand he was watching a last tear run down her cheek.

"Julie?"

His thumb came up and gently wiped away the droplet, searing her skin as it went. She wanted to flinch away, but she couldn't, snared by the heat flaring in his eyes.

"Julie?" he said her name again, as if it were a question. A question she didn't know how to answer.

He lowered his head, slowly but surely. She'd forgotten how tall he was. Or was that how short she was? She couldn't remember. All she knew was that his mouth was coming closer and closer. Then his lips crashed into hers.

The short stubble around his mouth tickled her lips, rasped at her skin, but God, she wanted more. She went up on her toes and pressed her hands to his chest and kissed him back. His teeth nipped at her lower lip and then his tongue was in her mouth, and it felt like he was delving the depths of her soul. Her fingers ran over his firm pecs. Jesus, he was hard in all the right places. Not that he hadn't been hard before, but now he was big, and solid and so much more...powerful.

She moaned, a husky sound that surprised her, the hunger clearly evident in her sigh.

Somewhere in the distance, a ringtone sounded.

"Ignore it," she mumbled into his mouth.

"It's Lance," he mumbled back, then tore his mouth from hers. "I need to answer it."

With one hand, he reached around and retrieved his phone from his pocket, but he didn't let her go completely, for which she was quietly grateful. As it was, she suddenly felt unsteady on her feet, as if the earth had just moved beneath her.

After a few seconds, she felt strong enough to take a step back, out of the shelter of his arms. With one final glance in her direction—was that regret in his eyes?—he brought the phone to his ear. "Tell me you got him, Lance."

Julie knew this call was important, but she couldn't seem to concentrate on what Aaron was saying.

Jeezes. What had she been thinking? Anyone could've walked in on them. How would she have explained that? And besides, she wasn't supposed to kiss Aaron. Wasn't supposed to want him. Bastard. How dare he still have such an effect on her?

She wandered over to the window, wanting to look out over the billabong, the view always helped to calm her mind. But she'd forgotten the curtains were drawn and cursed silently.

Aaron stopped talking, and she turned to see him grimace. It didn't look like good news.

"What did he say?"

"He said that we should've kept him talking longer," Aaron growled, taking a dig at her lack of self-control. Then he held up a hand as she began to protest. "But he also said it wouldn't have done us much good, even if we'd kept him on the line for half an hour. The guy was using a burner. It can't be easily traced. And if he's as smart as I'm starting to think he is, even if we do trace it, he'll probably have already ditched it."

"Wow." Julie wasn't sure what to say. It seemed they were no closer to catching this guy, or even finding out who he was. "What are we going to do now?"

"We have a private detective on retainer. Nicolay is good at what he does, and I've already got him looking into identifying this guy. He's talking to that group you saw outside the clinic, to see if they know who he is." Aaron took two steps toward her and slung an arm around her shoulder.

"Don't worry, we'll catch him. Soon."

She wasn't so sure. "And in the meantime, I have to stay cooped up inside. Is that right?"

Aaron pursed his lips, the scruff of his short stubble highlighting the line of his firm mouth. "I'm sorry, I know you hate it."

"What about the muster? Have you thought any more about that? It starts in two days." Julie wasn't going to give up hope that she could go. A chance to spend a week out in the Queensland outback would be good for her soul. She'd been looking forward to it for months. Some of the ringers were due to arrive tomorrow. The rest would rendezvous with them out at the campsite.

"I'm still not keen on you going."

At least he understood not to tell her *no* outright. Because she might have a melt-down.

"Surely, it's safer out there. Away from the guests and the delivery men, and the staff who you don't trust?" Julie still couldn't believe that Aaron didn't even trust the Stormcloud staff. People she'd known and worked with—some of them for years, now. It obviously came with the territory when you were a bodyguard, not trusting anyone. But Julie would be dammed if she'd go down that path.

"You keep saying your trust your staff implicitly, but you seem to have forgotten that one of them embezzled money from Stormcloud and murdered a fellow teammate." He stared at her and for a moment she was lost for words, squirming uncomfortably. He was right. But that was in the past. She was *sure* no one who now worked at Stormcloud could be doing this. "And there's also a whole other raft of other people who we'd need to clear," he added into the silence.

"What? The ringers? They're all old hands at this. They keep coming back year after year. Do you honestly think this stalker guy has any hope of masquerading as a battle-scarred, work-roughened, hard-bitten, bronco-riding stock hand?" The idea was completely laughable. The safest place for her right now would be on that muster. But how did she convince Aaron of that?

There was a knock at the door, then Dale entered. "The locksmith is here. I'll stay with Julie, if you want to show him what you need." Dale looked between the two of them, then the smile dropped from his face when it became obvious he'd just interrupted something.

"Thank you." Aaron grabbed his sports jacket from the back of a chair, slinging it on over his gun holster and said nothing more as he exited the door.

"Great, just what I need. A babysitter." Julie plonked herself down onto the sofa and crossed her arms. This whole hiding away was wearing very thin, very quickly. The stalker's phone call had scared her. But it'd also made her mad. And the more she thought about it, the more the anger rose to the surface, overpowering her fear. She needed to go on that muster. Would she get away with defying Aaron? Technically, she was his client, and he had to do what she wanted. Didn't he?

Dale sat on the other end of the sofa and regarded her. "You need to stop blaming Aaron for all of this. He's just trying to keep you safe. You're treating him as if he's punishing you by making you stay inside. This is the stalker's fault, not Aaron's."

Dale made sense, but Julie found it hard to wipe the glower off her face. It was easy to blame Aaron for her predicament, but Dale was right, he was merely doing his job the best way he knew how. Deep down, Julie understood that she was probably transferring some of her anger at him, surrounding her current situation. He'd broken her heart when he left, and she couldn't forgive him for that.

* * *

Julie stretched and yawned, but didn't open her eyes. She knew it was daylight because the increasing high-pitched hum of cicadas permeated even through the thick, wooden walls of the lodge and her closed window. The window she usually left open at night, so she could hear the peaceful night sounds that lulled her to sleep. But last night she hadn't heard a thing. Although something had disturbed her sleep at one stage. She remembered rolling over and vaguely wondering what that light, fluttering sound was. But it'd stopped, and she dropped back asleep.

Sitting up in bed, she blinked a few times and ran a hand through her hair. It was later than she normally woke, she could tell by the strong light filtering in around the bottom of her curtains. But what was there to get up for? She wasn't allowed outside, was hardly allowed to do any work at all. Usually, by this time of the morning, she'd be helping Skylar prepare breakfast, or be out with her father, feeding the horses.

Would Aaron still be asleep? Somehow, she doubted it. He was like a robot these days. So serious and straight-faced. All work and no play. Part of the reason she'd found it hard to fall asleep last night was knowing he was sleeping right across the hall. Images of Aaron lying stretched out on the mattress assaulted her mind. Did he sleep in his underwear? Or naked, even? Back when they were together, he'd always slept with a pair of underwear on, nothing more. How different would he look in a pair of those tight black boxer briefs today? Back then, she'd loved the long, lithe lines of him, toned stomach showing off a fit set of abs. But now, he was much more heavily muscled. Those abs would still be there, she had no doubt about that, she'd felt them beneath his T-shirt yesterday as they kissed. But they were way more defined, more pronounced, the muscles more substantial and solid. He'd definitely filled out and grown into his height. Her mind flittered back to the kiss they'd shared yesterday. It'd been so hot; she'd thought her panties might melt. Nothing had changed; they still had amazing chemistry. Aaron was capable of setting her insides aflame with just one touch of his lips.

Jeezes. Where had that thought come from?

Running a hand across her eyes to rid her brain of the unwanted images, she kicked off the sheet and swung her feet over the side of the bed. Padding on bare feet over to her large dresser drawer, she stood staring at the large wooden piece of furniture, but not really seeing it. What should she wear today? It'd been a nice change to get out of her jeans and shirt yesterday. Should she wear the capris again? Why not? She wasn't going to be allowed out of her cage, luxurious as it might be. Aaron had seemed to like the capris, if the flash of desire she'd seen in his eyes was anything to go by. He'd smothered it quickly enough, but he forgot, she'd seen that desire before, recognized it, even from twelve years ago.

A slight sound caught her attention.

It took her a few seconds to pinpoint where it was coming from. Outside her window. The same fluttering sound she'd heard last night. It was odd, like something was tapping on the glass pane.

Aaron had told her that under no circumstances was she to open her window, or the curtains. But surely a little peek wouldn't hurt.

Sneaking over to her window—although why she was creeping on silent feet, she had no idea, Aaron wouldn't know what she was up to—she took the edge of the curtain in between her finger and thumb and gently lifted it away so she could peer outside. Something was stuck to the outside of her window. It was a piece of paper, one corner flapping idly in the light breeze. Why was there paper stuck to her window? Julie drew the curtain open wider to get a better view and let out a scream before she covered her mouth and stared at the image someone had drawn on the paper.

Oh, God. The top half of the page contained a hand-drawn image of a fetus, an enlarged head and enormous eyes staring at her. A knife had been stabbed through the baby's heart and blood dripped from the gaping wound. Below the dead baby was an image of a large, wooden crucifix, with a woman stretched out, hands and feet nailed to the cross. The message was clear.

There was a knock at the door. "Julie, are you okay? I heard something." Without waiting for an invitation, Aaron barged into her bedroom, his large frame filling the room with its comforting presence. His gaze sought her out, checking to make sure she really was unhurt, before he scrutinized the rest of the room, searching for any perceived threat. It'd only taken Aaron a few seconds to get there. He must've rushed across the hall as soon as he heard her scream.

"Look at this," she said in a small voice, beckoning him over.

Aaron walked over and studied the image quickly. "Holy shit," he mumbled quietly. Without asking her permission, he gathered her in with one arm and briskly flicked the curtains closed with the other. He led her over to sit on the edge of her bed, kneeling on the floor before her, so he could look up into her face.

"I'm sorry you had to see that," he said gently.

"How did it get there?" But she didn't really need to ask, she knew. "More to the point, how did he know which window belonged to my bedroom?" Her mouth suddenly felt dry, and she licked her lips, but to no avail.

Aaron said nothing, merely looked serious. Oh, God, the stalker knew where she slept. Thankfully, he hadn't tried to break into her room. But leaving that horrifying message was bad enough.

"What's going on?" Dale barged into her room, breathing heavily, as if he'd run to get there. "Bindi said she thought she heard a scream."

"The stalker left her another message." Aaron waved his hand toward the window. Julie watched her stepbrother twitch aside the curtain, but turned her head away at the last second, not able to bear looking at that terrible picture again.

Dale came over and sat on the bed next to Julie. "This guy is some sort of twisted sicko," he said, resting a comforting arm around her shoulder.

As Dale sat, Aaron stood and went to prowl around the room, looking like a caged jaguar, ready to pounce. An angry caged jaguar. Anger seemed to radiate off him in waves. He was pissed off that this man had managed to get past him again.

"Don't let this shithead get to you," Dale continued gently. "We won't let him hurt you."

Julie should've been comforted by her stepbrother's words. Why then did she feel so hollow and inadequate inside?

"We need to get her out of this room," Aaron said. "And I don't want anyone touching that..." He waved a hand in the direction of the window. "We need to preserve the scene until we can get the police to come out and take a look."

"I'll go and phone Nash," Dale said helpfully, getting to his feet. "Then I'll post a guard outside so no-one tampers with the evidence."

"Great, thank you," Aaron agreed. He walked over and offered Julie his hand, helping her to her feet, and she suddenly remembered she was still wearing her pajamas. A little set of purple cotton shorts and a tank top. Comfortable to sleep in, but she noticed Aaron's gaze rest a tad too long on the skimpy outfit. She needed to get dressed. And get away from that horrible picture.

"Grab some clothes and bring them with you," Aaron directed. "You can get dressed in the lounge." She pulled her hand out of his and stared up at him. "I promise, I won't look," he added, seeing her glare.

Dale was already halfway out of the room. "Should I tell everyone about this?" he asked, poking his head back around the door. "I mean, should I let the staff know?"

Aaron deliberated for a second, then nodded. "Yes, everyone needs to be on high alert. This person is playing with us. Almost as if it's a game for him. And this shows they definitely have access to the property." Aaron's face was grim, and Julie wondered what this meant for her. Would he try and get her to move to a more secure location this time? Perhaps she might even agree to leave the lodge now. If not to protect herself, then to protect her family.

Ten minutes later, she sat on the sofa, nursing a mug of coffee Skylar had brought to her. Breakfast was being served in the great room right now. They couldn't very well keep the guests cooped up in their accommodation forever. Aaron had said that Julie shouldn't attend breakfast this morning, and for once, she agreed with him.

Aaron had indeed done as he promised and kept his back turned while she got changed. It'd been an odd, awkward few moments, as she stood naked in the corner of the room, her back also to Aaron, but with a strange desire to walk over and plant herself in front of him, show him exactly what he'd been missing all this time. To see his eyes widen with…what? Panic? Lust? Regret? All of those emotions would make her feel vindicated.

Aaron also sipped on a coffee, but he stood over by his desk, one butt cheek perched on the edge as he considered her. He'd already been out to inspect the scene outside her window, but he was keeping tight-lipped about it.

"I've been thinking," Aaron said, breaking the tense silence.

"Mmm," she replied noncommittally, a little afraid of what he was going to say. She knew the picture on her window was bad. Knew it meant this crazy man was escalating, getting closer. And knew it might also force Aaron's hand. It might oblige him to take this protection thing to the next level. She didn't want to leave the station. But she was starting to think she might have to.

"I think we should go on the muster."

"What?" She sat up straighter in her seat. "Really?"

"Yes," he mused, rubbing his thumb over the stubble on his chin. "Dale and Wazza, and even your father, are going. And you're right, I don't think this stalker will be able to blend in as well with a bunch of rough and tough, cattle mustering, bronco riders. We might even be able to enlist some of them to help in your protection detail."

"Woohoo!" Julie jumped out of her seat. Her day was suddenly looking much brighter. Without overthinking it, she ran over and put her arms around his neck, surprising him with a kiss on the cheek. "Thank you."

He turned his enigmatic gaze on her, one blue eye and one brown, both regarding her with a veiled expression, and she suddenly wished she hadn't followed her first impulse and kissed him. Because now she was standing way too close, arms still around his neck as he studied her with an air of predatory grace.

CHAPTER ELEVEN

An air of expectation hung over the station. Aaron had forgotten what this felt like. The anticipation of the start of a muster was suspended in the air; he could almost see it in the dust rising like a cloud above the stables.

Aaron undid the button on his sleeve, and rolled it up to his elbow, then did the same with the other one. He figured he may as well blend in with the rest of the crew. His black trousers, shiny shoes and expensive sports jacket would've screamed townie, and he didn't want to appear out of place to the ringers right from the get-go. His borrowed blue shirt with the Stormcloud logo on the top pocket—a gift from Wazza, as he was the closest in size to Aaron—was well-worn, the fabric soft and pliable. Aaron was surprised at how easily he'd slipped back into the uniform of jeans, boots, and hat. It hadn't been hard to find him a pair of boots; there were always plenty of pairs left hanging around on a station. Previous staff left them behind, or they'd been outgrown and replaced by one of the family members. Julie had dug around in a corner of the tack shed, beneath all the saddles stacked along a long wooden rail, and come up with a pair that fit him almost perfectly. Julie had also found an old Akubra for him in the back of Steve's closet. Aaron still owned an

Akubra, as long as his mother hadn't thrown it away. The gray felt hat had been his pride and joy. But there was no way he was going to get in touch with his mother to ask her to send it to him. Because then she'd inquire why he needed it. And he wasn't going down that path. He kept his contact with Donna to a bare minimum. There was no need for him to talk to her anymore. She had her life, and he had his. Besides, she would never change. No matter how much he'd tried to get her to love him as a kid, she'd always remained detached and aloof, and it was only getting worse as she got older. Aaron was happy to keep his estranged mother at arm's length.

It'd been two days since the drawing taped to the window incident. Since he'd agreed to let Julie go on the muster. There'd been no letters, phone calls, or texts in that time. Almost as if the stalker was indeed playing a game with them, and had decided it was their move.

He and Julie stood next to the Land Cruiser, waiting for Steve to finish his last-minute preparations so they could hit the road. The rest of the crew also bustled around, tying down loose ropes, and checking their loads. The sky was starting to turn lilac on the horizon, but the sun was yet to peek over the hills behind them, and he smothered a yawn. They'd been up since four am. Aaron had forgotten about the early starts during muster. A battered, old caravan was hitched to the back of their Land Cruiser. Aaron had helped Julie kit it out with all the cooking utensils, mounds of non-perishable food, and other supplies she'd need to cook meals for upwards of fifteen people for the next week. The caravan was also crammed full of camping equipment, including tents, pots and pans, and a large metal grille and other steel appliances for cooking over the fire. They were taking everything, including the kitchen sink, it seemed.

He glanced down at the petite woman standing next to

him. The look on Julie's face was priceless, almost worth the cost of admitting he should have agreed to let her go on the muster right from the start. It was as if she'd come alive again; she was almost the same Julie he remembered from before, bubbly, and jovial, laughter lighting up her face.

"You look...good," Julie said quietly from her position beside him. She'd been studying him from beneath lowered eyelashes for the last few minutes, banging her hat thoughtfully against her jean-clad thigh.

"What?" Where was she going with this?

"Less serious and businesslike. More like the old Aaron I used to know." Her compliment pulled him up short. Was that a good thing? Maybe it was in her eyes. But not so much for him. He certainly felt more at ease in jeans and a shirt. But he needed to keep reminding himself he was on the job; this wasn't a holiday, it was serious.

"Well, we can't have that," he replied gruffly. Then, on a spur-of-the-moment impulse, he ruffled Julie's hair like he used to do, and grinned down at her, while stepping away so she couldn't whack him with her hat.

"Hey." She pouted up at him, lips all plump and luscious, blue eyes flashing. Aaron felt a stab of an emotion he hadn't felt in a long time drive deep into his guts. He turned away to hide his surprise.

After the picture in the window, Aaron had insisted he sleep in Julie's bedroom. He'd dragged the mattress from the lounge area into her room and placed it at the foot of the bed. It was the only solution he could see, because he wasn't going to let her out of his sight again. Not until they'd caught this guy.

But he hadn't been prepared for the excruciating form of invisible torture he'd had to endure over the past two nights. Aaron had lain awake most of the night, listening to Julie breathe. Soft and deep. Every now and then, she would snuffle and turn over. She seemed to sleep the deep, dreamless sleep of the innocent. Whereas he was the exact opposite. He found himself wondering what she would do if he gave up on the near irresistible urge to crawl into bed with her. Would she reach for him like she'd used to? Drag his mouth down to hers, entreating him for more as she had the other day when they'd kissed?

Aaron still couldn't banish that kiss from his mind. Memories of it would sneak up on him when he'd least expect it, often at the most inappropriate times. Once, he'd been chatting with Daniella about a new batch of guests arriving the following day, and he'd glanced up to see Julie staring at him intently from the other side of the room. She'd licked her lips, an unconscious move, and turned away, but in that instant, he'd seen the heat behind her eyes, and his cock had sprung to attention. A highly unsuitable situation to be in, with his cock straining against the zipper of his trousers and Daniella staring at him, waiting for an answer. He'd kept his libido on a tighter leash after that, but there'd been other times when he'd caught himself thinking about her.

During the night, Aaron had taken to counting sheep to try and distract himself. And in a desperate attempt to stop thinking about how soft her skin would feel against his, he'd even considered rehashing the events of the night he'd left Dalgety. The way his mother's gaze had bored into him, spewing her venomous words in order to hurt him. Make him feel a little of the pain that she'd been feeling all those years. That'd worked. He'd stopped thinking about Julie for a while after that.

Earlier this morning, while Julie had been packing the last of her things into her duffle bag, ready for the muster, Aaron had approached and handed her a small canister of pepper spray.

"What am I going to do with that?" she'd asked after

examining it for a few seconds.

"It's for self-defense. You hold it up and spray it in an attacker's face." He took her hand in his, directing her thumb, showing her how to flick up the safety cover on the top, then pointed it away from them and mimed pressing the trigger with her thumb. "Short, sharp bursts are better than longer sprays."

"I know what it is," she said haughtily, recoiling from his touch. "And I've seen how they're used." She held the canister in front of her, pretending to examine it more closely. But Aaron caught the way she surreptitiously rubbed the back of her hand where his palm had covered hers.

"Where am I going to keep this?" she added, shooting him a confused look. "I won't be carrying a bag most of the time out there."

"I know. Just try and keep it close by." Aaron realized that muster wasn't your normal everyday situation. This wasn't like Julie would be going for a leisurely stroll down a city street with a handbag slung over her shoulder. She'd be constantly on the move. Flitting from the cooking tent to the cattle yards. There were a million things to do out on muster, and he knew he'd be doing his best just to keep up with her. "You can clip it on your jeans." He turned the canister over and showed her how it was attached to a keyring on one end, with a fastener that would clip onto a belt loop on her jeans. "It's even small enough to put in your pocket. Have you got a small backpack you can take? If you don't, I'll see if I can get you one." Aaron knew it'd be too much to ask her to wear a backpack all the time, but if she ever left camp for any reason —she'd mentioned riding out and helping the ringers muster the cattle if she had any spare time, although she wouldn't be doing that if he had any say in the matter—then she could carry it in that.

"I've got one," she replied, still staring at the small can.

"You realize pepper spray is illegal in Queensland. Only cops are allowed to use it."

"Yeah, I know. Which is why it might be better to keep it out of sight." Aaron understood the rules around pepper spray; it was considered an *offensive weapon* in Queensland, unless you had a permit, which Aaron was entitled to because of his work with Shield. He had other, larger canisters of the spray in his go bag. They often came in handy in a situation when brute force was required to subdue a criminal, but the circumstances didn't require a lethal weapon. Shield Security protection agents were always told to use their common sense during any violent altercation, but a gun should always be a last resort, in Aaron's mind.

"I'd feel safer knowing you had it on you," he continued. He didn't add that the penalty for being caught carrying pepper spray could possibly include a jail sentence, because that would just freak her out and there was no need to be worried, in his eyes. As a first offense, it was highly unlikely that Julie would go to jail. "But perhaps don't let Nash know I gave it to you," he added.

Julie had scowled at him, but carefully tucked the spray into a corner of her duffle bag.

"I've got something else for you." Aaron hesitated, unsure how she'd receive this next gift. He held up a small, black box in the palm of his hand. Lifting the lid, he took out a slim, silver ankle bracelet with a tiny charm hanging from one end.

Julie drew back in horror. "Why on earth would you want to give me jewelry?"

"Oh. No. Wait...this isn't what you think." Uh-oh, he'd done this all wrong; hadn't even considered this sort of reaction from her. But now he could see he was an idiot not to have anticipated her feelings. "It's a highly technical piece of equipment," he added, trying not to sound overly pompous. Hell, he wasn't handling this well at all.

She eyed him suspiciously, not moving.

"It contains a tiny GPS tracker," he explained. "So, if you ever go missing…"

"Oh." Understanding flared in her eyes. Was that a flash of disappointment, as well? "I'm not sure I want you tracking me," she replied darkly, but there was relief in the easing of tension from her shoulders. Then she held up a hand to forestall any of his arguments. "But, yes, I will put it on if you think it's completely necessary. Although I'd never in a million years wear something like this." The last sentence was muttered under her breath. Aaron might beg to differ. While Julie had never owned much fine or intricate jewelry back when he'd known her—she'd always said there was no point wearing expensive jewelry, it'd just end up lost or damaged with her work on the farm—he'd bought her a delicate gold necklace a few weeks before he'd left Dalgety, with a tiny diamond dangling on a charm. She'd worn it with pride, tucked beneath the collar of her shirt every day after he'd given it to her. He wondered if she'd kept it.

The anklet was standard issue, Jake had them made specially for any of their female clients who might be at greater risk. It was a simple sliver chain, with a single heart charm. For their male clients, there was a choice of a lapel pin or a men's ring. This was purely for practical use only. There'd been no deeper meaning behind his offering. Not this time. He hoped Julie understood that.

Julie had refused his offer to help her put it on, and he stood back, watching her fasten it around her ankle, an indecipherable look on her face. A flash of guilt speared through him, but he quashed it quickly. These old emotions rearing their ugly head were only going to complicate things between him and Julie. He needed to keep reminding himself she was a client. A paying customer.

"Right, I think we might be ready to leave." Steve's

booming voice brought Aaron back to the present. Julie had opted to drive; she said she'd travelled the road a few times before and was familiar with it, and Aaron was happy with that. It left him open to keep an eagle eye on everyone else around them, and what they were up to.

Steve and Dale were also driving a Toyota Land Cruiser, but they were towing a long trailer with two quad bikes and one motorcycle tied on tight, along with a whole raft of other equipment squeezed in next to the bikes. It was a tangle of swags and folding chairs, a portable barbecue, large containers of fuel and all other sorts of odds and sodds. Steve gave the trailer one last quick glance while Daisy dashed over to give Dale a kiss goodbye.

Wazza and Bindi were in a third vehicle, towing a big, slab-sided horse trailer, onto which Steve and Wazza had just finished loading five horses. All sorts of gear was crammed into the front of the trailer—saddles, bridles, feed for the horses, blankets, buckets, farrier equipment in case one of the horses threw a shoe. The list was endless.

Aaron watched Bindi lean in and check on the horses one more time, then expertly shut the doors, fastening the latch with one last thump. Her long, dark hair was tied up into a plait beneath her battered straw hat. Aaron had learned that while Bindi was employed as Skylar's assistant cook, she loved spending as much time as she could with the horses. Skylar had agreed to let Bindi go on muster, but it meant she'd rope in Sasha to help over the coming week, as the lodge was over half-full, and the guests still expected their gourmet meals. Aaron was now intimately acquainted with all the Stormcloud staff, after having read up on their backstories. He glanced over at Bindi, who was hopping into the passenger seat, while Wazza got into the driver's seat. She was originally from New Zealand, but had moved over here with her family when they'd had to sell their farm. Bindi didn't say much, but she seemed to be far wiser than her twenty-five years. Blending in with the rest of the crew in her jeans and light-pink, long-sleeved shirt, Bindi seemed at home here on the station.

Aaron was quietly glad that Sasha would be staying behind. There was nothing in her background that raised any red flags in regard to an association with the stalker, but he still didn't trust her one hundred percent. While he was getting Julie away from all the familiar people and places on the station, he might also be breaking her away from any mole that could potentially be watching her.

The last vehicle in the lineup belonged to a mustering crew who'd arrived yesterday afternoon. Mick Scanlon, Scanner to his mates, and his three daughters, Sue, Beth, and Maddie; Aaron couldn't remember who was the eldest, they all looked so similar. They were already packed up and waiting, watching the commotion from beneath their battered hats with world-weary eyes. Julie had filled Aaron in on them last night over dinner. It seemed there were quite a few of these roving muster crews who went from one station to the next during the muster season. They could easily find work for eight to nine months of the year. Then they'd spend the rest of the year on their own farms or properties. It was a rough sort of life, but Aaron could see the advantages, as long as you weren't afraid of hard work. A life of freedom, with not too many responsibilities, spent out in some of the most beautiful country in the world.

Aaron already had Lance check them all out as soon as he'd decided they were going on the muster. He'd garnered a list of names from Steve and handed them all over to HQ two days ago. Lance had given the all-clear on the Scanlon contract crew, as well as clearing all the other riders coming in from around the country. This was the first year the Scanlons had worked for Stormcloud, but the other ringers would all be returning from previous years. The rest were due to meet up at the stock camp. Aaron had made a point of talking to each one of the Scanlon team, making his own impression of the girls and their father. They were all country people, through and through, with the slow, country drawl, and the roughened hands and dirt-encrusted nails to prove it. Aaron highly doubted they had anything to do with Julie's stalker, but he'd learned never to discount anyone. So, he'd keep an eye on them all.

Skylar, Daisy, Daniella, Sasha, and Alek stood together by the stabling yard fence, watching everything with practiced eyes. They'd be left to run the resort for the next week on their own. It was part of the harsh reality of living in the outback. Everyone just mucked in and got on with the job. Daniella and Alek could cope with operating the guest activities, which would run at a scaled-back version for the next week. Daniella was a highly capable woman, skilled in horsemanship, as well as being able to drive an ATV. Daisy had said she'd help out with the horse rides and a planned trip to the old, abandoned, gold mine later on in the week, as well. Daisy technically didn't work at Stormcloud; she had her own job, on a contract for a gold-mining company, finding ways to implement a more sustainable process at their mine site in North Queensland, as well as setting up a collaboration project with a local indigenous group, growing bush tucker. But being engaged to Dale made Daisy practically family, and she'd said she would juggle her commitments so she could spend more time at Stormcloud.

Aaron's small handgun was tucked safely into the glove compartment of the Land Cruiser, within easy reach if he needed it. Once he got to camp, he'd make sure he wore it at all times. The rest of his gear, including his larger SIG, was in his go bag in the back seat of the four-wheel-drive.

"Let's get this show on the road," shouted Steve.

Julie let out a whoop of joy, and the other staff followed her lead, until the air was thick with their excited calls. A shiver of anticipation ran through Aaron. Even though he hated to admit it, a small part of him was looking forward to this. He was a professional, and not for an instant would he allow anything to prevent him from doing his true duty; of protecting Julie. But a small part of him was also excited to be going on his first cattle muster. The seasoned part of his brain acknowledged that the setting—the middle of the isolated outback—might cause some difficulties, make it harder for him to do his job. Throw him a few curve balls, even. He hoped that wasn't the case, but he believed he was up to the task.

He let out his own whoop of exhilaration and jumped into the passenger seat.

CHAPTER TWELVE

Julie concentrated on the dusty road in front of her, making sure she followed the tire tracks of the other cars, keeping her wheels in the ruts and checking the caravan was traveling securely behind her. This was the first time she'd driven this particular track with a caravan attached, and it was taking all her skill to make sure she didn't get bogged in the sandy soil on either side of the road.

Last year, she'd come out to the stock campsite with Skylar, helping ferry replenishments and other supplies—a generator to replace the broken one, and extra water because the tank had been low—but they had returned to the lodge the same day. Julie remembered a few times over her childhood coming out here when she'd come to stay with Steve during the school holidays. But that was all.

Even with the air-conditioning going full blast, a rivulet of sweat ran down between her breasts. It was physically hard work guiding the four-wheel-drive over the rutted ground. She glanced over at Aaron in the passenger seat. He looked totally cool, calm, and relaxed. Maybe she should've made him drive, instead. But no, she was enjoying this challenge. There was a creek crossing coming up soon that heralded the last stretch before they arrived at camp. She was the third vehicle in the cavalcade, followed by the Scanlons in their enormous semi-trailer in the rear. The family had everything in that truck, all the supplies they needed to live for months at a time. She hoped they'd be able to negotiate the creek crossing; it could get tricky if you didn't know what you were doing. But then again, they were probably used to driving under all sorts of bad road conditions.

Almost on cue, Aaron asked, "Are we getting close?"

"Yes, about ten minutes away." She almost bounced in her seat at the thought of getting to camp, the last three hours of hard driving forgotten. "I can't wait till you see it," she said. "It's quite beautiful."

"Really?" Aaron's glance at the surrounding countryside was skeptical. They were traveling through dry, dusty, open woodland. Trees were sparse, and offered little shade, and the long grass was already turning brown and dead. Most people didn't realize that the withered grass was what kept the cattle going through the long months of the dry season. It still held nutrition and even moisture, enough for the desert-hardened cattle, at least.

"Yes, really," she replied, not letting his skepticism rattle her happy mood. "There's a permanent water source out here. A billabong that hardly ever dries up, except in the deepest of droughts. It attracts so much bird life. We set the permanent camp there because of the water. It's great."

"Sounds nice," Aaron said noncommittally. He'd been uncharacteristically quiet on the drive out. Which she hadn't minded at the time, because she needed most of her focus for the road. She could feel the weight lifting from her shoulders with every mile they got farther away from the lodge. Getting away from the constant threat of her stalker. The letters, the phone calls, none of that could touch her out here. Aaron had seemed more cheerful as well, for the first half an hour, at least. But perhaps the weight of responsibility hadn't lifted so much from his shoulders. He still had a job to do. Aaron had warned her there would be rules she needed to follow, precautions that needed to be taken; just because they were moving location didn't mean she was suddenly safe. Her head understood the continued risks, but her heart wanted to soar up to the cloudless, blue sky.

They'd decided to keep Aaron's true role under wraps. It was easier not to have to explain to everyone what was going on inside the family. Aaron had concocted a story that Julie wasn't one-hundred-percent happy with, but as she couldn't come up with anything else, she went along with it. Aaron was supposed to be her boyfriend, as well as the assistant cook. It gave him the excuse he needed to stay close by her side at all times, and a reason not to join the other ringers out on muster. Julie had argued that people might not believe their story, because as far as she was concerned, there would be no public displays of affection. He was to keep his distance and she would not, under any circumstances, be treating him like a boyfriend.

"Have you had much to do with cattle before?" she asked, not taking her eyes off the road.

"Nope. Only the sheep on Tony's farm, I'm afraid," he said with a shake of his head.

Julie had wondered if he'd continued his love of the land after he'd departed. Because he'd left without any explanation, and she had no idea where he'd ended up, she sometimes imagined him riding off into a faraway sunset somewhere, horse galloping swiftly beneath him as he pushed a last wayward sheep into a waiting yard. It seemed those fantasies had been completely wrong, and he'd forsaken country life for a job in the city. Which was a shame, because he was wasted in the city. He'd been such a skilled rider; had an empathy with the horses that made them want to please him. He'd been able to get even their grumpy old gelding, who'd managed to buck her off twice, to behave beautifully when he rode him. She'd loved to watch him ride. Would he still have that special ability? Or had his time in the city turned him soft, buried his talent beneath that professional exterior?

"Sheep are very different animals from cows," she said, with a smile attempting to corral her wayward thoughts. Which was a bit of an understatement, especially when it came to these top-end cattle, who were left to roam wild for the whole year without ever seeing a human being. They were untamed and hard to handle, often contemptuous of these puny men trying to corral them.

"Hmm, I'm sure I'll get the hang of it," he mused, then he shot her a sharp look. "But I won't be dealing with the cattle, and neither will you," he warned. "Remember, you promised to stay in camp. There will be no riding out and chasing cattle. I can't protect you properly out there."

Julie pouted at him. Spoil sport. But she was determined not to lose her good mood. At least she was away from the lodge, would be sleeping under the stars, breathing the free air.

The vehicles in front slowed, they were at the creek crossing. Julie watched as first her father, and then Wazza, negotiated the rocky creek bed. They took it slowly and carefully because of the steep incline on the opposite side, with deep wheel ruts left by vehicles crossing when the track had been wet and muddy.

Aaron stared out the window. "Are you sure…?"

She smiled at him gaily. Of course, she could do this. Shifting into first gear, she let the vehicle roll forward slowly. Aaron grabbed at the handle above his head, and Julie suppressed a giggle. This was the first time she'd seen that steely façade of his crack. A small part of her liked that she made him nervous.

The four-wheel-drive bumped slowly down the embankment, and Julie negotiated her way over the flat river rocks on the bottom. Then she lined up the wheels and gave the diesel engine a little gas, so it growled as it climbed the steep side on the opposite bank, straining to pull the heavy load behind it. *Please don't let her get stuck.* The last thing she needed was the indignity of Steve or Wazza having to help pull the car and caravan out. The wheels slipped as she went over a patch of gravel, but she eased the clutch just a little and let the torque and the car's momentum carry her forward. A few more agonizing seconds later, they popped over the edge of the embankment and were out on level ground once more. Julie let out a breath she hadn't even known she was holding.

"Impressive driving." Aaron let go of the grab bar above his head and nodded slowly. "Remind me never to underestimate you," he added, and her chest ballooned. Which was stupid, because she didn't need compliments from Aaron Powell.

Julie slowed down and watched in her rear-view mirrors to make sure the Scanlon's truck made it through. Their articulated truck had a long wheelbase, and there was a tricky moment when Julie wondered if they might get the rear end stuck on the far embankment as their front wheels climbed the near one. But Scanner was clearly an old hand and angled the semi sightly to the left, so that his tailgate just cleared the rocks at the bottom as he began his climb up the other side.

Julie signalled the vehicles in front to keep moving, and the convoy rolled on again. In the distance, a flock of birds took to the sky, and she could see a rising plume of dust, which meant some of the other ringers had already arrived and were setting up their tents and hopefully clearing the area around the camp of debris that'd built up since they were here last.

A tract of grassy plain opened up before them, and Julie pointed out the window to the left. "There's the billabong," she said. A shallow expanse of water stretched away toward a stand of trees on the far horizon. The grass around the edges remained green, with sedges and other tall, water plants growing around the fringes. Spindly eucalyptus trees gathered around the periphery in great clumps, all jostling so their roots could reach the permanent water source.

"This is a long-term stock camp," she explained to Aaron, although he'd probably already heard it all before. She pointed to their right, at a bunch of taller trees in the distance, beneath which nestled a maze of steel yards, ready to be filled with wild cattle. "We always start our musters here. Depending on our stocking rates, we might move camp later on, out to a couple of mobile sites."

Steve's four-wheel-drive was already pulling into a spot of shade beneath the trees. Some of the figures straightened up from where they were setting up a stretch of canvas to stare at the newcomers. They'd arrived at the camp right at nine am, but they still had a big day ahead of them.

"Looks like those other roving ringers you mentioned are here already," Aaron said, his astute eyes checking them all out, as if he could somehow tell from this distance if they posed Julie any harm. She wanted to remind him that Lance had already done background checks on them all, and as far as he was concerned, they'd passed with flying colors.

"Yes," she agreed. "Some of them got here last night." A large canvas tent was already set up over near the water tank they used to run their showers and get fresh water. The tank should still be full, as the last rains of the wet season had been less than a month ago. Folding chairs and a table gave the site an air of semi-permanence. Whoever owned that tent had claimed prime position.

There were five ringers meeting them here today, bringing

the total crew to sixteen. Julie had met some of them last year, when she'd come out to camp with Skylar. There was Lee, the indigenous stockman, who barely said two words, but watched everything around him with his ageless eyes. Carrot —a redhead, of course—and Dave, who often travelled together and were the larrikins of the bunch. Then there were Bazza and Rosie, a husband-and-wife team, whom she'd met when they'd come back to the lodge to carry out more stock work on a short-term contract straight after the muster last year. She and Rosie had struck up a friendship, she liked the woman's laconic manner and easy smile that split her freckled face whenever Julie told one of her jokes.

Steve was already out of his vehicle and waving wildly at Julie, directing her over to a dusty, flattened area where they could position the caravan. She drove around in a half-circle, watching her load through her side mirror until Steve held up his hand and she stopped.

Julie jumped down from the cab and stretched her back, kicking out her legs and giving them a shake. God, it was good to get moving again. Aaron did the same on the other side of the vehicle. She watched covertly, as he tipped his head backward and rubbed the side of his neck, then rolled each of his wide shoulders, one at a time. Funny, but Julie didn't remember this shirt ever looking so good on Wazza. It stretched nicely over biceps that bulged through the fabric. Then Aaron leaned into the cabin of the vehicle, and it took Julie a second to figure out what he was doing. He'd flicked open the glove compartment and quickly and efficiently retrieved his gun, bending down and slotting it beneath his jeans. Julie made a small noise of annoyance. He didn't need to carry a weapon, not out here. They'd had more than one heated conversation about it over the past few days. After much wrangling, Aaron had finally conceded that instead of wearing his large handgun in his shoulder holster—which

would be obvious to anyone who knew what to look for—
he'd wear his smaller, tactical SIG Sauer 9mm in an ankle
holster instead. In her eyes, Aaron was taking his
responsibilities to the extreme. What would he say if someone
became suspicious? Aaron had shrugged off the question,
clearly not worried about what the ringers might think of him
carrying a gun. But he should be worried. They were a tight-
knit bunch. In some ways, they were more accepting of
people—it took all types to live the life they did—but in
others, they were less tolerant, especially if they thought there
was a threat to them, or their way of life.

"Have you got your pepper spray?" Aaron asked, coming
around the front of the vehicle.

She frowned and put her hands on her hips. Really? Was
that all he thought about? They'd only just arrived, and he
was already thinking the worst. Why did he have to bring her
mood down by reminding her she was a target?

"Well, have you?" he asked again, staring her down.

With a sigh, she patted the front pocket of her jeans. "Yes,"
she said, rolling her eyes. She'd popped it in there early this
morning, just as she was leaving her bedroom.

A low buzzing sound filled the air, then a small white
speck appeared on the horizon.

"Here comes Tony, the helicopter pilot," she said, happy
for a change in subject. "Right on time. Now we can really get
this muster under way." The little chopper landed lightly on
the ground, raising a plume of bulldust around it. Aaron
craned his neck, as if to get a better look at the chopper. Or
the pilot, Julie wasn't sure which. Steve ran over to chat to
Tony, who alighted from the chopper, both of them ducking
beneath the spinning blades, probably giving him
instructions as to the best spot to start driving in the cattle.
The chopper would round up the cattle in the farthest
paddocks and drive them toward the waiting ground crew on

horseback and on quad bikes, who would then gather them up into larger and larger groups and drive them toward the waiting yards, often a distance of up to twenty kilometers away. Chopper mustering had revolutionized this game. Made it possible to muster thousands of cattle in days instead of weeks.

"Give me a hand to unhitch the caravan," Julie said.

"Will the chopper stay at the camp?" Aaron asked, placing his Akubra firmly on his head and following her around the back of the vehicle to help unhitch the safety chains and then loosen the tow ball, ready to uncouple it.

"Yes, for the next few days, at least," she replied, struggling to undo the bolt holding the safety hitch. All the fine, red dust from the track had worked its way into the screw, making it near impossible to turn. "Why?" She straightened so she could regard him.

"Helicopters interest me," he replied, regarding her from beneath the brim of his hat. "I've got a pilot's license."

"You can fly a helicopter?" She couldn't hide the surprise in her voice.

"Yep," he said in an offhanded manner. "It's a hobby. Not something I need for my job," he added in a hurry. "Purely for fun."

"For fun, huh?" She regarded him through narrowed eyes. It was good to hear that Aaron could actually do something for fun. She'd been starting to believe he was deadly serious all the time.

"Want a hand?" Aaron tipped his chin in the direction of the caravan's tow bar.

"Nope. I can do it." She grunted as she hit the nut with a hammer and then tried it again. This time it moved, and she used a pair of pliers to untwist it completely. Success. But try as hard as she could, she couldn't quite manage to lift the coupling hitch off the tow ball. It was stuck, and no matter how much she twisted it and grunted, lending all her weight to heaving upward on the handle, it wouldn't budge.

"Now, do you want a hand?" Aaron said, not bothering to hide his smirk.

"Go ahead," she huffed in a disgruntled tone. Sometimes brute strength won out in the end. He may as well put all those glorious muscles to work for once.

It was going to take a while to unpack the caravan and get it set up for the mammoth task of cooking for sixteen people. But Julie was glad for the convenience; she'd rather have the caravan to store all her foodstuffs, than have to set up under one of the large, white canvas awnings some of the ringers were already erecting. It was easier to keep the caravan clean and organized just how she liked it—no one else was allowed in without her permission. She could also sleep in the van if she liked. A double bed took up one end of the long caravan. But Julie would rather toss her swag down on the ground and be able to stare up at the stars.

"First things first. I need to get smoko organized. Then the riders can get going and we can set up everything else," she said, watching as Aaron, with seemingly no effort, unhooked the caravan, pushed it back from the car a few inches and positioned the dolly wheel with the brake on, so it wouldn't roll away. Smoko was already taken care of for this morning. Skylar had packed some of her famous pumpkin-and-wattleseed scones, which she'd baked this morning. Poor Skylar must've had to get up at three am to get them done in time. Julie hoped that the ringers who'd arrived last night had taken the initiative to get the campfire going this morning and hopefully set up a billy full of hot water so she could make tea and coffee.

"Right," Aaron replied. "What can I do to help?"

"You can put chocks around the caravan wheels to keep it in place. Then get the fold-away tables out of the back of the

Land Cruiser and set them up over there." She pointed to where the ringers had almost finished setting up a large canvas awning. "Once we've had our morning break, we can set up the mess tent over the tables, so there's shade for people to sit and eat," she continued. "We'll drive lunch out to them today. I'll only have time to make sandwiches. But Skylar put in a couple of her delicious quiches as well, she always keeps some in the freezer, just in case. That should be enough to keep everyone full until dinnertime."

"When you said that being the cook was a full-time job, I didn't imagine that it would actually take up *all* of your time," Aaron said with a twitch of his lips.

Julie grinned as he made his way around to the driver's side of the Land Cruiser. His grumbling was becoming amusing. Today was considered a late start for them. They wouldn't get a full day's muster in; the stock hands were usually in the saddle just after sunrise.

"Wait until the hard work begins, you'll love it," Julie sang out as she climbed the stairs into the caravan. If he'd forgotten what it was like to be out on muster, then he was about to appreciate a good day's hard work. Which might be good for him, bring him down a peg or so off that high horse of his.

"I can do this all day." She turned in time to see Aaron raise his arms and strike a pose resembling a prize fighter. That sounded like another Captain America quote. Her heart lifted even higher as she laughed at his silly antics.

CHAPTER THIRTEEN

Aaron took a seat next to Julie around the campfire, and asked himself for the umpteenth time today, why he'd thought bringing her out on muster might be easier. He rolled his shoulders gingerly, feeling the ache deep in his bones. Aaron liked to think he kept himself super fit and healthy, with three to four gym visits a week, and regular, ten-kilometer runs whenever he had a spare hour. Today had been spent carting boxes of equipment as they unloaded the vehicles, erecting numerous tents and awnings, banging steel pegs into the ground to hold up the tents, helping Dale to get the bore pumping water to fill the tank for showers—which ended up with him covered in grease and dust—carting feed for the stock horses gathered in the makeshift yards, and running back and forth between the caravan and mess tent with endless food collection errands for Julie.

But even when the ringers arrived back at camp, they weren't close to being finished. The first job once the cattle were in the yards was to draft out the weaners, calves, and dry cows. Some cattle would be sent for processing to the meat works, and they were kept in the large pens ready for the trundling trucks to come and collect them in a few days. The micky bulls—male calves—would be castrated, dehorned, ear clipped, branded and vaccinated before being let loose again. And the female calves given much the same treatment, so they could be released to fatten up and get ready for breeding next year. Aaron had watched the ringers doing this dusty, arduous job and suddenly didn't envy them quite so much.

He was more physically fatigued than he'd been in a long time. The most frustrating and surprising part of it all was that Julie kept up with him—perhaps had done even more than he had. He'd forgotten how strong country women were, how hard they worked. It was a good lesson in humility.

He'd done it all while keeping a close eye on Julie, of course. He never let her out of his sight, and if anyone approached her, he would hover like an overprotective father. Even though he was now pretty sure Julie was safe. Grudgingly, he admitted that it'd take a hell of a lot of skill and pre-planning for the stalker to be one of these ringers sitting around the campfire. You couldn't just pretend at this job. You were either a ringer, or you weren't, there was no in-between, as he was beginning to discover the hard way. Because he wasn't one, and knew they only accepted him because of Julie, and because the boss said they had to.

Even so, he wasn't going to let his guard down. Just because he was pretty sure no one at this camp was the stalker, didn't mean the offender couldn't still infiltrate somehow. It'd be almost impossible for someone to find her out here, and even if they did, they wouldn't be able to just swoop in and abduct her, because where would they take her? It was the middle of nowhere. Aaron had persuaded Steve not to let any guests come out to muster this year. Some of the hardier guests, with a good standard of riding, would often request to join the crew for a day. Steve had admitted that the guests were more of a liability and usually got in the way rather than being any help. But they liked to say they'd partaken in a truly top-end experience. So, Steve had agreed with Aaron almost right away regarding not involving the guests this year. Daniella had been harder to convince, however. She'd had a request from at least three couples to come out and watch the muster. But the fewer people who knew exactly where Julie was, the better. Part of the idea of getting Julie away from the lodge was to separate her from anyone suspicious, including the guests.

"Can I get you a drink?" Julie asked, bringing him back to the present with a jolt. "I'm going to make me a cup of tea, but I'm getting Dad and Dale a whisky. Do you want one?"

Aaron shook his head. He never drank alcohol while he was carrying a weapon. Some agents allowed themselves one or two, but he hated to think anything might impair his judgement. "Do you need a hand?" he asked, half-levering himself out of the chair.

"No, you stay here." Julie put a hand on his shoulder to keep him from standing. An instinctive gesture perhaps, but Aaron felt the tingles spread down his arm from her touch. She withdrew her hand quickly and Aaron let his gaze follow her shadowy figure over to the mess tent. He should go and help her, she'd been on her feet all day, as well, and she must be as exhausted as he was. He was about to get up and go over to her, when the familiar figure of her stepbrother joined her at the table, a bottle of whisky in his hand, and he resettled himself into the chair.

"How was your first day?" The male voice came from beside him, and Aaron swivelled his head to take in the lanky guy sitting next to him in a folding chair that was too small for his tall frame. Aaron wracked his brain for a name.

"Great, thanks, Brian." Aaron had made sure he'd been introduced to all the crew before they went out on muster this morning. Brian sat next to his wife, Rosie. They were a husband-and-wife team from down near Walgett, a small town in New South Wales. Julie had told him that the young couple were contracting out to other stations so they could earn enough money to stock their own small property. It was a hard life, but they hoped to do it for a few more years, then they'd have enough to call it quits.

"Call me Bazza, everyone else does." Brian waved a hand in the air and Aaron noticed it was clean. When the team had returned to camp this afternoon, they were filthy, red dirt from head to toe, grime embedded in every fingernail and skin crease. This country was nothing like the lush, rolling hills of New South Wales. It didn't take long before all the ringers were covered in a fine layer of bulldust. Some of the other ringers didn't seem to be as fastidious—perhaps because they didn't have a wife to nag them—but Bazza had washed his hands and face before he sat down to eat dinner. "It's a bit of an eye-opener, your first time on muster, hey?" Brian added.

Was it that obvious? Aaron sighed. "Yes, this northern end of Australia is very different from most things I've experienced," he agreed.

Aaron looked up as Julie returned to her chair and sat with her hands wrapped around a metal mug of tea. Dale took a seat on the other side of his stepsister, handing Steve a mug, which presumably contained a measure of whiskey. Aaron acknowledged Dale with a nod.

"What's different?" Julie asked, taking a sip of her tea.

"I was just saying this country is a complete contrast to what I'm used to," Aaron admitted. "I mean, Dalgety could get dry in the summer, but this is something else again."

"Wait until the wet season," Julie said with a smile. "The country goes from dry as a chip to a sea of mud, to grass so green and tall a grown man could get lost in it."

"Hmm," Aaron answered with a raised eyebrow. He really

hoped he wasn't still at Stormcloud by then. If he was, it meant they'd failed in their job to find this stalker and eliminate him.

"How did you guys meet?" Rosie spoke for the first time, leaning around her husband.

"What?" For a second, Aaron didn't understand the question.

"You and Julie," Rosie said with a cheeky smirk. "You make such a cute couple and I just wondered how you met."

"Oh, ah…that. You want to know how we met?" Damn, his tongue was suddenly stuck to the roof of his mouth.

Rosie nodded, taking a sip from her bottle of beer.

He and Julie had worked out a vague story before they left the lodge, just in case anyone asked, but Aaron was still unprepared for the forthright question.

Images of the very first time Aaron had laid eyes on Julie came back to him. Julie had only been sixteen at the time, and him eighteen. Aaron had worked odd jobs on local farms in the area on weekends and after school. But now he'd finished school, he was looking for something more permanent. Old Joe, who ran the IGA supermarket in town, had mentioned that Tony Benitez over at Roseby Downs might be looking to hire. Aaron remembered arriving at the front of the homestead and stepping out of his ute to see a whirlwind charge past him in a nearby paddock; a slip of a girl on a palomino horse racing to the end of the field to try and shut the gate before a herd of sheep escaped. He'd watched, mesmerized, as she made it to the end just in time, leaping off her horse and shooing the sheep away while she dragged the metal gate closed. Then she'd trotted up to him and speared him with her blue eyes from beneath her hat, asking him what he wanted. In that second, he knew he wanted her. But it'd taken another couple of months, until after she'd turned seventeen, that he'd finally allowed the raging attraction sizzling between them to turn into a physical relationship. And even then, they'd kept it a secret from Julie's mother and stepfather.

"It's not a very interesting story, really. Around nine months ago, I arrived out at Stormcloud for a job interview, but I ended up getting lost," Aaron said to Rosie. It was always better to stick as close to the truth as possible. And this part was true, apart from the timeline. "Julie found me wandering around and pointed me in the right direction, that's all." Aaron gave a shrug.

"But I bet it was love at first sight, though, hey?"

"Yes, it was," Aaron admitted. "She drew me in with those gorgeous blue eyes and her amazing smile. And after I got the job, it didn't take long for me to woo her into my arms." Which had also true been true, twelve years ago. But now…? Julie had made it very clear she wanted nothing more to do with him, in a romantic fashion, at least.

"Aww, that's so sweet," cooed Rosie. "And did you know the first time you saw him that he was the guy for you?" The woman's eyes lit up with enthusiasm as they landed on Julie.

Now it was Julie's turn to squirm uncomfortably in her seat.

He scooted toward her chair and put an arm around her shoulders. "Of course, she fell head over heels for me, didn't you, honeybun?"

Her eyes turned arctic blue as she speared him with her gaze. Perhaps he'd crossed a line, but they had to make this relationship seem believable, didn't they? Dale gave a muffled grunt of amusement and then hurriedly took a sip of whisky when Julie turned to glare at him. The Stormcloud staff were in on the ruse, but Dale obviously found it awkward to watch.

She turned back to Rosie. "Sure did. We've been madly in love ever since." She gave him a sickly-sweet smile and touched his face with her fingertips in an intimate gesture. "Aaron is my knight in shining armor. He looks all big and rugged on the outside, but on the inside, he's as vulnerable as a newborn calf. It's what I love most about him."

Even if she was overdoing the saccharine smile, Aaron had to hand it to her, she was a hell of an actor. Damn, she even had him believing they were together.

"What about you two? How did you meet?" Julie asked, smoothly deflecting the conversation away from them, and he gave a quiet sigh of relief.

A strange musical jangle suddenly erupted from the side pocket of his chair. It took Aaron a second to realize it was the satellite phone ringing. "Sorry, I'd better get this," he said, picking up the phone and walking away from the fire. Normal cell phone reception out here was practically non-existent. Steve had furnished him with a satellite phone so he could stay in touch with HQ.

"Aaron, here," he answered efficiently, once he was out of hearing range of the circle around the campfire. "Jake, is that you?"

"Yeah. Sorry to be calling so late, but I've got some good news I think you might want to hear. As well as some not-so-good news."

"Great, I could do with some good news." Aaron's heart rate spiked. Perhaps he'd be out of here sooner than they all thought.

"We think we have a name. Travis Mailmann." Jake paused, letting the information sink in. "We tracked down the Christian group, that often protests outside the clinic Julie attended. They were there on the day she attended."

Aaron turned the name over in his head. It didn't ring any bells, but he'd ask Julie if she'd heard it as soon as he got off the call.

"The church pastor, William Spencer, was more than happy

to speak to Nikolay. He even tried to palm off some of their pro-life pamphlets onto him." Jake laughed at that, but Aaron just wanted him to get on with it, and when he didn't respond, his boss soon sobered. "Anyway, the old guy wasn't going to give out names of his parishioners, which is fair enough. But when Nicolay told him a guy was stalking Julie, had crossed the line, and was threatening violence, that his whole protest group might be charged as accessories to a crime, it didn't take long for the pastor to come up with a name."

"Good," was all Aaron said. Nicolay might be gruff and somber, but he certainly got the job done. He was very particular about details, so Aaron believed him. If he thought this was the right guy, then it probably was.

"William seemed to be almost grateful to spill the beans on this Mailmann. It seems he was even creeping the pastor out with his overzealousness, at times. They tolerated him because he really embraced their Christian morality and seemed harmless. But then, some of his intense ideals were starting to frighten them. He even—"

"Do you have an address for this guy?" Aaron asked, cutting through Jake's explanation. Aaron didn't need the fine details right now. Jake could send that through in an email. Aaron wanted to know if they were close to catching this guy. "Did you get any hits on the name?"

"That's the not-so-good news. This guy is a ghost. No address, no phone number. He does have a small online presence. A Facebook page where he spouts versus from the Bible and condemns women who have abortions. But that's all we can find at the moment."

"Damn," Aaron muttered to himself.

"It may even be an alias," Jake said down the line. "The pastor did give Nicolay a photo of this Travis guy, but I'm not sure how much help it'll be. I'll email it to you. It's not very clear, Travis is standing with a group of other protesters. He's got a beard, and a cap pulled down to cover his eyes."

"Thanks, I'll make sure Julie gets to see the photo, asap." Aaron turned the new details over in his head. "That new legislation can't come in soon enough," he added. The Queensland government was due to pass a new law in the next few weeks, granting a safe access zone of one-hundred-and-fifty meters around family planning clinics. Aaron hadn't really thought about it before he'd become involved with Julie again, but it was a heinous thing that people were allowed to harass and belittle women, making an already hard choice even harder. The new law might not stop protests all together, but at least it'd keep them out of the faces of the women who needed to use the clinic. "Hopefully it will stop this kind of thing from happening again."

"I agree," Jake replied, but Aaron heard the weariness in Jake's voice. They both knew that a piece of paper with a new law written on it wasn't going to stop sickos from attacking innocent women. They'd just find another way to do their hunting.

"Nicolay is looking into everyone in this group, of course. Leaving no stone unturned. But as you'll see from the photo, most of them are women in their fifties and sixties, and don't really fit the profile of our stalker," Jake said.

"Right. Thanks Jake. Let me know if Nicolay comes up with anything else." It wasn't what Aaron had been hoping for, but at least it was a start.

"Will do. I'll get Lance to work some of his magic and see if he can come up with any more on this Travis guy. He might be able to find stuff that Nicolay can't. Talk to you when I have more info."

"Cheers." Aaron rang off, his mind still processing all the information. He'd need to find somewhere he could get reception around the campsite, so he could download his emails and show Julie the picture of the man called Travis Mailmann. On the off chance that she recognized him, they might be able to solve this case after all.

CHAPTER FOURTEEN

Aaron helped Julie up the step and into the caravan. The touch was conciliatory, unconscious, but Julie's stomach still tightened at the contact. She and Aaron had strolled back to toward the caravan on the outskirts of the camp, after she'd said goodnight to Dale and Steve and the rest of the crew. Everyone else was retiring for the night. The fire had been doused and lights were going off one by one around the campsite. Bazza and Rosie had their own tent set up on the opposite side of the fireplace nearest the water tank, and she saw Bazza duck into the tent and draw down the zip. The Scanlons also had a large tent—more of a marquee, really, with only three sides enclosed, the fourth side left open to let in the air. Lee, the indigenous stockman, took himself off into the bush, where he'd set up his swag under cover of a large stand of bloodwood trees. It seemed like he was a bit of a loner, but then, so were a lot of people you met up here. Carrot and Dave had been the last to leave the fire, ribbing each other quietly about the day's mustering efforts, while they headed toward their modified trailer, which served as a way to carry all their belongings, and also had an extension on top, which folded out to one side of the trailer and functioned as a sort of roof over their heads, under which they set up their own swags.

It was early by most people's standards, just after nine pm, but she had to be up by five to get breakfast ready for the crew, and everyone else was in for a long day's work tomorrow. Steve had wanted to walk her over to the caravan, but after a few moments of hushed whispering, hoping that Aaron wouldn't overhear, she'd convinced him that it was Aaron's job, and that he should go and bed down in his swag near their large horse trailer beside Dale and the rest of the Stormcloud crew. Which he finally did, but not before giving her a quick, awkward hug. He was clearly still worried about her.

The team had spent an easy evening chatting beside the campfire. Carrot had even brought out an old guitar and started strumming it, a beautiful backdrop to the stars and peaceful night around them. Aaron had seemed fairly relaxed, at least until Rosie had asked them how they'd met. Julie had nearly lost it at the flash of naked fear on Aaron's face. But then she'd quickly sobered when he'd started telling half-truths about how they'd met, and the memories of their first meeting back in Dalgety came back to haunt her. Afterward, Aaron had moved off to talk to Tony, the helicopter pilot. She'd watched as his features had become animated in the firelight while he chatted, leaning forward eagerly to hear what Tony had to say. Vaguely, she wondered what they were talking about. By the enthusiastic waving of hands, she decided it had something to do with flying helicopters, and she was glad that Aaron had something else beside her safety to fill his mind.

Glancing up, she noticed low clouds sliding over the horizon, blocking out the moon. They'd been rolling in all afternoon, causing the humidity to rise. It was stuffy inside the caravan, and one glance at the double bed tucked down at the end made her recoil in dismay. She didn't want to sleep cooped up in this tin box, with Aaron sleeping on the floor at her feet. It'd been Aaron's plan all along, but not hers. The past two nights sleeping—or not sleeping, as had been the case—with Aaron in her bedroom was enough to cure her of any more time confined in close quarters with him. She had another plan in mind.

"I'm going to sleep under the stars tonight," she stated, not looking at him.

"What? That's not what we agreed on, I—"

"I brought you a swag, you'll be safe from snakes and spiders, if that's what you're worried about," she said, cutting him off.

"I'm not worried about the vermin," he growled. "I've spent plenty of nights in a swag before. Remember—" He cut off abruptly. Julie was sure he'd been about to mention the times they'd slept down by the river, and she grabbed the tabletop with her hand to steady herself. "What about those clouds?" Aaron pointed skywards, changing the subject.

"Oh, it won't rain, don't worry." She forced a giggle and turned on her heel, glad to be able to hide her face. "We sometimes get what's called a dry storm up here in the north," Julie explained. "The clouds build up because of moist air from down south, but it won't rain. We might get some lightning and thunder, but no rain. It's actually not a good omen, because the lightning can cause bushfires. We'll need to stay alert."

"Great." Aaron didn't sound at all pleased. "Thunder and lightning, did you say?" What was that look that flashed across his face? Apprehension? Aaron removed his Akubra and scrubbed a hand over his face, and the look was gone.

"Yep. It can be quite a show." She went to head out the doorway, but Aaron's large frame still filled the entrance. He frowned at her. "The swags are in the back of the Land Cruiser," she explained.

"Do you really think that's a good idea?" He wasn't moving an inch.

"Yes, I do. Can't you feel how hot and airless it is in here? We won't get any sleep, we'll be tossing and turning all night." She took a step closer, only a foot from his face now, and put her hands on her hips, willing him to get out of the way. They stayed like that, locked in a stalemate. The urge to glance down at his strong, masculine lips was immense, but she wasn't giving in. He wasn't going to win this one.

"Fine," he finally conceded, backing down the steps and onto the ground.

Julie released a quiet breath. Jeez; she was glad he'd moved when he did. Because she wasn't sure exactly what might've happened if he hadn't. Staring into his face mere inches from hers had given her time to reacquaint herself with the little idiosyncrasies of his features. The blue eye was the color of a stormy ocean, the brown eye more like a piece of rare amber. Square jaw, set at a jaunty angle, covered with a week's worth of scruff. Resolute mouth set into a hard line, but with the ability to quirk upward with amusement at the most surprising times. His tawny hair was still the same, a little longer on top, fashionably swept over to one side, but shorter around the back and sides. The darker slash of his expressive eyebrows riding up his high forehead. And that scar was intriguing, it leant him an almost pirate-like look.

Aaron held up his hand. "I'll get the swags. You stay there. Grab a flashlight, will you? And have you got your pepper spray?"

Julie sighed; he was in overprotective mode again. She merely gave a weary nod and then puttered about in the caravan, taking care of her nightly ablutions, like washing her face and brushing her teeth. The caravan had a large water tank, which allowed her the luxury of running water at her fingertips. But she'd still have to shower over at the water tank like everyone else, where Dale had rigged up the makeshift shower bays using hessian bags as screens. That was a task for the morning, after everyone else had left for the muster, and she might have a little privacy. As long as Dale didn't try and hang around, demand that she stay within sight, like he'd been doing all day. She stared out the small window, watching a sudden flurry of lightning strikes on the horizon. They lit up the nighttime sky, sending everything into stark relief for a millisecond.

A sudden image assaulted her brain, of her and Aaron standing in the outdoor shower together, her hands running over his soapy shoulders, down his back, over his superb buttocks, and then… *Hold up, girl*. What *was* she thinking? She needed to switch off her libido right now, because that was never going to happen. Aaron Powell was never going to have another chance to break her heart.

She picked up the pack of cards sitting on the rear of the countertop and began to shuffle them absentmindedly. It soothed her to have something to do with her hands, helped her to think. Plus, she liked to do magic tricks to pass the time or to entertain people. It was fun and often helped break the ice. The cards slipped between her fingers, the familiarity of them letting her mind wander.

"I've set up the swags over by the old river gum," Aaron said, stepping up into the caravan.

Julie's hand flew to her heart. "Jeezes, you scared me."

"Sorry." But the look on his face said that he wasn't really, and his next statement proved it. "You should be more aware of your surroundings, you know."

She threw her hands up in the air, almost losing the cards. Was this guy ever going to take a break from serious protection agent? She was safe out here. As safe as she could possibly be.

Keeping a lid on her temper, she instead asked him, "Do

you want to brush your teeth?"

She stood and watched as he did so quickly and efficiently, then they shut up the caravan and he showed her where he'd set up the swags with a swing of his bright flashlight. The old river gum spread its protective limbs above them, leaves rustling gently in the breeze.

"I wasn't sure if you wanted to join the others over by the fire," Aaron began to say, but she waved her hand.

"No, no, this is great," she replied. They were close enough to the others that if they called out, they'd hear, but far enough away to have a little precious privacy.

"It's pretty flat under here, not too many stones," Aaron started to explain. Then another flash of lighting lit up the sky, followed by an ominous rumble of thunder and Aaron flinched and ducked his head.

Julie stood for a second, contemplating first the overarching sky above and then Aaron, as he too glared at the sky, then mumbled something too low for her to hear.

"Don't tell me you're afraid of thunder?" she asked, unable to stop a cheeky smirk. She wracked her memory banks to see if she could remember a time she'd spent with him during a thunderstorm, but came up blank.

"No, I'm not." Aaron purposefully dropped his hat beside his swag and began to remove his boots one at a time.

"Yes, you are," she crowed, suddenly delighted to find something this big, strong, no-nonsense man was afraid of. "Don't worry, I can hold your hand, if you like." What could Aaron possibly find scary about a summer storm? She thought it was wild and beautiful.

"Just get in your swag, so I can turn the flashlight off," Aaron growled, not quite able to meet her eye.

She did as she was instructed, unzipping the swag and laying it open, but couldn't keep the silly smile off her face. It'd cool off during the night, but at the moment, with the clouds keeping in the heat and raising the humidity, she was going to sleep with the swag open and only a sheet to cover her. A lot of the modern swags were almost a miniature tent; they had a roof and a small fly. But at Stormcloud, they used the basic version that bushies had been using for decades. It was essentially a large sheet of waterproof canvas wrapped around a thin mattress made up with sheets, blankets, and a pillow, which could be rolled up and tied into a bundle. If it rained, you pulled the canvas over your head to keep you dry. It was simple, but it worked like a charm. Her swag had a slightly more modern twist, in that it had a zip to keep it closed and a small metal tripod that could be erected over her head to keep the canvas off her if it rained. Aaron had laid out the beds side by side beneath the white tree trunk. She toed off her boots and put them near her head, so they were easy to find in the morning.

"Just so you know, I'll be sleeping in my underwear tonight," she said sweetly, then slowly undid her jeans and teasingly wiggled them down to reveal her thighs, then calves, then finally she kicked them off. She had no idea why she suddenly wanted to act the provocateur. But whatever had prompted her, the way Aaron's eyes widened with surprise—and something else—was more than gratifying. In another exaggerated move, she took the small canister of pepper spray out of the front pocket and held it aloft, for him to see, then placed it inside one of her boots, within easy reach should she need it during the night, which she wouldn't. Folding her jeans, she shoved them down the bottom of her swag; it was the only sure way to keep the creepy crawlies out of them. Prudence got the better of her at the last second, and she decided to keep her T-shirt on. She'd remove her bra once she was in bed. Then she hunkered down into her bed with a sigh, propping herself up on her elbow to watch him.

Without a word, Aaron unsnapped the small gun and removed the ankle holster, and then he also shucked his jeans in one efficient movement, revealing powerful thighs tapering down to muscular calves. Her mouth went suddenly dry at the sight. Uh-oh, she should've thought about that before she chose to tease him. Then, in an equally methodical move, he pulled his T-shirt over his head, so that he was standing in only boxer shorts. A flash of lightning lit up the sky, showing off his Adonis chest and muscular arms to full extent. *Oh, shit.* Julie licked her lips. He was absolutely stunning.

It was his turn to smirk at her as he stepped into his own bed and slithered into it. But then another loud crack of thunder rumbled overhead, and Aaron ruined his sexy pretense by grimacing and ducking his head.

"Are you sure you don't want to hold my hand?" she said again, meaning it this time. Poor guy, he really did seem to be afraid of thunder.

"No, thank you." His voice was deep and gravelly, which did nothing to quell her lustful thoughts.

To distract herself from her contemplation of his impressive chest, she asked the first question that popped into her head. "Where did you get that scar? The one through your eyebrow?"

"This?" Aaron touched the scar with his finger.

"Mmm-hmm. You didn't have it back when... I was just curious," she finished haltingly.

He hesitated for a split second, as if deciding how to answer. "I hit my head on the steering wheel when I crashed my car."

"You crashed your car? When?" She leaned toward him on her elbow, fascinated.

Again, that slight hesitation. "The night I left Dalgety."

"What?" Julie was flabbergasted. "How?"

"I was angry, and I misjudged a corner, that's all."

"What were you angry about?" This was the essence of the problem. If he'd only tell her what had made him so angry that he'd up and left without saying goodbye. Was it something she'd done? She doubted it, he'd kissed her sweetly on the lips as he'd climbed out of her window that night, promising to see her in the morning. But he'd never returned. Something had happened that night, and she needed to know what.

"That's my secret, Captain. I'm always angry," Aaron answered in a deep, accented voice.

What? He was quoting The Hulk at her, now? "That's bullshit, Aaron, and you know it," she replied. "Tell me what really happened," she demanded.

Aaron narrowed his eyes at her challenging tone. She was becoming angry, too, and he could probably see the conflict in her eyes. How dare he be so flippant?

Another flash of lightning illuminated the scrubland, followed by a growl of thunder a few seconds later. The storm was moving away. Soon, it'd be dissolving on the far horizon, all that hot air and pent-up emotion finally spent. Because she was watching Aaron's face intently, she saw him flinch at the sound. He really was afraid of thunder. The realization flushed all the building anger from her veins. Aaron rolled over with a grunt to face away from her, and she was left in no doubt that was the end of the conversation.

But she was determined it was only just the beginning.

CHAPTER FIFTEEN

"Is there anywhere I can get cell reception in this bloody backwater?" Aaron held his phone to the sky and shook it, but then regretted his impatient words as soon as they left his mouth. It was only ten in the morning, but it'd been a long day already, and he was letting the stress get to him. It was imperative for him to check his emails and messages, especially the one with the supposed photo of this stalker guy, otherwise he was working half-blind on this job.

He'd been on the go since just before five, helping Julie prep the food for breakfast. The hungry hoard had descended at five-thirty, devoured everything in sight, and then left him and Julie alone in the suddenly empty campsite. But that was only the beginning. Julie had to clean up from breakfast and then prep for lunch and dinner, and even though his job was to protect her, she had him running around camp like a personal slave.

Julie lifted her head from where she was kneading the dough to make damper and studied him. But instead of some clever retort, which he probably deserved, she said, "There's a repeater tower up on that hill over there." She pointed a flour-covered finger to the left of the campsite.

"What's a repeater tower?" He was pretty sure it wasn't a

cell tower, so why on earth would he get reception up there?

"It's for the UHF radios," she said, as if that explained it all.

Aaron had noticed all the staff out on muster wore a portable radio in a specially made pouch slung over their neck and around one shoulder, so they could talk into it hands free if need be. But that still didn't make him any the wiser, so he stared at her blankly.

"UHF radios only work if they have a line of sight. If a hill or mountain get in the way, they don't receive so well. So, in those areas, we put a repeater tower, which helps strengthen the transmission."

"Oh." That was all fairly logical. But it still didn't answer his question about cell coverage, which used completely different technology.

"You can also get some mobile reception up there, because it's the highest point for miles around," Julie said, putting him out of his misery.

"Oh. Good."

"If you help me get this damper in the camp oven and stoke the fire for me, I should have half an hour or so free before the silverside is ready to be carved up, and the damper is cooked. We can saddle up the two spare horses and ride up there."

"Thank you," Aaron replied, and he meant it. Julie didn't have to take time out of her busy day to help him. "I'm on it," he added, heading toward the campfire. He felt more at ease now they had the camp to themselves. No one could approach without him seeing or hearing them. He ran a perimeter check every hour or so, just to make doubly sure nothing was out of the ordinary. Which meant he was happy to give Julie a longer leash and not hover over her, like he had last night. He walked to the firewood stacked high in a pile, ten meters behind the fire pit. Grabbing a few large pieces, he expertly slotted them around the edges of the red-hot coals. Julie wanted the coals to cook over, but not a roaring flame, as that would only burn things.

Aaron was getting a fast lesson about what cattlemen liked to eat; plenty of simple, high-protein, high-carb meals to keep them going all day. But it seemed here on Stormcloud, they were fed at almost a gourmet level. For breakfast this morning, Julie had served up huge piles of bacon, fried eggs, toast, and baked beans. The lunch menu today consisted of an enormous side of corned beef—Stormcloud beef, of course —done over the campfire, which would be sliced thinly and laid out on a plate, homemade damper, an enormous bowl of coleslaw on the side, and a fresh fruit platter, all neatly sliced so the ringers could eat it and go. For morning smoko, Julie had already baked up a huge batch of scones, which would be served with a slathering of strawberry jam—no butter, it melted in the unforgiving heat. He and Julie would stack all the food in the back of one of the Land Cruisers and drive out to meet the team, to deliver lunch and this afternoon's snack and save the crew time and energy, so they didn't have to come back to camp. Luckily, there were no vegetarians or vegans out here. They wouldn't fare well.

Ten minutes later, Julie was still fussing around the damper, making sure it was in the perfect spot on the fire, and testing the meat to see how much longer it needed.

"I'll go and saddle the horses," Aaron suggested helpfully. Anything to get them up that hill a little quicker.

"Would you mind? That'd be great," she replied, still preoccupied with the food. "I got Dad to bring Chester, the chestnut, for you to ride."

Aaron strode over to the horse yard, a makeshift construction of steel fences erected beneath the shade of a cluster of river gums. It was the first time he'd taken a good look at the horses. Most of the ringers brought their own mounts, but some, like the Scanlon crew, preferred to ride the four-wheeler ATVs. Aaron peered over the top of the fence at the two horses standing together in the far corner. The big one must be Chester, and...hang on... For a second, he thought it was Cloud, Julie's beloved palomino from Roseby Downs, and his heart did a double-tap in his chest. But no, that'd be impossible. Cloud would be in horse-heaven by now, or at the very least deep in retirement back in some lush paddock in Dalgety. Julie and Cloud had been a spectacle to watch together; they almost seemed kindred spirits. He'd loved to watch them, Julie's long, blonde hair flying behind as she urged Cloud into a full-on gallop through the green grass.

But he'd promised himself no more memories. So, he banished those untrustworthy thoughts and went over to the trailer where all the horse's tack was stored, glancing back to make sure Julie was okay. Her voice raised up in a song he didn't recognize, and he smiled to himself. She had a good voice, but she only sang if she thought no one else could hear.

It'd been a long time since he'd saddled a horse, but it came back to him as if it were yesterday. Both horses were well-trained, and while Chester sighed as he slipped the bridle over his ears, he walked docilely enough beside him across the yard to be saddled. The horse's hooves kicked up a haze of dust in the mid-morning sunshine. Now and then, he caught the sound of Julie singing, and was reassured she was safe. Chester nuzzled Aaron's hand, probably looking for a treat, and he let the horse's whiskers tickle his palm for a moment. A flock of parrots flew overhead, squawking lazily, bright colors flashing, headed to the billabong for a drink. He brushed a fly away from his face and tilted his head back to stare at the dappled light streaming down through the leaves.

Julie kept saying that it was beautiful out here. Peaceful. But this was the first time he'd really stopped to experience it.

And she was right.

He could see the attraction of this place. Of this lifestyle.

The ankle holster would get in the way when he was riding, so he leaned down and slipped it off, tucking the gun into the front of his jeans. Julie seemed to think she was completely safe out here, untouchable. But he wasn't confident enough to leave the weapon behind. It was his job to be cautious.

"Come on then," he said in a low voice, clicking his tongue and leading both horses through the yard gate, then shutting it behind him.

Julie was waiting for him as he led the horses over to the campsite. Her Akubra was firmly clamped down over her forehead and she was holding up two UHF radios. "We need to wear these, so we can hear what's going on out there, in case we're needed."

Handing Aaron one of the radios, she took the reins of the palomino from his other hand. "Thanks for saddling Dusty for me. She's a great little mare. Dad bought her for me when I started working here," she said, slipping the radio pouch over her shoulder.

"She reminds me of Cloud."

"Yes, she does look a little like her," Julie replied, a strange look passing over her face.

Aaron wanted to ask what'd happened to Cloud, but thought better of it.

"How long since you've sat on a horse?" Julie asked with a cheeky grin, swinging lightly up into her saddle.

"A long time," he admitted, letting his gaze find hers. His stomach suddenly fluttered with nerves, and he wondered if he'd be able to do this. Julie had assured him earlier that it was just like riding a bike, your body never really forgot how to do it. Some of his nerves must've transferred to Chester, and he danced a few steps sideways. Aaron took a deep breath and chided the horse in a low voice. "Oi, settle down." Then he lifted his foot into the stirrup and swung his leg over the horse's rump.

Julie was right, his muscle memory kicked in and he began to move with the horse, as it walked after Dusty. He was riding in a western saddle, almost like sitting in an armchair, and his legs stretched and loosened, feeling the gait of the large animal beneath him.

Julie turned and flung another cheeky grin at him. "How's it feel?"

"Great." He threw a grin back at her and urged Chester to walk up, so he came alongside Julie. "It feels great," he admitted.

"You can take the cowboy out of the country, but you can't take the country out of the cowboy," she remarked.

Aaron lowered his eyebrows. Perhaps long ago, he'd thought of himself as a cowboy. But not anymore. His life was in the city now.

"Chester's a great horse," Julie said, waving her hand in his direction. "He used to be dad's stock horse, but he's got a new young gelding he's training up, so you get to ride him instead. He's practically bomb proof, and really patient. He's only got one flaw; he hates snakes. Dad told me one time Chester bucked him off when a snake slithered in front of them as he was walking down a dry creek bed."

"Good to know." He patted the chestnut's warm neck. He didn't blame the horse, snakes were nasty, evil creatures.

"Are you up for a trot?" Julie didn't wait for an answer, however, she merely squeezed her heels into Dusty's side and took off, leaving him to follow in her wake. Oh, he was going to be sore tomorrow, and he'd probably regret this, but right now, he may as well enjoy it.

Fifteen minutes later, they crested the top of the low escarpment, and Aaron reined Chester in and drew in a deep breath. Scrubby floodplains spread out around them as far as the eye could see. Here and there a bottle tree reared majestically into the sky, clumps of smaller Acacia dotted in between, the billabong near their camp a bright jewel in the midst of the dry, brown country. The stock camp almost looked idyllic from up here, the parched clearing and the unadorned austerity softened by the distance and heat haze.

Away in the distance, a plume of dust rose into the sky. "Is that...?" He pointed in the direction.

"Yep, that's the muster," Julie concurred. "Looks like they've already got quite a large bunch gathered up." She removed her sunglasses and squinted into the distance. "I guess we'll find out when we take lunch out to them." Pulling off her Akubra, she ran her hand through the short strands, rubbing away the sweat and dust. Her eyes were crystal blue today, reflecting the sky. He'd enjoyed the view as they'd climbed the small hill with Julie in the lead, watching her neat, jean-clad ass move with the rhythm of the horse, hips rolling almost hypnotically in front of him.

A metal tower soared around ten meters into the sky, right above them. It was a basic structure, with what looked like an antenna on the top. Aaron had just tilted his head back, holding onto his hat, so he could see right to the top when something pinged in his back pocket. His phone.

"I've got coverage," he crowed with delight. Dismounting, he let Chester's reins drop onto the ground—Julie assured him the horse was well trained and wouldn't wander away—and pulled out his cell. It pinged again. And then again. Absurdly, Aaron felt a swell of relief, like an addict taking a drag of a clandestine cigarette. He was obviously becoming way too attached to his phone. But this was for work, so he could feasibly justify it.

Julie remained atop her horse, drinking in the vista below. Her phone began to make pinging noises, as well, but she ignored it. If only he had her self-control.

Aaron opened the email app and hungrily began to scan through the incoming mail. There were at least four emails from work. But it was the two from Nikolay he was most interested in. He opened the newest one first, sent only an hour ago, which was a succinct summary of what Nikolay had found out about the rest of the church group. As far as Nikolay was concerned, this Travis guy fitted the profile of their stalker the best. But he reiterated Jake's concerns from last night, stating that it was highly likely Mailmann might be an alias, as it was unusual for any real person to have such a small online footprint, with so little information out there in the world. And while he couldn't discount the pastor—which made Aaron stop and think for a second—the man with the beard seemed to be the most obvious suspect. Then Aaron opened the email sent last night, scanning it quickly before downloading the attachment and clicking on the photo. Jake had been right, the photo wasn't great. It was of a group of around ten people, all holding up signs with pro-life slogans on them, three of them men, but except for one younger goth woman dressed all in black, the rest were older women wearing cardigans and sporting gray rinses. Nicolay had circled the image of a man standing at the rear of the crowd. Jake zoomed the photo in to see if he could make out any features, but he already knew that he didn't recognize this person. The hat hid his eyes, and the scruffy beard hid most of the bottom third of his face. It could be half the men in the inner city of Brisbane, for all he knew. The guy was wearing a white shirt, buttoned up to the neck, and a dark-gray cardigan, also buttoned up, but that was all Aaron could see of his outfit, as a short lady with a purple, knitted jumper blocked out the rest. Would Julie recognize the guy? It was a long shot.

Aaron approached Julie, who was in the process of

dismounting. He hadn't mentioned his discussion with Jake last night with her yet. But now he had the photo, he needed her to look at it.

"I want you to see something," he said, standing beside her and holding up the phone. "Our private detective has tracked down that group of protesters outside the clinic on the day you were there. And we have a list of names and some photos."

Julie froze, her hand lifted halfway to her face to take off her sunglasses. "He did? You do?" Her face paled beneath her Akubra.

"Yes." Perhaps he should've broken the news to her a little more subtly, but it was too late now, so he plowed on. "There's one guy we're especially interested in. His name is Travis Mailmann." Aaron searched her face for any signs of recognition. "Is that name familiar to you in any way?"

Julie removed her sunglasses and hat, and tapped them lightly against her leg, then bit her lip, her eyes taking on a faraway look. For a second, he was distracted by her white teeth worrying at her lip, and for a mad moment he had to fight the urge to rub his thumb gently over those plump lips to soothe away her concern.

"No, can't say that I have," she said eventually.

Aaron held his phone up in front of her. "What about this guy? Have you ever seen him before?"

Julie stared at his phone, leaning in close to get a good look. She started to shake her head, but then frowned and pursed her lips. She took the phone from his hand and zoomed in on the photo. "He looks…" She shook her head. "I don't know why, but I feel like I've seen him somewhere."

Aaron's blood pounded through his veins as he watched her scrutinize the image. Could this be the break they were looking for?

"It's something about his eyes. No, wait, maybe it's the

beard, and the way he's dressed," she mused. "Like he's some kind of nerdy hipster. But that hat. Why would a hipster wear a baseball cap?"

To cover his identity, Aaron wanted to say. But he let her roll things over in her mind. They were close, he could feel it.

"The cap is one of those stupid touristy ones, like the ones my local newsagent used to sell back in Brisbane—Wait." She held up a hand. "I think I remember where I saw him. I was at my local supermarket buying some fresh fruit a few days after I went to the clinic. It's only a block from my house and I used to walk up there all the time. I wasn't looking where I was going, and I turned around and bumped right into him. My apples went everywhere. He was most apologetic and helped me to pick them all up." She tapped a finger against her lips. "I didn't really look at him, I was too busy collecting my fallen fruit. Probably the only reason I remember the incident was because he said something that struck me as kind of strange at the time."

"What did he say?" Aaron encouraged.

"He kept saying he was sorry, over and over again. But then he said something like, *fate works in mysterious ways, and I should thank God for his merciful hand.*" Julie lifted her gaze to Aaron's face. "At the time, I brushed him off as some harmless quack. I got my fruit together, paid for it, and headed home." A shiver ran through Julie. "I remember feeling a little creeped out the whole way home. I was so glad when I finally walked through my front door and shut it behind me. At the time, I put it down to still feeling guilty over the whole termination. But now…" She put a hand over her mouth. "Oh, God, he could've followed me home. I led him straight to my place and I never even knew it." Her blue eyes brimmed with tears. "How could I have been so stupid?"

"You weren't stupid, Jules. You hold no blame for any of

this." Aaron put a hand on her shoulder to comfort her. He'd seen it so many times before; the victim feeling in some way responsible for bringing down the violence onto themselves. "This is a good thing. It means we're closer to catching him."

But his words had no effect, and her tears began to fall. "I made this happen. If I'd never met Judd. If I'd hadn't had that damned abortion. If I'd been a bit more aware of my surroundings." She swiped at her eyes angrily, but it didn't stop the sob from breaking free.

"Oh, Jules, it's okay." He pulled her into his arms. "None of this is your fault," he soothed, his hand automatically coming up to stroke her hair. "We're going to get you through this, I promise." This was the second time she'd broken down and cried in his arms. The first time had ended in a kiss. This time, he was determined to only be there for her support, nothing more. He held her lightly against his chest and let her rest her head in the crook of his shoulder. A horse snorted softly nearby, and the sunshine beat down on his shoulders as a trickle of sweat ran down his spine. She was pliant and soft in his arms. They were standing out in the middle of the desert in the blazing sun, while Julie's heart was breaking. The incongruity of his surroundings wasn't lost on him.

He'd left her so long ago because he knew she deserved better. But now it felt like they'd come a complete circle. Here he was, holding the woman he'd once thought was his one true love while she lamented the failings of her life so far. A small voice kept asking what might've happened if he'd stayed. Could he have saved her all this pain and heartbreak? Or would he have been the cause of so much more?

CHAPTER SIXTEEN

Julie searched the skies above for a sign. A sign of what, she wasn't sure. A sign that she was doing the right thing, perhaps. She went back to beating the cake mix and gave a secret smile. Today was the fourteenth. It was Aaron's birthday. Did he think she wouldn't remember? He certainly hadn't mentioned anything to her, and she got the distinct feeling he'd be quite happy to let it slip on by unnoticed.

This day was bittersweet. Because it was also on this day twelve years ago that he'd disappeared from her life. And she still hadn't forgiven him. Had she?

"Do you need a hand?" Aaron's deep baritone broke through her musing.

"No, no, all good," she said, half-turning away. Most likely he wouldn't ask what she was cooking, but she didn't need him getting suspicious.

Aaron raised an eyebrow as if he were about to argue, the one with the white scar bisecting the dark hair. That scar was also a reminder of the day he'd left her, but somehow, she didn't mind it. In fact, she wanted to run her finger over it, to feel if the skin was smooth and healed, or was it still slightly raised after all this time?

"What did Dad say this morning before he left?" she asked,

to distract him, and herself. This morning, Steve had beckoned Aaron over and leant down from atop his saddle, talking earnestly into his ear.

"Much the same as he did yesterday afternoon," Aaron replied. "He was just making sure that... I, ah...kept you safe."

Julie snorted. She could just imagine the conversation. Steve worried about his daughter, even though she was fully grown. But then, what parent ever stopped caring about their kids? When they'd first arrived, Steve had suggested he or Dale stay behind at camp, as well, to make sure Julie had adequate protection, but Aaron had convinced him that he was very good at his job and Julie was in capable hands. Steve had headed out on the first day with a frown darkening his features and had radioed in more often than was strictly necessary throughout the day to make sure she was okay.

Then yesterday, after Aaron had shown her the photo of Travis Mailmann, her stalker, and after she'd finally pulled herself together—she couldn't believe she'd broken down in his arms twice now, what was happening to her—they'd taken lunch out to the crew and relayed the new information to Steve and Dale and the other Stormcloud staff. Steve had sobered and interrogated Aaron as to what they were going to do with the new facts. Aaron had told her father that this was a step in the right direction. His man, Nicolay, was onto it, delving into all the tiny details they could find about the stalker. He'd also passed the information onto Nash, to see if the police had this guy on file, but they were still waiting to hear from the senior constable. Steve had seemed slightly more at ease after Aaron told him all this and had stopped calling her on the UHF every five minutes. There'd been no more contact from the stalker, no more threats or innuendos, it was almost as if he'd been a figment of her imagination. But Julie knew her father wouldn't relax completely until they'd caught this guy.

Last night had passed in pretty much a mirror image of their first night out in the bush. She and Aaron had set up their swags under the tree and gone to bed early, ready for another early start. The rhythm of living and working in the stock camp was starting to get into her blood. It was hard work, but she loved falling into her swag, exhausted at the end of the day.

She and Aaron had worked hard all day, with no time for a short ride up the hill, like they'd done yesterday. They made a good team, falling back into the same easy camaraderie they'd been used to at Roseby Downs. Perhaps not quite so easy, Julie amended silently, because there was always that matter of trust between them now. She didn't think she'd ever allow that wall she'd put up around her heart to come down, not when it came to Aaron.

The muster crew was farther out today, and it'd taken them longer to drive lunch out. Plus, she might have to admit that she'd perhaps overextended herself a little, and her menu might've been a tad ambitious. She'd made quiche and roast beef sandwiches with mustard and lettuce for lunch and homemade sausage rolls for smoko. And she was now in the process of putting the finishing touches to her two large pots of shepherd's pie; a special request from Dale, as it was his favorite. It was helpful to have the oven in the caravan, as it gave her the added ability to be able to cook things like biscuits, cakes and other pastry products. Adding another level of complexity by deciding to bake a cake for Aaron—she was going to surprise him with it after dinner—probably didn't help.

Julie had talked to Skylar this afternoon; her stepsister had called on the sat phone to check that all the meals were going as planned, and to make sure her supplies were still sufficient to keep the camp going for the next few days. Julie had held in a sigh. She was more than competent at handling the camp mess tent, she'd proved that when she'd taken over the kitchen for those few weeks while Skylar had been hiding from a crazed gunman. But Skylar was a perfectionist and a bit of a control freak, so Julie let her talk and made the right noises at the right times, not wanting to antagonize her.

After they'd sorted out the finer details of what to cook for the crew, Julie asked, "How are things going back at the lodge?" What she really meant was, had there been any more signs of her stalker while she was gone.

"Pretty good," Skylar answered. "Nothing out of the ordinary, if that's what you mean." It was Skylar's way of telling Julie they'd heard nothing more, which was a good thing. Julie was beginning to wonder if her stalker had just given up. Perhaps knowing that Aaron was guarding her had warned him off and he'd gone home with his tail between his legs. "We're run off our feet, of course, with you guys all out there," Skylar continued. "Mum is in a flap half of the time. You know how she gets."

Julie could imagine, Daniella was very organized and efficient, but when she got stressed, she often became extra demanding and ran around trying to do everything herself. "Hang in there, sis," Julie replied. "Only a few more days, and we'll be back."

"Yeah, well, I don't think those guests leaving in the dead of night, two days before they were due to check out, helped Daniella's mood."

"What? What do you mean? Who left?" Julie was puzzled. It was highly unusual for anyone to leave early, everyone loved staying at the lodge, and they were paying a premium to do so.

"That newly married couple, the older guy and the cute little younger woman," Skylar said disinterestedly. Skylar never took as much time as Julie did to learn the guest's names. She was much more interested in hiding away in her kitchen than fraternizing with the clients.

"You mean Chase and Maya?" That was odd. "Why would they do that?"

"Yeah, that's them," Skylar said. "And I have no idea, they just packed up their four-wheel-drive and took off really early yesterday morning, without letting us know. Daniella was pretty mad when she found out, but she's got the guy's credit card details, and she said she's going to bill him the full amount, anyway."

"That's pretty weird," Julie mused. But then it took all types. From what she remembered about the couple, they were going to do some exploring after they left Stormcloud, head north and check out more of the *outback*, as they called it. She hoped they'd be okay. A lot of city folk drove up here in their big cars and thought they were invincible, but the land could be harsh and unforgiving if you weren't prepared for it. And Maya especially seemed sweet and a little naïve. She might not do too well camping rough in the severe conditions of the outback. "Did you tell Nash about it?" she asked suddenly, as a prickle of concern ran down her back.

"Yeah, I did. He said he'd keep an eye out for them. But he's a busy man, you know."

That was for sure. Nash and his partner, Constable Willow, ran the small police station in Dimbulah and were the only two cops for hundreds of miles. Their jobs were so much different to those cops in the city, and they were often away from the station for hours, or even days, at a time. But that wasn't exactly what Julie had meant. They'd been told to keep their eyes open for anything different or out of place, and this was both of those things.

Julie had spoken to Skylar for a few more minutes and then ended the call so she could go and get the Anzac biscuits out of the oven. She'd mentioned the call to Aaron, and he said that Nash had already passed on the information, so Julie soon forgot about it. As long as Nash and Aaron knew about the guests' slightly odd behavior and neither of them seemed worried, then she wasn't troubled, either.

It was now getting on toward late afternoon, the orange rays of sunshine flashing through the tops of the trees, setting the billabong on fire. The bird life around the body of water was amazing, and the lowering of the sun toward the horizon was bringing in thousands more birds for a final drink before they retired for the night.

"They'll be back soon," Julie called out to Aaron, who was over by the fire, stoking the coals to keep the two large camp ovens sufficiently hot. "I heard Scanner on the radio a few minutes ago. It sounds like they're only ten minutes out." Julie ducked back into the large canvas annex they'd erected as a makeshift mess tent. Where had she put those cake tins?

"Yeah, I can see the dust plume coming closer. I think I can hear them as well," Aaron added, standing on tiptoe and craning his neck. Was that a look of longing on his face? Don't tell her that Aaron Powell might actually want to be out there helping them bring in the recalcitrant bush cattle, rather than standing guard over her? She knew that once he got out here, he might remember some of his idyllic lifestyle from his teenage years, but of course, he was still denying he missed it.

She took the chance to examine his profile while he was distracted by the oncoming muster. He'd barely left her side over the past two days. Which was both annoying and somehow comforting, all at the same time. And he continued to carry his small gun in his ankle holster, which was also both annoying and comforting. The more she got to know this new Aaron, the more she could see so much of the old Aaron still hiding inside.

"You can saddle up Chester and go and meet them, if you like," she offered. "I'll be fine here for ten minutes on my own." It'd give her time to get the cake in the oven without him seeing what he was doing.

Aaron's blue eye flashed at her from beneath the brim of his hat, and he studied her for a few seconds before replying. "Thank you, Julie, but that's not my job. My job is protecting you, remember?"

She wanted to stick her tongue out at him, but huffed out a breath and turned her back instead. She was only trying to be helpful. He'd looked so much like the Aaron she'd known back in Dalgety, with that eager yearning on his face to be off helping the crew, that she'd almost let her old feelings surface again. She'd remember not to do that from now on.

After dinner, the crew sat around the fire, satiated and worn out, chatting about the wild scrub bull that'd charged at Sue on her ATV. She'd only just managed to swerve out of the way in time. They all laughed, as if the danger had been part of the fun of it all. Julie began washing up the plates and cooking pots. Maddie, the youngest of the Scanlon team, pulled out a battered, dusty, old radio from the back of their truck and set it up on a wooden stump near the fire. There was no radio reception out here, but she'd come prepared, and had a stash of old-fashioned tapes on hand. She'd chosen a mixed tape of well-known Australian country singers. Slim Dusty was now warbling about the pub with no beer from the speaker.

Surprising everyone, Bazza and Rosie got up and began to dance to the beat, kicking up a small dust cloud on their makeshift dance floor beside the fire. Julie smiled as she watched the married couple swing each other around with a familiar intimacy that almost made her jealous. Then Carrot asked Maddie to dance. At first, she said no, but the redhead kept patiently reaching for her hand until she finally conceded and got up to sway to the music self-consciously with him. Julie left the bowl of sudsy water and wandered to the front of the mess tent to get a better look at the dancing couples oscillating in the flickering firelight.

The song finished and then changed to a more upbeat one by Troy Cassar-Daley and Dave gave a whoop and asked Beth Scanlon to get up with him, ignoring her father's low scowl in his direction. Julie tapped her foot along with the music. They sometimes ran a version of a country bush dance at Stormcloud for the guests, and more often than not, it was Julie's job to get them all up and dancing, showing them some country dance moves to get them going. She loved to dance, loved to lose herself in the music. So, when Dale got up from his chair and gave her a cheeky wink, offering her his hand, she wiped her palms on the back of her jeans and took it, moving out on to the natural arena with a gleeful skip. They stomped up a dust storm with their cowboy boots, Dale whirling her around like a pro; her stepbrother was a good dancer and liked to participate almost as much as she did.

"Yeehaw," she yelled, allowing the pure pleasure of the moment to infuse her. Everyone else who wasn't dancing clapped along from their seats, adding their own voices to the music. Even Wazza took Bindi by the hand and dragged her out of her seat, joining in the merriment. As she danced, she caught glimpses of Aaron standing, watching her from the sidelines, arms crossed and a small frown marring his handsome features. She threw him a wicked smile and redoubled her efforts. This was the first real fun she'd had in days; weeks, even.

The song changed again, this time to a ballad, sung by James Blundell, and he began to croon the words about living out west where the rain don't fall. Julie dragged in a few ragged breaths, she was nearly worn out. The other couples changed their dance style and came together for a slow waltz. Dale took her hand, ready to guide her around the dance floor, when, much to Julie's astonishment, Aaron suddenly materialized beside her.

"Do you mind if I cut in?" he drawled to Dale.

"Be my guest," Dale replied with a knowing grin, passing her hand over to him before she could protest. Her heart kicked like a mule at the touch of Aaron's palm against hers, the heat of him burning through to her soul. She was about to protest when Aaron drew her in close, placing a hand in the small of her back and she lost her ability to speak as her face came to within inches of his broad, muscled chest. He was so warm, like a small furnace burned deep in his chest. It was so Aaron.

"What are you doing?" she squeaked, then cleared her throat and tried again. "You don't like to dance," she amended.

"I didn't used to like to dance," he replied. "But you don't know everything about what I do and don't like anymore."

It seemed not, because Aaron was now a very proficient dancer, and he took the lead, twirling her lazily around between the other couples without even stepping on her foot once. His proximity was doing strange things to her head. She could barely think straight, was scarcely conscious of the others moving to the beat around them. Her world narrowed until it was just her and Aaron, her palm resting in his, their thighs touching as they swept around the arena, his breath quiet, but feverish in her ear. Why was he doing this?

She didn't dare look up at him, because that'd be her downfall. He'd see it in her eyes in a second, how her body reacted to his, and how the chemistry was still there, stronger than ever. She'd never responded to any other man quite like she had to Aaron. Not before she'd met him, nor after he left her. And she was scared she might see the exact same emotions reflected back in his eyes. He captured her hand in his and lay it gently on his chest, then returned his palm to middle of her back. She could feel his strong heart beating beneath the shirt. She was suddenly lost in the feel of him, how his heartbeat drummed in time with the music; in time with hers. It drummed through her chest and down her stomach and thighs, setting her core on fire.

The song came to an end, but she almost didn't notice, until another more upbeat one took its place and everyone broke apart to shimmy and shake to the music. Wazza declared he was beat and retired to his chair, Bindi following behind him. It was Wazza's deep voice that finally broke through Julie's trance-like state. She withdrew from Aaron's grasp slowly, and he let her go, although with a hint of reluctance.

Looking around the stock camp, her mind cleared, and she almost slapped her forehead. The cake, she'd nearly forgotten about the cake.

"I need to go and ice the..." she stopped herself just in time. "I need to get something from the caravan. I'll be back in a minute," she added breathlessly.

"I'll come with you." He was beside her in a split second.

"Stay here and enjoy the music," she cajoled, "I'll be quick, and I'll be fine, you can see the caravan from here."

He was about to argue, she could see it in the set of his mouth—his delectable, kissable mouth—but after a second, he let her go. She scampered off toward the caravan, stopping to whisper in Bindi's ear as she went. She needed an accomplice to this plan of hers. Bindi smiled and nodded as Julie spoke quickly.

The rich chocolate cake was cooling on a rack in the caravan, all it needed was icing and a few candles. Aaron was thirty-one today, but Julie didn't have that many candles, so she formed what she had into the shape of a three and a one. Five minutes later, Julie was fairly pleased with her efforts. She grabbed a box of matches and walked back to the fire.

Bindi came to meet her just before she broke into the circle of firelight, hiding the cake with her body and helping her to light the candles. Then with a flourish, Bindi stood back, and they began to sing Happy Birthday at the top of their lungs, walking toward Aaron with the cake held high. After a few seconds of surprise, others from the crew joined in and they all looked in Aaron's direction.

Julie saw the exact second Aaron figured out the cake, and the song were for him. His handsome face blanched white, and he took a step away from her and the advancing cake. Julie faltered, but she couldn't stop now, so she kept singing at the top of her voice, even though her heart had sunk to the pit of her belly. Everyone got up from their chairs and formed a semi-circle around her and Aaron, singing *for he's a jolly good fellow* in raucous bellows.

Aaron plastered on a false smile and blew out the candles as everyone congratulated him.

"Why didn't you tell us it was your birthday?" Steve asked. "We would've organized something more for you."

Aaron shrugged and gave an enigmatic smile as Wazza came up and slapped him on the back, but the quick flash of pique in his eyes wasn't lost on Julie.

"Yeah, never let an opportunity for cake go by, mate," Scanner drawled. "Or any other sort of birthday favors," he added with a sly wink in Aaron's direction. The innuendo wasn't lost on Julie, and she felt her ears burn. She placed the cake on the table at the front of the mess tent and everyone crowded around, all wanting a piece of the tasty delight. Aaron hovered at the back of the crowd, frowning.

"Bindi, would you mind cutting the cake?" She asked, shoving the knife in the other girl's hand. "The plates are over there." She indicated a stack of crockery at the end of the table. "I just need to..." What did she need to do? Even she wasn't sure, but she'd upset Aaron somehow and she felt like she needed to fix it.

"Sure, no probs." Bindi gave her a skeptical smile, while her eyes strayed to where Aaron stood in the shadows. It seemed even she could feel there was something wrong.

Julie made her way unobtrusively through the throng all clamoring for the largest piece of cake, and stopped in front of Aaron, looking up into his face. "Don't you like cake? I thought chocolate was your favorite." She was at a loss for words. Why was he acting like this?

"It is," he replied with a growl. "But...I'm sorry. I just don't like to celebrate my birthday, that's all." He spun around and headed away from the fire. What had she done wrong?

"Aaron, wait." She had to run to catch up with those long legs of his. "I'm sorry, I didn't realize. I thought you'd be happy with my surprise." Happy that she'd remembered his birthday, but she didn't add the last part.

"Well, I'm not," he growled. "I don't like surprises, and I don't like remembering my birthday. It's just one more day on the calendar. Nothing special."

Whoa, where had that come from? It obviously had something to do with him leaving Dalgety on the day of his birthday. But what? Perhaps she should've checked with him, before embarrassing him—and her—in front of everyone like that. But how was she to know?

"Tell me why you hate your birthday so much? It has something to do with you leaving without saying goodbye, doesn't it? I need to know what happened. Dammit, I deserve to know what happened." They'd tiptoed around it long enough. It was time Julie extracted the truth, once and for all. She put her hands on her hips and glared up at him.

He cocked a scarred eyebrow in her direction. There were a multitude of emotions swimming through his eyes, she could almost see each one come to the front and then be replaced by the next one, but she waited, not going to be fobbed off this time. The last emotion to register in his eyes was hard to decipher. Was it resignation? Mixed with a dash of pain?

"Fine. But I don't think we should do it here," he said in a low voice, gaze drifting to the crew now re-taking their seats around the fire. One or two of them cast a questioning glance in their direction. "Shall we take this to the caravan, instead?"

"Sure," she replied curtly, and followed his shadowy form to the outskirts of the camp. He stopped next to the large river gum where they normally set up their swags. It was dark out here, away from the fire and the battery-operated lamps they used in the mess tent. Now and then, she caught flashes of reflected firelight in Aaron's eyes, but his face was full of shadows, and she could no longer read what was going on in his mind.

He leaned back against the large trunk and crossed his arms. Julie felt a nervous tickle of anticipation run down her spine. She was finally going to find out his secret. Discover why her whole world had been turned upside down.

CHAPTER SEVENTEEN

Aaron drew in a breath and looked up to the sky, anywhere but at Julie. She was right; she did deserve to know. At the time, he'd been so caught up in his own pain that he'd thought it best if he just left Dalgety, rather than inflict any of his shit on her. It'd all been too much for him to handle. All those years he'd told himself that Julie would get over it, she was young, and that kind of puppy love didn't last forever. But he could see now that he'd been wrong. It wasn't mere puppy love. It'd been much deeper and stronger. Julie had suffered, he was beginning to see that now. Suffered the agony of being abandoned by an asshole like himself. She'd revealed during one of their many talks that she hadn't had a single long-term relationship since he'd left, and while it was possibly supreme arrogance to think she'd been pining over him, it was also the plain truth. He'd hurt her deeply, cut her to the bone and left her scarred and wretched. She did deserve to know why he'd abandoned her, he owed her that much.

"Do you remember that night?" he began, tipping his head farther back and concentrating on the stars. "We had a great night." He sighed with the memory of it. "You made us a picnic, and we took it down by the creek. And you stole a bottle of champagne." He smiled. It'd been her first taste of the bubbly liquid and she'd got tipsy and giggled all night.

"Yes, I remember all of that," she replied, impatience obvious in her voice. "Very clearly," she added, not hiding the snark in her tone. "It's afterward that I want to know about."

"Okay." He held his hands up, palms outwards. He was hedging, he knew that. "Afterward, I went home." He hesitated. Here it came, she'd never look at him the same way ever again. "When I got home, my mother was waiting up for me. Sitting on the couch, drunk as a skunk." It wasn't uncommon for him to come home and find his mother practically unconscious on the couch. She'd start on the cardboard box of wine around five every afternoon, and usually by nine would take herself off to bed, swaying and incoherent. But the night of his nineteenth birthday, something had been different. He saw it in her eyes the minute he walked through the door. Something spiteful and cruel, as if all that bottled-up misery she kept hidden from him was finally screaming for an outlet.

"She stood up and wished me a happy birthday. But there was nothing happy about her smile. It was kind of cruel, and she laughed, but there was nothing funny that I could see…" Aaron hesitated again. Julie was still staring at him, but she'd taken her hands off her hips now. "I'd always known my mother begrudged celebrating my birthday. She would've happily let it slide on by without even acknowledging I'd ever been born, most of the time." His chest contracted at the thought, as something heavy lodged inside. Julie was never aware of his mother's ambivalence toward him, he'd been careful to make his childhood seem completely normal, as if his mother was the most caring person in the world. But he knew he hadn't completely fooled her by some of the probing questions she sometimes asked.

"I'm sorry, Aaron, that must've hurt you." She took a step

closer.

"Not really. Well, perhaps it did," he added, as an afterthought. And he'd turned that pain into something he recognized, something he could deal with. Anger. "Whatever, I suddenly got really enraged, like someone had flicked on a light in a room that'd been dark my whole life. I finally asked her what her problem was. Why my birthday seemed to cause her such pain?" Aaron remembered the moment so clearly; it was etched into his brain forever. The way his mother's face had twisted into a sneer. But it was more than contempt he saw in her eyes, it was loathing.

"And what did she say?" Julie prompted.

There was only one way to say it, so Aaron recounted his mother's tirade, word for word.

"Because I regret having you," Donna had spat at him. "You should never have been born. I thought I could go through with it, but after you were born, every time I looked at you, I saw *him*."

Aaron had been so shocked at his mother's outburst that it took a few seconds to understand that she meant his father.

Donna continued, as if she hadn't just broken a pact of silence she'd held sacred for the past nineteen years. "The truth is, I never speak about your father, because he's no father at all. He's a rapist. He raped me. He was some stupid bouncer at a nightclub where I used to work, and he caught me walking out late one night. No one else was around. No one heard me scream." His mother seemed to run out of steam after that and sat awkwardly on the couch. "You're a bastard child. Conceived in hate, not in love. That's why I never enjoy your birthday. Because you have a rapist's blood running through your veins and every day is a reminder of what happened to me," she ended heavily.

Aaron had stood for uncounted seconds, dumbfounded, watching his mother calmly take another gulp of her wine, as if she hadn't just ripped his whole world to shreds.

He drew in a breath and brought his mind back to the present. "So, you see why I had to leave. I'm a monster in sheep's clothing, I just didn't know it."

"Oh, no, Aaron." Pliant arms wrapped around his waist and a soft body pressed up against his. "I'm so sorry. That's terrible." Julie lay her head on his shoulder and held him. His first reaction was to push her away; he didn't need her pity. He was only telling her his story so she'd understand. That he was damaged goods, he was contemptible, not worthy of her sympathy. But it wasn't pity he felt flowing through her, as she pulled him in closer, her hips coming to rest against his; it was tenderness, kindness, acceptance.

"You're nothing like a monster. Look at you, you protect people for a living. Protect them against people like you father," she said, lifting her head and staring into his eyes. "You could never in a million years hurt someone. And you're certainly no rapist, that's for sure."

Her words took a grip on his heart. She understood him like no one ever had. Why hadn't he been able to see that back then? There was no condemnation or outrage, just pure clarity that he was more than what he made himself out to be. Even if he didn't agree with her, he felt the veracity of her emotions, felt her optimism wash over him.

"I think the great Yondu said it best," Aaron said stiffly. "He may have been your father, boy, but he wasn't your daddy." It was another Avengers quote, but as soon as he heard this one, it'd hit him like a steam train. It was just like his mother had said, his father was no father at all.

"I'm sorry you grew up without a true father's influence," Julie said. "But I think you've turned into a wonderful man, despite all that."

As he stared down at her, her lips parted ever so slightly, his fury at himself, at his mother, at his father evaporated as he was captured by her gaze. Time seemed to slow, and his heart jolted in his chest. A night owl hooted somewhere in the distance, soft and haunting. He wasn't sure how long they stood like that, wasn't conscious of anything other than the pulse in her neck, and the scent of the warm, sweet woman in his arms. She hadn't reproached him as he expected; she'd done the exact opposite and embraced him. Embraced his pain. Used her body to soothe him, just like she'd done when they were younger. And his body wanted more. The spark was still there, and one touch from her fanned the flames into a bonfire.

He didn't want to talk about his mother or his sad little life anymore. He wanted to press his body all along hers. Feel the softness and heat of her. He'd missed her so much. His hands around her waist drifted lower to cup her ass through her jeans. She drew in a small gasp, but didn't try and stop him.

"I couldn't take my eyes off you tonight," he said, voice suddenly husky. "When you were dancing, something inside me just needed to be out there with you. Touching you." His lips buzzed down the side of her neck, as he breathed in the smell of her warm skin. "You smell good, too, by the way," he mumbled into her neck. Unexpectedly, she tipped her head to the side to give him better access, and his cock tightened immediately. She wanted this as much as he did. He pushed his thigh gently at the apex of her legs, until she let him settle between her thighs, the hard length of his erection pushing into her belly.

Slowly he turned her, sidling around the trunk, so it was between them and any prying eyes that might see them from the campfire. Using the trunk to hide them, he rested her back up against the bark and captured her mouth with his.

It was as soft and pliable as he remembered. He recalled this same kiss. He knew this feeling, as if kissing Julie had been imprinted on his mind. Something he could never forget, no matter how hard he tried to erase her from his memories.

His tongue ran over the seam of her lips, and she opened her mouth to him, just as he knew she would, and he became lost in her. Their kiss deepened, became hot and delicious and familiar. He hungered for more, almost as if he could make up for twelve years of not kissing Julie. No other woman had been like her. He'd dated other women, of course. Not one of them had ever left him with this feeling of…inevitability.

Julie groaned, low and soft in the back of her throat and he crushed her to him, wanting to get close; closer still. Julie welcomed him in, deliberately rubbing herself against the hard ridge of his erection. It felt so good, so right. He grabbed her hips, letting his hands slide under her shirt and explore her waist and the curve of her lower back. Oh, God, he needed her. He wanted to take her here, up against the old river gum.

"Julie? Are you out here?"

Aaron tore his mouth from hers. Shit, it was Dale. Immediately he stepped away, but didn't let go in case she toppled over, letting her find her equilibrium first.

It took a few seconds for her to open her eyes, and when she did, they were dazed and still full of longing.

"Dale's coming," he whispered.

Finally, she seemed to grasp the situation, and drew in a deep, shuddering breath, then frantically tried to straighten her hair and her shirt at the same time.

"Yeah," she called. "I'm right here." She stepped out from behind the tree, Aaron lingering behind her. If he stepped into the light, Dale would know by the bulge in his pants what they'd been up to. Would he mind his stepsister was out here kissing the hired bodyguard? Aaron preferred not to find out, at least not tonight.

"Oh." Dale stopped when he saw Julie emerge from the

shadows. "Ah, sorry…I just wanted to check you were okay." His gaze traced Julie's features and then flicked to Aaron. Shit, they'd been busted. The look on Dale's face said he knew *exactly* what they'd been up to.

"Yep, we're all good." Julie stared at her stepbrother, and Aaron was impressed at how implacable she seemed. She wasn't going to let him ruffle her feathers, and she wasn't going to give him any more info than was absolutely necessary.

"That's good…" Dale hesitated, then he must've come to a decision, because he said, "Right, I'm off to bed. Shall I turn out the lamps in the mess tent?"

"Yes, please," Julie replied sweetly. "I'm going to hit the hay, as well." She stretched her arms above her head and gave a mock yawn, and Aaron had to hide his smile.

"Goodnight, then." Dale still looked dubious. "Goodnight to you too, Aaron," he called, as he turned on a booted heel.

They stood and watched him saunter away over the dusty clearing toward the fire. Aaron could see the rest of the crew milling around, also getting ready to go to bed.

Julie turned to Aaron and covered her mouth to stifle a giggle. "Jeezes, he nearly caught us making out like sex-starved teenagers," she whispered.

"Maybe I still am a sex-starved teenager," he said, gathering her back up into his arms. The moment might have been interrupted, but he wanted nothing more than to go right back to what they'd been doing. "You make me feel truly alive for the first time in forever," he admitted. He dropped his lips to the delicate spot right behind her ears where he remembered she was ticklish and she purred, her body melting against his, sending a shot of heat straight to his groin. "I haven't been able to think about anything else but you, from the very first time I saw you again, all fired up and ready to send me packing in the hallway."

"This is crazy," she muttered into his ear. "But when I'm with you, all propriety seems to go out the window." Her fingers ran around the top of his waistband, then one hand reached around to cup his butt cheek and gave it a cheeky little squeeze. It was nice to see that she hadn't lost any of her confidence when it came to seduction. She'd always been feisty and imaginative. One of her best qualities. "This past week, with you around, I forget who I am. Forget I'm supposed to stay away from you." As she spoke, she palmed his cock through the fabric of his jeans.

"Oh, sweet Jesus," he groaned. What was she doing to him?

As if coming to a decision, she suddenly stepped away from him. "Go and get the swags," she commanded. "I'll meet you back here in five minutes."

"Okay," he drawled, uncertain of what that meant. Was she saying what he thought she was saying?

Then she kissed him, hard and deep, and he was left in no doubt of what she meant. That kiss was a promise of what was to come.

He had the swags set up in record time and was leaning as nonchalantly as he could against the tree trunk when Julie returned. In the past few minutes, once his blood had returned from down south of his waistband, and he regained a measure of common sense, he'd come up with a million and one reasons they couldn't do what he thought they were about to do. She was a client, and he had strict rules when it came to fraternizing with a client. But Julie had smashed down all those walls of protocol and procedure with one easy smile. Perhaps he should've asked Jake to swap him out when he still had the chance. Then he might not be about to compromise all his morals and hard-won ethics just to spend one night with a woman he used to be in love with. When Julie came back, he was going to give her every excuse to allow her to back out of this. No, he'd tell her they couldn't do this.

A twig snapped and his attention zeroed in on the dark space between the caravan and the swags. He could just make out her lithe figure walking toward him. It was hard to see any details in the soft starlight, but when she finally got close enough, he gulped down a breath when he saw she was only wearing a towel wrapped around her like a toga.

"Hi," she said, a seductive, husky note to her voice. Then Julie dropped the towel, and his mouth went dry and couldn't form a single, coherent word.

She was completely naked.

And still as gorgeous as ever. And as daredevil as ever. All his reasons not to go ahead with this evaporated.

His gaze roved over her as he closed the gap between them, still lost for words. He stopped a few inches from her, drinking in her glorious body. Pert breasts, nipples taut, shimmering in the pale light offered by the stars. His cock went so hard he thought it might burst through his jeans.

The space between them hummed with potential, sweet and sensual and full of unspoken hunger.

"God, Jules, you're beautiful."

"Really?" she breathed, and he caught a hint of uncertainty. The fact that she was unsure of herself made him that much more attracted to her.

"Of course." He traced a finger lightly over her cheekbone.

He loved that she was so daring. But he was also aware that prying eyes may be able to see her creamy skin glowing in the starlight, so he scooped her up and carried her to his swag—it was a king-size, and while it'd be snug, they'd both be able to fit. A little sound of surprise left her lips, then she slipped her hands around the back of his neck, and looked up at him, so sweet and trusting. Lowering her into the cover of his swag, he pried her fingers away from his neck and hastily

shucked his boots, jeans, and shirt in three quick seconds—
he'd already stowed his weapon beneath his swag—so he
was now as naked as she was. Then he went to slip in beside
her.

"Wait." She put a hand on his chest. "Fair's, fair," she said
with a cheeky smile. "I need to see what I've been missing
out on, too."

He rocked back on his heels and squared his shoulders,
letting her look her fill.

"Holy…Jeezes. Wow, you're so…" She couldn't finish her
sentence, but he took it to mean that she liked what she saw.

"Can I get in now?" he asked as she continued to gawk at
him. He could hardly believe they were going ahead with this
crazy scheme. He'd been dreaming about this from the first
moment he'd laid eyes on Julie; dreaming about re-living old
passions.

"Oh, yes," she murmured, shifting slightly, to allow him
room in the cramped space. He began to wonder how they'd
used to achieve this when they were younger. Having sex in a
swag had seemed so easy back then. Now…he wriggled
lower, his legs twining with Julie's in a glorious tangle of skin
on skin. She giggled as they struggled to untangle
themselves, then all of a sudden, she pushed on his
shoulders, pinning him to the ground, and squirming around
until she was lying on top. Memories of her doing the same
thing years ago surged back; this was how they'd done it
before.

Lifting the sheet to cover her shoulders, she sat up, using
the fabric to shield her from anyone who might be looking
their way. Although, even if anyone was looking in their
direction, Aaron was sure they wouldn't see anything but a
dark, amorphous shape in the deeper darkness beneath the
tree. He sucked in a sharp breath as she slithered up his body,
her core coming to rest hot and slick above his erection. Her

skin was like silk sliding against his. His gaze snared on her face. It was too dark to see the pale blue of her eyes, they were now only dark pools reflecting the starlight.

"You're so much...bigger, than I remember." Her hands traced small circles over his pectoral muscles, smoothing over his shoulders, then running, feather-soft down the well-defined ridges of his abs, feeling for each individual bundle of muscle under the skin. Then her nimble fingers dropped lower and found the tip of his cock and began to stroke it gently. "Bigger in every way," she added.

He was losing all ability to do anything but feel, his body was alive, an array of hot flashes going off beneath his skin. He was a single nerve, aware of every touch of her fingers, every breath across his skin.

He was unsure where this might lead. Unsure of what this all meant. Perhaps they'd have this one night together and then go their separate ways. But he was too far gone to care. Tomorrow would take care of itself.

He stared up at her as she sat astride him, the stellar backdrop surrounding her with a crown of stars.

"God, you're so beautiful," he sighed. *Why did I ever leave you?* He kept that thought to himself.

CHAPTER EIGHTEEN

Julie lay awake, staring up at the sky above. Dawn was creeping her golden fingers over the horizon, turning the heavens light purple at the edges, fading to a bewitching teal blue higher up, reminding her of an aquamarine crystal she'd seen in a gem shop once. Crystal skies, that was what hung over her on this wonderful morning. A morning so full of promise and fulfillment.

Aaron twitched beside her, and she smiled. He'd always been a twitcher in his sleep. She let the warmth of his big body invade her soul, as memories of what they'd done last night invaded her mind.

She'd sat astride him, his chest rising and falling beneath her, and it'd felt so very familiar, but also intensely different at the same time. The way his gaze held hers, without wavering, was just about the sexiest thing ever. It didn't feel real that she was touching him again after so long. But at the same time, it couldn't get more real, her whole body was zinging with electricity. His big hands were all over her, stroking the back of her neck, down her spine, over the globes of her backside, along the length of her thighs, until she felt like she was going to melt from the inside out. She wanted him inside her, then. Luckily, Aaron had a condom in the pocket of his jeans. She loved a man who was prepared. Hovering above him, his erection pulsing at her entrance, she couldn't hold out a second longer and she lowered herself onto him, exquisitely slow. Loving that fact that she held the power, she was the one in control. She could stop it right now if she wanted to. But oh, God, there was no stopping this steamroller of pent-up emotions and needs overwhelming her. It was a waterfall of sensations running through her, sweeping away those years of unhappy feelings. And for those few pure moments, it was perfect.

Now, it was morning, and she was back in the reality of her life. She shouldn't have done it, but at the same time, had been powerless to stop it. How many times had she told herself over the past week that she was *never* going to let Aaron back into her life? Then what had she just gone and done?

She wasn't sure she could answer that question. All she could say for sure was that things could change in an instant, and last night was a testament to that. But now, she was back to being Julie, living on a cattle station in far North Queensland, with a stalker making her life hell. And Aaron was her bodyguard, with a life in the city, far away from her.

At that thought, she squirmed, deciding it was time to get up and face the day. She was already running late to serve the crew breakfast; she could hear them starting to stir. It'd be toast and beans for breakfast this morning. Where had Aaron put her towel? She was going to have to do the walk of shame back to the caravan with only a towel wrapped around her so she could get dressed. What had she been thinking?

"Morning, beautiful," Aaron murmured, but she was already half-way out of his swag.

"I have to get breakfast," she said by way of reply.

He tried to snag her ankle as she stood up, wrapping the towel around her, but she shook him off, not needing to do this right now. "See you over there," she said, and fled, barefoot across the dusty clearing.

An hour later, the crew had left for the day and Julie was doing the pile of dishes from breakfast, her mind already filled with everything on the menu she had to cook. She needed a shower, but was loath to ask Aaron, because the last thing she wanted was him to stand guard outside the hessian enclosure like he normally did, while she was in there, all naked and soapy. Her body would betray her, she knew it would.

"We need to talk." The sound of Aaron's voice, so close to her ear, startled her.

"Jeezes, will you stop creeping up on me." She almost stamped her foot.

"Like I keep telling you, you need to be more aware of your surroundings," he fired back.

"I am aware of my surroundings," she said, barely holding on to her anger. But it was good he was being a dick about this, because it made what she had to say a little easier. She turned and wiped her hands on a dishcloth, avoiding his gaze. Throwing the cloth on the table, she moved out from under the mess tent toward the caravan. "I need to get a change of clothes," she said over her shoulder, "And then I'm going to grab a shower. I've got lots to do today. If you want to talk, then walk with me." Not waiting to see if he followed, she strode toward the oblong shape at the edge of the clearing. It was going to be another perfect Queensland day. Hot and dry.

He was by her side in an instant. "Look, Julie, this is as awkward for me as it is for you." Grasping her elbow, he tugged her around, so she had to stop walking and face him. "I don't regret what we did last night, but I'm getting the distinct feeling that you do."

She almost laughed out loud. Regret? No, she didn't regret

it. Her complicated emotions went much deeper than that.

"I guess we both got what we wanted," she said in an even, measured tone. "But it won't be happening again."

"Why not?" His tone was slightly belligerent, but his eyes told her he already knew the answer.

"Because you hurt me, Aaron. And I can't forget that."

His multicolored gaze fixed on her face. "I know, and I'm truly sorry. But I had good reasons. Well, they felt like good reasons at the time," he qualified.

"I'm sure they did." Yes, she'd been horrified by his story. Horrified that any mother could think those things about their child, let alone say them to his face. And now she finally knew that Aaron had been dealing with his own feelings of inadequacy and guilt, as unfounded as they were. She felt sorry for him, wanted to help him heal from those terrible scars. But it didn't wipe away the fact she'd spent months, years even, crying over him, wondering what she'd done wrong, never able to truly trust another man with her heart again. The sex had been out of this world, as she knew it would be, but now she was left feeling oddly empty and bereft.

"And I know you're sorry for what you did, but it doesn't wipe away those twelve years of heartache I had to endure." She shook her elbow free from his grasp. "I think it's better if I just go back to being your client and you, my bodyguard. It's simpler that way, and then when this is over, you can go back to the city, like it never even happened."

Aaron's jaw tensed, and his eyes narrowed at her words. He opened his mouth to argue, but she held up a hand to stop him.

"You're good at your job, Aaron, and I trust you to protect me. But I don't trust you with my heart."

It was as simple as that. Or was it? If she kept telling herself that, then perhaps it would be. Besides, this was no time to be delving into the depths of her emotions that were better off left untouched. Aaron didn't need to know about her decision not to have children, because it was of no consequence to him. She pirouetted on her heel and stalked toward the van.

Five minutes later, Julie stepped into the shower, the stream weak and lukewarm, but it felt wonderful on her bare shoulders. Water was a scare commodity, and she needed to lather up her hair and body and wash it off as quickly as was humanly possible. Instead, she stood beneath the trickle of water, letting the emotions overcome her. All the way from the caravan, her eyes had prickled with tears, but she'd held them at bay, forcing down the lump building in her throat. Now, in the relative privacy of the shower, she let her tears fall soundlessly. Aaron stood guard beside the water tank as he always did, mere meters away, but the gulf between them now felt insurmountable as she cried and cried.

Vaguely, she became aware that Aaron was speaking to someone, and she choked back the sobs so she could listen to what he was saying. It sounded like he was on the satellite phone, perhaps to his boss back at Shield. His voice was tense, and had a strange quality to it. Hurriedly, she washed the soap away and turned off the water, suddenly needing to know what was being said.

"What's up?" she asked a few minutes later, emerging from the shower cubicle with her hair still wet, boots pulled hastily on to damp feet. Aaron's face looked like it was carved from stone. "What's the matter?" she asked again, concern turning to alarm as she saw the steely glint in his eyes.

"I've just been talking to Jake," Aaron said. His body was rigid, radiating tension, and he'd lost all the loose casualness he'd adopted since they'd come to the stock camp. Protection-agent Aaron was back in full control. This didn't bode well.

"Let's go and sit in the caravan. There are some things I need to tell you."

Uh-oh, she was really nervous now, but she followed him, meek as a lamb, as he kicked his way through the dust to the van, head rotating in every direction, on the alert.

"Right, tell me," she demanded, once she was sitting on the edge of the bed inside the van. It was already heating up in here, even though it was under the partial shade of the scraggly stand of trees.

"So, you know we've had our private detective, Nikolay, looking into finding out as much as he can about this Travis guy?"

Julie nodded for him to continue.

"Nicolay has some contacts in the police force in Brisbane, and so he's been hitting them up to see if there's any record of this guy at all, but so far, they haven't managed to find anything suspicious."

"Okay." None of that sounded bad. Not serious enough to make Aaron stare at her as if he was about to impart the worst news ever. "And...?" she said impatiently. What the hell was he not telling her?

"He also asked his contacts to look into other reported stalker cases, whether they were solved or unsolved, to see if there was any similarity between yours and others. See if they could link other cases to a pattern." Aaron sat on the bed next to her, a move that momentarily distracted her. Up until now, he'd been keeping his distance, her barbed words from earlier clearly making an impact on him. "Nicolay needs to look more deeply into this, but it seems that he's found...some disturbing cases that could well be related."

Julie froze beside him. What was he saying? Had this stalker done this before? Wasn't that a good thing, though? Because if he had, wouldn't it make it easier to find him? "Define what you mean by disturbing," she said quietly.

"Over the past eighteen months, since you left Brisbane, there've been four reported cases of women being stalked, all connected to the fact that they'd recently had an abortion."

Julie's skin began to crawl, and Aaron lay a comforting hand on her knee. Jesus, this was her worst nightmare. But at the same time, a sort of twisted relief also flowed through her; she wasn't the only one. In a strange way, it was a kind of vindication; she wasn't going completely mad.

"Before that time, there's been nothing that seemed to fit this same profile, so if the stalker was active back then, he was flying under the radar," Aaron continued. "Perhaps learning his trade, so to speak. You seem to be his first victim, but then you disappeared, and he had to concentrate on others."

She didn't like that more women had been targeted by this psycho. It hadn't been her intention when she left that he pick on someone else. All she knew was she needed to get away. "What happened to the women? Can any of them identify the man?" she asked, half-hopeful.

Aaron shook his head. "I'll get to the identity part in a moment. The first two women reported similar things to what you've been experiencing, notes in their mailboxes, texts and phone calls, but when they told him they'd involved the police, the harassment stopped. But the third woman…" He squeezed her leg tightly. "…she was taken hostage and tortured for over an hour, before she managed to get away."

"What?" Julie covered her mouth, shocked beyond belief. "What do you mean by tortured?" she asked from behind her hand.

Aaron winced. "I'm not sure you want to know—"

"Yes, I do," she said, dropping her hand. "Tell me, Aaron." She needed to know. She was no shrinking violet that needed to be protected from life's atrocities, and he more than anyone should understand that.

He looked directly into her eyes. "He beat her quite badly and also drugged her. But then…" Again, Aaron hesitated, and she ground her teeth together impatiently. "This guy had a large cross, and it seemed he was going to nail her to it, like some sort of fanatical religious nut."

Which sounded exactly like something the guy who'd been stalking her would do. "What happened then?" she asked, unable to look away from his face, seeing his eyes full of loathing at the appalling deed this man was prepared to commit.

"It seems he wasn't very good at hammering in the nails, and after a few aborted attempts, even though she was drugged, the pain must've been enough to get her up and moving, and she took him by surprise, kneeing him in the crotch and then making a dash for it. A good Samaritan found her wandering down the street an hour later that night."

Julie expelled a loud breath. Thank God the woman had escaped. But this was bad. Julie was finding it hard to assimilate everything Aaron was telling her. He moved closer, letting his leg rest up against hers, and draped an arm around her shoulder. The comforting touch helped center her a little. "So, they never caught the guy?" she asked in a whisper.

Aaron shook his head. "No. He was wearing a balaclava and clothing that completely covered his skin. And the street where she was found was in an industrial area of Brisbane, with lots of warehouses and abandoned buildings. They never found the place she'd been held, and all the DNA evidence they collected gave them nothing. That was about eight months ago."

Call it fate, or whatever you liked, but Julie was so glad her father had called when he did, and she'd left Brisbane. She shuddered to think that it might've been her they found wandering, dazed, and beaten down the street.

"That's terrible. Horrible." Julie didn't know what to think, her mind was numb. But then she remembered Aaron's words from earlier. "Hang on, you said there were four women. What happened to the last one?"

"Ah…" Aaron looked stricken, and his hand clenched tightly on her shoulder.

"What, Aaron? Tell me, please," she pleaded, but a sick feeling rose up in her stomach.

"Around a month ago, a woman was found nailed to a cross in an abandoned warehouse. She was dead, Julie."

No. The caravan seemed to swirl around her, and her vision narrowed to a pinpoint, the room going dark.

CHAPTER NINETEEN

"But we're still not sure if these cases are connected," Aaron hurried to add, holding Julie tightly into the side of his body. She'd gone completely immobile, like a frozen doll sitting next to him. "Julie, did you hear me?"

A shudder ran through her entire body, but then she seemed to come back to herself. "Of course, they're connected," she said, her voice flat and devoid of all emotion. "And it means he's escalated. It means he's capable of murder."

She'd got it spot on, that's exactly what Jake had said over the sat phone earlier. She was eerily calm. He'd expected hysterics, or at least some sort of explosion. Julie was always so full of energy. This unemotional woman scared him a little. This was the worst possible news, and it made him want to throw her over his shoulder, stick her into the car and drive her somewhere that he knew she'd be safe. It was killing him that he couldn't do that for her. But she had a life to live and was determined not to be cowed by one vicious asshole. So, he'd protect her with everything he had, even if it had to be under her rules.

Her words from earlier still stung, but in the light of this new information, he'd packed all that hurt away to be analyzed later. She'd wanted to push him away, pretend that last night had never happened. And maybe that was for the best. Although the fact that his heart felt more like a stone in his chest than flesh and blood made him think twice about her declaration that they weren't meant to be together.

"How is he getting his information?" Julie's voice broke his contemplation. "Surely he can't be following them all home, or just getting lucky, like he did with me."

"No, you're right. We think he might have recruited an accomplice on the inside," Aaron answered. There was no other explanation. It might be a coincidence, once, perhaps twice, but this guy had found names, addresses and phone numbers for five separate women. That was more than a mere fluke.

Julie sat in silence, again seeming to evaluate his words as he sat with her.

"So, what happens now?" she finally asked dully.

"We redouble our efforts to find this guy," he said.

"Yeah, like that seems to be working well now, doesn't it?" At least her apathy had morphed to cynicism. He'd take that as a small win.

"That's not completely fair," he countered. "Nicolay has been going above and beyond to get all the information he can. And this new lead might be the vital clue we need to finally confirm the stalker's identity."

"Hmm." She didn't sound convinced, but moved away from his comforting embrace and then stood. "We should let Dad and the rest of the team know." Her eyes drifted to the woodland outside the window. "But I don't want him getting all uppity and calling off the muster, or anything stupid. This doesn't change anything, not really." She walked over to the window and stared, unseeing, at the vista beyond. "Perhaps we should wait and tell him tonight."

Aaron was inclined to agree with her. But Steve Clements

was his client, and he had a policy not to withhold anything from a client. Sometimes the smallest bit of information could lead to a memory, or a clue, help save a life, even. Information was power. "I think we should tell him when we take lunch out today?"

She turned and fixed him with her gaze. Eyes that reflected the blue of the sky looked back at him. He was still amazed at how they seemed to change color along with her mood. Arctic when she was mad, deep indigo when they darkened with desire, and bright blue when she was determined. Two steps brought her back to where he remained seated on the edge of the bed, her thigh touching the tip of his knee. His cock reacted in an instant, thinking about how her firm, lush thighs had gripped him with her need last night. Banishing the thought, he looked up to meet her gaze.

"I'm glad you're here, Aaron." She touched his cheek quickly with her hand, and his heart skipped a beat. "I'd be terrified out of my wits if you weren't." He was surprised at her candor. And she really seemed to mean it. A complete turnaround from when he'd first arrived on the scene. And from her harsh words earlier this morning. "I also want you to know, I don't regret spending the night in your swag. That was one night of pure pleasure, and I'm glad we shared it. I'm sorry if I was more than a little blunt this morning. I didn't mean to hurt you."

He could feel the *but* coming, so he remained silent.

"But what I said is true. We can't and shouldn't be together. We're just not right for each other. Perhaps we never were."

He wasn't sure how to answer. All the reasons he'd left her in the first place still stood. He was the by-product of a rape, unwanted and unloved by his mother. He was determined he'd never pass on those monster genes to his children. He never wanted his offspring to be born with the stigma of what he'd had to endure. There would be no children in his future, he'd decided that long ago. So why would anyone in their right mind want to have anything to do with him? At least not long term, anyway. It'd been madness to let himself believe even for one second that he could possibly have a normal life with a normal woman. Last night he'd been in a dream, today the clarity of reality burned clear and bright.

"It's fine," he replied. "I agree, I'm not the sort of man you need in your life." He tried to keep the bitterness out of his voice. Unsure if he'd succeeded, he stumbled on anyway. "You need a man who can give you stability, who fits in with your lifestyle and your family. Who can give you children of your own, someday. I don't blame you for not wanting to have anything to do with me and my...past."

"My reasons have nothing to do with what you told me about your...parentage. That's not it at all, Aaron." Julie looked stricken, and he almost believed that she meant it. But then she hurried on to say, "And what do you mean, *can give me children of my own*? Is there something else you're not telling me? Are you unable to have kids, or something?"

They were getting onto unstable ground here; it was a deeply personal choice he'd made, and not one he'd shared with anyone else. But perhaps it was time to clear the air once and for all. Once Julie knew the truth, then there would be nothing left to tie them together.

"Not physically unable, no," he replied. No longer able to sit still, he got up and pushed past her toward the door. It was getting stifling in here. "I just don't want kids, that's all. Ever." There, he'd said it.

Julie didn't answer, merely stared at him as if he'd suddenly sprouted horns out the top of his head. He could see it in her eyes that she was confused, but also relieved. A slight breeze drifted past his shoulder, and he was aware of flies buzzing lazily in the growing heat. How much time had passed since the call from Jake? Julie would need to get moving if she was to have smoko and lunch ready to go in time. His mind drifted back to his more urgent agenda, acting on this new intel. He had more calls to make, things he needed to check with Nash, contingency plans to be put in place.

"I think we should get—"

"Well, I'm not ever having kids, either," Julie said over the top of him. "So that makes us even."

"Why not? You'd make an amazing mother," he blurted out, before he had time to think. Why would she not want to have children? The idea surprised him, made him inexplicably sad.

"I have my reasons, just like you." Her eyes became shuttered, and she turned away for an instant. Then turned back to say, "I could say the same thing about you. You'd be a great father."

They stared at one another, caught in a stalemate of shared disbelief and indignation. Suddenly, he had an inkling as to why she didn't want to become a mother. Did it have something to do with the abortion? He'd heard of women who suffered unresolved grief and guilt over the loss of a child, even though it was their decision initially. Or perhaps she was physically unable to have more babies? Aaron was unsure how to voice these questions, or even if he had the right to ask.

Before he could say anything, Julie seemed to recover her composure. "I've said way too much. This is neither the time nor the place to be discussing all our deep and meaningful decisions. Let's just agree to drop the subject, shall we?"

He continued to stare at her for another ten, long seconds, but in the end, he was a man of action. Words scared him. It was better not to have to bare his soul, and here she was, giving him an out, a way to avoid all this conflict and emotional pain.

"You're right. We have bigger problems on our list of priorities to solve at the moment." He wasn't being a true coward; he did mean to re-visit this conversation at a later date. Just at a more appropriate time.

"Right, you do what you do best. I trust you to keep this situation under control." She waved an arm in his direction. "And I'll do what I do best, which is getting the next meal ready." Without waiting for him to agree, Julie pushed past him and was down the caravan steps before he could stop her. The mere brush of her shoulder past his was enough to make him catch his breath. He turned to follow her across the grassy clearing. She strode, shoulders back, legs encased in those jeans that hugged her backside just right, striding out, taking her to the mess tent. Her short hair, wet from the shower, had dried in the time they'd been in the van, and she ran a hand distractedly through it, leaving a few tufts standing upright, which he wanted to smooth down with gentle fingers, much the same as he'd done last night. But she was getting on with it, and so should he.

Julie began to clatter around in the tent, so he found a spot just beneath the shade of the large canvas where he could stand and see her, as well as the surrounding stock camp, with one sweep of his gaze. He mulled over Nicolay's unsettling news. Nothing here at camp had changed, yet everything had changed. He was more on edge than ever, leery and unsettled. But the camp was as quiet as it always was without the rest of the crew here. The unruffled surface of the billabong reflecting the serene sunlight, the scattered trees silent in the growing heat of the day. The soft snort from Chester, and the swish of a tail to drive away the flies as the two horses rested in the shade. Nothing was out of place. But all of a sudden, it felt sinister.

Aaron was sure—as was Nicolay—that the four other cases

were connected to Julie, but as yet, they had no proof. Nothing to give them any hint of where to start. It was all so maddening and frustrating. Nicolay had been staking out the family clinic during over the past week, but there'd been no more protest groups hanging around outside. He'd gone back and questioned the pastor again about the man they called Travis, but had come up with no more information. The pastor had told Nicolay that after his group had heard about the stalking episode, they'd decided to stop their protesting. They never wanted to harm anyone, merely help them change their mind, if they had indeed been wavering, unsure of whether to go through with the abortion. The pastor also added that with the new legislation due to be passed shortly, their protests were bound to come to an end sooner or later, anyway. They may as well stop now.

Would Julie be safer back at the lodge? It was a question Aaron had weighed up time and time again since they'd arrived out here. At least if she was there, he could keep her locked up and out of sight. The stalker would find it hard to penetrate the building. It depended on just how determined this depraved individual was. If he was responsible for the murder of that woman back in Brisbane, then it meant he was capable of almost anything. Aaron's gaze flicked endlessly around the camp, afraid he was going to miss something. They were exposed out here, anyone could be hiding in the bush, just out of sight, and he'd never know. But wasn't that the whole point? This camp was isolated and out of the way, no one knew they were here apart from close family and staff, it'd be almost impossible for someone to find Julie in this remote corner of the bush.

This was a completely unique situation. He'd never had to guard a client in the wilderness before. He was used to having solid walls and sturdy buildings around him in which to shelter. Along with fast cars and high-powered weapons, if they needed to make a speedy getaway. Out here, Aaron was reduced to the small SIG on his ankle. It was less than ideal. Perhaps he should start wearing the large handgun in his shoulder holster, and be damned if the rest of the crew noticed. Julie's safety was more important than keeping his identity a secret. Jake had agreed with him, however, that this was the best place for her to be, unless of course he could convince her to move to one of the various safe houses Shield had scattered around the state, and hide her out there until this had been resolved. He glanced over at Julie, who was slicing cold cuts of meat and making a stack of sandwiches for lunch. It made sense, because she didn't have time for anything fancier, like her delicious sausage rolls or potato salad today. Would she listen to him this time if he asked her to go with him to a safe house? She'd been so determined that she wasn't going to disrupt her life, or that of her family, to bow down before this crazy stalker. But maybe now she knew what he was capable of... Would she change her mind?

The sat phone buzzed from his back pocket. It was Nash, calling from the police station in Dimbulah. Nicolay had called him earlier and filled him in on the newest details, and now he wanted clarification from Aaron, as well as to let him know he wasn't happy with this new turn of events. And that perhaps it was time the police took over. Aaron didn't like the way Nash insinuated he was somehow not up to the job; as if he were inferior. Even though he was probably as highly trained as most police officers and had more freedom when it came to bending the rules. Aaron was used to it by now, the subtle, and not so subtle, put downs. There was a lack of faith within the police force when it came to protection agent skills. Nash was worried about Julie, and he had every right to be, she was going to be his sister-in-law if he and Skylar got married. So, Aaron let Nash ramble on, because the senior constable had a vested interest in making sure that Julie was kept safe. Aaron also wanted to keep the cop on side. If he got in a tight spot—though God forbid that happened—Nash and his junior constable were the closest form of professional help to be had out here.

"I'm going to do a perimeter check," Aaron said. It was more imperative than ever he keep up his stringent protocol, make sure nothing had changed around the camp. "Make sure you stay on the UHF," he added, when she flicked him an uneasy glance. And he'd make sure he kept her in his line of sight at all times.

* * *

The mood in the Land Cruiser was decidedly tense. Julie drove, keeping her eyes on the ground in front, but her mouth was twisted into a scowl of displeasure. They were on their way back to the stock camp after dropping lunch off to the crew. Steve's words after he'd told him the news from Nicolay replayed in Aaron's head.

"That's it, Julie. This changes everything. You're leaving tonight. I want you out of here, and somewhere safe." Steve had turned to glance at Aaron. "I'm assuming you have a house, or something where you could take her?"

"Yes, sir," Aaron had replied, hiding his grimace at the way Julie's eyes had turned to shards of ice at her father's words. "We have a couple of safe houses in Brisbane and one in Cairns."

Julie took off her Akubra and slapped it against her leg. "I'm not—"

"Yes, you are," Steve had bellowed, and Julie had taken a step backward in sheer surprise at her father's outburst. "No more arguing. I've played along with your wishes this far, but no longer. Not now we know this man is a murderer." Steve held up a hand to forestall any more of Julie's arguments.

Aaron didn't disagree with Steve, but he'd never tell Julie that.

The rest of lunch had been spent in strained silence, Julie serving the crew with a sour look plastered on her face. No one was dumb enough to ask what was going on, but Aaron could see the questions in everyone's furtive glances.

As he and Julie packed up the lunch things and stowed them back in the vehicle, Steve had come up and put a hand on his daughter's shoulder. "I'm sorry, honey," he said, low enough not to be overheard by the rest of the group. "I don't like to get heavy-handed, but I don't feel like I've got any choice. I need to see you safe, otherwise…" Steve didn't finish his sentence, and Aaron looked up to see a gleam of tears in the other man's eyes. He'd walked away to give the father and daughter some privacy.

"Dad said he's going to drive us back to the lodge himself tonight. Like he doesn't trust us on our own, or something," Julie said, breaking the awkward silence in the vehicle cabin. "The muster will go on without him tomorrow, then he'll drive back out tomorrow night."

"That sounds like a good plan," Aaron replied carefully. Julie turned to glower at him for a second before returning her focus to the open plains ahead. Steve had had a quiet word with Aaron before they'd left after lunch, confirming that Aaron would take Julie away from the lodge as soon as was humanly possible and stash her somewhere safe. Aaron told him there was a safe house in Cairns, and he'd call in a helicopter charter to take Julie straight there tonight after they got back to the lodge.

"Of course, you'd agree with him," she said with a curl of her lip.

"Now, that's not fair, Julie. All we want is to keep you safe."

"Yeah, cooped up like a bird in a cage, more like it," she huffed.

He decided there was no talking sense into her, and so kept

quiet. The stock camp was just over the next low rise, if Aaron wasn't mistaken. He was beginning to learn the lie of the land after a few days out here. The hill with the repeater tower was off to the right, and he thought he caught a glimpse of sunlight sparkling off water at the far end of the billabong. Everything looked as calm and serene as when they'd left it an hour and a half ago when they rolled to a stop next to the caravan a few minutes later.

"I've got to get the beef on for the stew for dinner. And I'd better prep stuff for breakfast for Sasha. Then I need to get my things packed and ready to go." Julie hopped out of the vehicle, slamming the door behind her, and stalking off into the heat of the afternoon.

"Julie, wait," Aaron called after her. His normal routine was to clear the area before she was allowed to get back to work, but she didn't stop or turn around. Feisty and stubborn, as always.

He ran after her, tugging her back with a gentle hand on her shoulder. "Look, I know you're pissed off at the whole world right now, but I still need to do my job."

"Fine," she spat, and then stood, arms crossed, glaring at him as he walked in front. In her current mood, it'd be too much to hope that she'd stay safely in the vehicle until he'd finished. But at least if she stayed out in the open, he could keep an eye on her.

Two minutes later, she was still standing in the same spot, tapping her foot as he emerged from the mess tent.

"All clear," he said.

"Fantastic," came her snarky reply. Then she headed toward the canvas annex. "I'll go check the rest of the camp," he added.

"You do that," she called over her shoulder.

Steve had told Julie that Sasha would come out and replace her as cook for the last two days of muster, leaving Daniella and Skylar to carry the load back at the lodge. Aaron knew Julie was feeling guilty that she was now adding to everyone's burdens by leaving the station. Hopefully, she'd come around in the end.

Shaking his head, Aaron tugged the sat phone out of his back pocket. He needed to call Jake and give him the update, make sure the safe house was available and prepped for their arrival. He could walk and talk while he did his perimeter sweep, Aaron decided as he reached up to check the door to the caravan was locked. His go bag and handgun were in there, and it was a force of habit to check it on each boundary inspection. The handle turned, and the door swung open. What the…?

Before he could step inside, the sat phone rang in his hand, startling him so that he almost dropped it. Before answering, he peered inside the caravan. Nothing seemed to be out of place. Had he, or Julie, forgotten to lock the door before they left?

He pressed the answer button on the phone. "Aaron, it's Jake here," his boss said without preamble.

Talk about serendipity. "I was just about to call you," Aaron replied. "We need to get the house in Cairns ready for visitors. Steve wants her under full protection now. I'm bringing her in tonight."

Jake blew out a loud breath on the other end of the line. "That's great news. It's time the family comprehended how much danger that girl is in." Aaron agreed with his boss, but they both knew clients were often less than cooperative, even when their lives were in danger. Making it so much harder for Aaron to do his job. Some clients consented to do everything necessary to keep themselves and their families safe. They were the easy customers, allowing Jake and his men to protect them in the best way possible. But on the other side of the coin, a reluctant client couldn't be forced to do anything they didn't want to. They were paying for protection, but they often didn't perceive how difficult it was for Shield to maintain that protection in certain circumstances. This was one of those situations.

"That's good, because I have some info from Lance that makes it even more imperative Julie get to safety," Jake said.

Aaron stood a little straighter and waited.

"Lance has been doing internet searches on all the guests who've stayed at the lodge over the past few weeks, combining that with any details we received from the police, to see if we can come up with anything suspicious."

"Go on," Aaron said slowly, as the hair on the back of his neck stood up.

"Lance thinks he might've found something that needs more attention. One of the women guests, a Maya Graymann, used to work for a large doctor's surgery as a receptionist and medical typist. She quit her job when she married her new husband. But get this, the doctor she worked for consulted out to a couple of different family planning clinics, The Marie Stopes Family Planning Clinic being one of them."

Aaron's mind suddenly cleared, like a rain-spattered window wiped clean. That was the clinic Julie had attended. "That's the same couple who went AWOL from the lodge a few days ago." An image of the nerdy guy, with his much younger Malaysian wife, standing meekly by his side, assaulted his brain.

"Yes, it is," Jake agreed. "We've already handed the info over to your mate Nash in the force, let's see what they come up with. In the meantime, we're delving into the details of both Maya and her new husband's life."

This might well be the information they were looking for. Aaron felt a stab of adrenaline, fueled by elation surge through him. "Give Lance a big kiss from me," Aaron said. "I think he might have just cracked this case wide open."

"Agreed," Jake said. "I need to go. I just wanted to keep you up to date. I'll talk to you more when you land in Cairns. Call me tonight."

"Will do." Aaron rang off and stared at the phone. Could this be it? Could this be the clue they'd been searching for all along? Maya could be the accomplice, feeding the stalker the information he needed. Which potentially made Chase Graymann the stalker. But how were the couple connected to Travis Mailmann? If Nikolay was right and Mailmann was an alias, then was Graymann his real name? He needed to go tell Julie about this new development.

Something moved in his peripheral vision. But before he could react, he was hit in the chest, and he went down like a sack of potatoes, unable to move or speak, completely immobilized. In his groggy, half-conscious state, he realized he'd been tasered.

CHAPTER TWENTY

Julie crashed a saucepan down on the tabletop with a lot more force than was necessary. She was trying to control her anger, she really was. Because her father—and probably Aaron, as well—were only looking out for her best interests, even while they were taking over her life. A small part of her probably agreed that perhaps it was time she admitted defeat. It'd be safer for everyone involved, including herself, if she hunkered down somewhere for a little while. But she hated being told what to do.

Where was Aaron, anyway? Wasn't he usually hovering around like one of those infernal flies buzzing around her face?

Julie bent down to retrieve a large saucepan from beneath the table, muttering under her breath about men and their egos and how they should keep their arrogant ideas to themselves. When she stood up, she gave a squeak of surprise, and dropped the saucepan with a clatter onto the earthen ground.

"Chase? What are you doing here?" It took Julie's mind a few seconds to catch up. What was the mild-mannered guest doing all the way out here? But on a second glance, she noticed he was no longer so nerdy looking. The glasses and the button-up shirt were gone, replaced by a black cap and khaki shirt and pants, as if he were trying to mimic Steve Irwin, the crocodile hunter. What the hell? "Where's Maya?" she queried, her mind still whirling.

Chase didn't answer, merely raised a hand, and pointed something at her. What was that thi—

"Argh." A guttural groan was forced out her throat as her body went into spasms, over which she had no control. It hurt like hell, like fire ants were biting her all over, like flames were licking at her extremities. And even when the pain subsided, she was left floundering, like a fish out of water, with no strength in her muscles and very little conscious thought.

She felt his hands on her then, tying her wrists together, but there was nothing in her power she could do to stop him. Slowly the spasms subsided, and she lay gasping for breath on the dusty ground. Then Chase hauled her to her feet. He was stronger than he looked.

"Walk," he commanded.

But she was hardly in control of her legs, and she stumbled forward, falling flat on her face.

"Get up," he yelled, hauling her to her feet again. "And walk. We need to get out of here."

This time when her feet hit the dirt, she managed to stay upright, and she staggered in the direction he pushed her.

"What do you want?" she croaked, gaze madly searching the camp for any sign of Aaron.

"I thought that'd be obvious," Chase answered. "I want to rid you of your sins."

All those terrible things Aaron had told her came crowding into her mind. The way that woman had been tortured, and the way the other woman had been nailed to a cross and left to die. She let out a moan of fear.

"No. You can't. Please don't do this," she pleaded, turning

around to face him.

"You should have thought of that before you took your innocent baby's life," he replied. How had she never noticed his cold blue eyes before? Like they held no emotion. He pushed her in the back to force her to get moving again. She stood her ground. Why should she do as he told her? She should fight, he wasn't armed, as far as she could tell. The small can of pepper spray was still in her front pocket, if only she could reach it.

"Move," he said, voice low and menacing. Then he flicked the khaki shirt aside to reveal a gun in a shoulder holster hidden beneath. If she didn't know better, it looked a lot like Aaron's weapon. But how had this man found it? And did he even know how to handle it?

"Do you really want to find out if I'm prepared to use this?" he asked, caressing the handgun with a smile. When she hesitated, he said, "I didn't think so. That way. The car's over there." He lifted his chin to indicate a stand of trees over by the edge of the billabong, along the road leading out of the stock camp.

Where was Aaron? Had this man disabled him with the same technique he'd used on her? Or was he hiding somewhere, waiting for the right time to come out and pounce? Julie decided not to mention him, just in case.

Limbs still shaky from whatever Chase had done to her—was it a Taser?—she walked along beneath the blazing sun in the direction he told her. In her mind, she went over her options. There was still no sign of Aaron. If he had been incapacitated, or God forbid, killed—nope, Julie wouldn't even begin to entertain that idea—no one was due at the camp until the muster crew returned in around three hours. Which left no one to save her. She'd have to save herself. She catalogued all her available tools on her body or anything that could be used as a weapon. Stupidly, she'd removed her

UHF radio from her shoulder holster and laid it on the table in the mess tent. So, she had no form of communication. There was the pepper spray, but unless he untied her hands, that was out of reach. Her mobile was practically useless out here, so she'd left it in the caravan. Otherwise, all she had on were her jeans, with a belt, Blundstone boots, and shirt. Nothing that could help her defeat a gun-toting crazy man. The sun was hot on her face, and she wished she had her Akubra for shade. Her mouth was dry, and she needed a drink.

At last, they reached the small copse of trees. Julie caught glints of sunlight reflecting off metal through the gaps in the leaves, but from the camp the car had been well and truly hidden.

"Get in," Chase demanded, opening the passenger door. Hesitating, she looked around, hoping for some miracle. Hoping for rescue. Then a thought struck. Where was his wife? Was she in on this as well?

"Where's Maya?" she asked.

"Get in," he said, more roughly this time, ignoring her question.

What choice did she have? Awkwardly, because her hands were behind her back and the car was a long way off the ground, she levered herself into the four-wheel-drive. Then watched as he shut and locked her door and walked around to the passenger seat. It was the same rental the newlywed couple had arrived at the lodge in. She was already playing out different scenarios in her head of how she could possibly use her feet once they got driving to kick out at him, knock the steering wheel out of his hands, or boot him in the chin. If she could cause the vehicle to crash, then he wouldn't find it so easy to spirit her away.

Chase leapt into the driver's side, then picked something up off the floor and shoved it in her arm. A syringe full of some kind of drug, and even though she tried to fight him off, she could feel consciousness slipping away. It was a weird feeling, even while she fought to keep her eyes open, her body gave in to oblivion.

"Where's Maya?" she mumbled. For some reason, she needed to know where the other woman was. "What have you done with her?"

"She was a bad wife. Wouldn't do as I asked," Chase said, but she almost didn't hear his words. "It wasn't really my fault, she made me do it. But at least she's with Him now, she can rest in peace."

What had he said? But she lost consciousness before she could process his words.

* * *

The world was all dark shadows and swirling shapes. Julie's eyes were open, but they wouldn't focus properly. She tried to move her head, but it wouldn't obey. It wasn't that she was tied up; it was as if her muscles were paralyzed. Where was she? It was hot. The ground was dry and dusty beneath her. Flies buzzed around her face, but her hand wouldn't seem to obey her mind to shoo them away. One landed on her cheek and crawled toward the corner of her mouth, greedy for the moisture to be found there. Feebly, she blew a gust of air through her lips to scare it away. But her lips were cracked, her mouth parched, and it was a useless attempt. She lay on the dry earth and stared upward. Was this how it was all going to end? Was she about to die here?

Finally, her eyes began to focus, and she could see the shapes above were branches, the leaves raining down dappled sunlight on her face. How had she got here? The last she remembered was getting into Chase's car, then he shoved a syringe full of something in her arm. How long had she been unconscious? Squinting up at the sun through the leaves, she tried to see where it sat in regard to the horizon. It looked to be around mid-afternoon. She and Aaron had arrived back at camp just after one pm. So, that meant she'd been out of it for at least an hour, possibly more. Her dad and Dale and the rest of the crew would still be out on muster. They had no idea she was missing. No idea her stalker had finally got to her.

And what had he done with Maya? His half-remembered words returned to her, sending cold fingers walking down her spine. Had he killed her? Because that's what it sounded like. Surely not. Surely, he wouldn't kill his own wife. The thought was too horrific to contemplate.

What about Aaron? He couldn't be dead. She wouldn't believe it. If he were dead, she'd be able to feel it. There'd be some sort of seismic shift inside her. But if he wasn't dead, then why wasn't he coming to rescue her? A tear leaked from the corner of her eye. She wanted him to be alive so badly. She shouldn't have yelled at him this morning. Shouldn't have told him they could never be together. Because it wasn't true. She did want him. He was the only one she'd ever really wanted. If only she had the chance to tell him that.

Noises began to filter through to her mind, but she couldn't force her head to turn in that direction. There were muffled thuds and bangs, and now and then there was a grunt, as if someone was exerting themselves. It meant that Chase was still around. And he was up to something. But what? She needed to get out of here. Needed to get moving. Trying again to lift her hand, she willed her fingers to move, concentrating all her effort on that one tiny motion. At first, they refused to obey, but after what felt like an eternity, the thumb on her left hand moved. She felt the dust rub beneath the pad of her finger as she drew little circles on the ground. Soon, she was able to form a fist with that hand, but she still couldn't lift it off the ground.

A dark shape loomed suddenly above her. "Hm," he said,

as if talking to himself. "Looks as if the drugs are wearing off." He poked her shoulder, but she could do nothing but glare at him. "Good, I need you to be awake for this next bit. But not too awake," he amended. "Don't want to lose you like that other one. This has to be perfect."

He bent down and picked her up beneath the armpits, dragging her across the dirt, limbs dangling uselessly, like a puppet with no strings, head lolling forward on her chest.

Move. Do something, her mind screamed. She curled her left hand into a fist, but it was weak, she had no strength. Chase must've dragged her for around twenty meters, out from beneath the shade of the trees and into the afternoon sunlight. At last, he lay her down in the dirt, and she blinked up at the sun, wishing the bright, blazing ball of gas would go away.

"Let's get you ready," he muttered with glee, leaning over her again. "You need to be pure when you meet Him." This time Julie noticed his face was red, and dark sweat stains marked his shirt under his arms and around his neckline. He started to unbutton her shirt. What the fuck was he doing? He manhandled her like she was a mannequin, like she was nothing more than an object. Soon, her shirt was off, and then her bra. It was humiliating and degrading, and she closed her eyes, unable to endure it. Then his fingers found the button on her jeans, and he began to strip them off, as well. Panic rose in her throat. Was he going to rape her? Aaron hadn't mentioned anything about the other women being raped. But that didn't mean he wasn't going to do it.

Anger, hot and urgent, surged through her. She wasn't going to let him get away with this. With every fiber of her being, she willed her muscles to work. This time she managed to get her right fist to form a ball, as she stared up at him.

"Hm, you're surprisingly beautiful," he murmured. "Our child would have been amazing, if only you'd allowed him to live." He touched her then, his fingers surprisingly gently and reverent. What the hell was he talking about? The baby she'd aborted wasn't his. He was delusional.

"You will be my crowning glory. Once I've redeemed you, then He will surely welcome me with open arms." Chase stared down at her, eyes alight with some inner lunacy. She curled her lip at him, but he merely smiled. "I guess it was fitting that you were also the hardest of them all to retrieve. I had to bide my time, watch you until He told me it was right. Hide out in the scrub on top of that hill and observe you." He gave a little laugh and stroked her hair. "You never even realized how close you came to me that day on the horses."

Julie wanted to spit in his face. He was a disgusting pig. It sounded like he'd been watching them at camp for days, studying her, like an insect under a microscope. The only time she'd ridden a horse was when she'd taken Aaron up to the repeater tower. Had this snake been hiding up there and spying on her the whole time?

She never got the chance to ask him, because he stood swiftly and disappeared out of her range of view. The hot sun beat down mercilessly on her fair skin. She practiced tensing both her fists again and again, trying to pump blood into her muscles and get them working. All of a sudden, her arm twitched, and she managed to lift it a few centimeters off the ground. Her body was coming back to her, but would it be quick enough? Her pepper spray was still in the pocket of her jeans, which he'd discarded in a pile a few feet away. Could she roll over and reach it? If she could get her body moving, she might be able to use it to blind him long enough to…

There was a loud thud next to her ear, and she managed to turn her head far enough to see what had made the sound. Her breath froze in her lungs.

No. No. No!

It was a crudely manufactured cross made from dead limbs

from the trees nearby. Her heart pounded so hard in her chest, she thought it might explode through her ribcage.

But when he came for her, she feigned paralysis, as if she were still completely unable to move.

He picked her up awkwardly, but she remained limp and pliant, even while he puffed and strained over her. When he draped her inexpertly over the top of the wooden cross, it took all her will to remain unmoving, even though he dropped her head, so it banged painfully on the branch below. Time. She needed as much time as possible to regain her strength so she could get away. She could feel it coming back now, feel the numbness leaving her veins.

But when he positioned her arm along one of the spans of the crucifix, placing a nail in her palm and raised a hammer over his head, she could no longer stay still. With a yelp of pain and fright, she pulled her hand away, and rolled off the cross to lie face-down and prone on the ground. But then she feigned weakness again.

"Shit." Chase swore, the word sounded foreign coming out of his mouth. He stood above her, his shadow a blessed relief from the sun. "Shit," he swore again, but Julie remained still, as if her effort in rolling off the cross had expended what little strength she had left. "I don't want to drug you again," he muttered to himself. "But I can't have you getting away." It was like he was having a one-sided conversation with himself. Finally, he dropped the hammer in the dust a few feet away and said, "I'll be right back," and marched off toward the trees, where he must've parked his vehicle. Was he going to get more drugs to sedate her? She couldn't take that chance.

Carefully, she rolled over onto her back and lifted her head to watch him walk away. It was now or never. Painfully slowly, she managed to drag her feet underneath her, until she was on her hands and knees. With a superhuman effort, she surged upward to stand on her feet, swaying dangerously. Escape. Run. Run away. But to where? Anywhere was better than here. She stumbled forward, heading toward a low rise of hills she could see on the horizon. One foot in front of the other, she managed a few steps, then stooped down to pick up Chase's discarded hammer.

A huddle of scrubby acacia bushes beckoned her onward. If she could make it there, she'd at least be out of sight. Her legs began to move faster now, until she was almost jogging, her head still lolling to one side a little. If only she wasn't naked, but there was no way she was going back for her clothes. It was hard going with her bare feet, but she ignored the small stones and sticks that dug into her soles. Faster than she imagined, she was behind the blessed cover of the small trees. In front of her, more open woodland stretched to the faraway hills, dotted with eucalyptus trees and the remains of the dry tussock grass. Quick, he'd be back any second, Julie shuffled forward, looking for a better place to hide. In her mind, if she could hide long enough, then perhaps she'd buy time for someone—Aaron—to come to her aid.

"Oh no, you don't," Chase said from behind her, appearing around the side of the bushes. There was a cruel twist to his mouth, and Julie knew she wasn't getting away this time. She took off at a sprint—which was probably more of a slow trot in reality—headed in the direction of a shallow creek bed running toward the hills in the distance. But after only ten or twelve steps she felt a hand grasp at her arm, whipping her around, and she fell backwards onto the dirt, with him on top of her. She screamed and hit him in the head with the hammer as hard as she could. He cried out, and she pushed him off her, where he lay in the dirt clutching his head.

Using her hands to push herself up, she took off again over the red dirt, hammer still gripped tightly in one hand.

Angling down into the creek bed, she stumbled along the dry bottom, where the flat rocks made it easier on her bare feet. There was a roar of rage from behind her. She didn't look back, merely tried to run faster. This time she made it a good fifty meters or so, before he caught up with her. He grabbed at her, but couldn't hold on. It was enough to knock her off her balance, however, and she tripped and fell, as he also landed heavily, grasping at her ankle to stop her from crawling away on all fours.

Her knees and elbows were scraped and bloody, but she kicked out at him with all her strength. She felt something tug and then release on her ankle and looked down to see him holding up the anklet Aaron had given her. With a surge of adrenaline, she sat up and rammed the hammer down on his head again. This time there was a satisfying crack, and he made a sound like a wounded wolf, almost a howl of pain.

Scrambling to her feet, she looked down at the man groveling on the ground, one hand holding his head, while blood oozed between his fingers. She could hit him again. Would that put an end to this? He looked up at her, his face contorted with pure hatred. Moving faster than she would've anticipated, he got to his knees and fumbled for the gun in the holster.

She turned and took off at a gallop.

Julie made it up onto the far side of the creek bed, jumping behind the trunk of a large river gum as the first shot rang out. She ducked but kept moving from one tree to the next, using them as cover, as two more bullets whizzed past her.

Oh fuck, was this guy never going to stop? She ran, and ran, and ran, her breath pounding in her lungs, as more bullets flew through the air.

CHAPTER TWENTY-ONE

Sweat ran freely down the side of Aaron's face, trickled down his back and chest. Dust rose to mingle with the moisture, causing streaks of red on his skin. He grunted and rolled onto his other side, furiously working at the ropes around his wrists. They were getting looser. This guy was an amateur when it came to tying knots. And it was going to be his downfall. A few more minutes and Aaron would be free.

"You should've killed me, you fucker," he swore at the sky. "Because I'm coming to get you."

Aaron had no clear idea how much time had passed. The guy had hit him over the head after he tasered him—with Aaron's own Taser, what's more—and he'd been out of it for quite a while. At least an hour, if the alignment of the sun was anything to go by. The guy might not have realized it, but he'd done him one small favor—leaving him lying beside the caravan, at least he was shaded from the merciless sun. It was already hot enough; he was glad he wasn't lying directly in the scorching rays.

His wrists burned where he was twisting and contorting them, working the ropes to get the knot loose enough. But it was a small price to pay.

Aaron wasn't sure exactly what had transpired during the

ambush. He'd already called himself all the names under the sun, and then some, at his own stupidity, at his lack of vigilance and the sluggish way he'd carried out protocol over the past few days. He'd been lulled into a false sense of security that they were safe out here. That, and the way Julie filled his mind, his every waking thought, took over his logical brain. If—no, when—he got Julie back safely, and this was all over, he was going to resign from Shield. No bodyguard doing their job properly would've let his client be abducted like this. At least, he hoped that was what'd happened. Since he'd recovered consciousness, he called out continuously to Julie, but the camp had remained stubbornly silent. Nothing and nobody moved. And if this stalker was the same one who'd taken the other women, then he had a pattern he liked to follow. He'd take his prey somewhere quiet and isolated, where he could carry out his sick little games.

Aaron sucked in a sudden breath as one of the knots gave way slightly and he was able to slip the loop of rope over his thumb.

He was free.

Whipping his hands around in front, he shook the ropes off his other wrist and quickly untied his feet. Then he was up and running. The stalker had taken Aaron's sat phone, but he was hoping against hope that he hadn't taken his cell phone, which was on the counter in the caravan. Everyone knew there was no reception out here. But Aaron knew better.

Racing into the caravan, he found his cell exactly where he'd left it, and he let out a gust of relieved air. Then he leaned down to check his go bag. He already knew his Taser and SIG Sauer would be missing. The bastard had also taken the small gun and the ankle holster while he'd been unconscious, which left Aaron with no weapon. But at this moment in time, he didn't much care.

Sprinting to the mess tent, Aaron did a quick search, calling Julie's name. Nobody answered. The table where he and Julie had dumped their UHF radios after they came back from the muster was empty, which meant the abductor had probably taken them as well.

Aaron stood in the middle of the camp, turning a three-sixty-degree circle. Where had the fucker taken her? It'd be like trying to find a needle in a haystack, which was exactly what the stalker must've been thinking; that he could hide out in the bush for days without being found. But Aaron had an ace up his sleeve, and he prayed with all his might that the little GPS tracker was still transmitting.

He turned to stare up at the hill with the repeater station on top. It was rocky and would be hard to get up there in a standard vehicle, even with a four-wheel-drive. But Aaron had a better idea. He ran to the horse yard, surprising the two resting horses when he vaulted over the railing.

"Come on Chester, I need your help," Aaron said, grabbing a bridle and catching the sleepy chestnut. Aaron had him saddled in record time and the pair took off, straight through the camp, Aaron crouched low over the horse's withers, urging him into a gallop. He'd lost his hat somewhere in the scuffle with the stalker, and the wind whipped through his short hair as he urged the horse to go as fast as he dared over the red dirt. They had to slow half-way up the hill when the ground became rocky and treacherous, but they still made the trip in a third of the time it'd taken him and Julie a few days ago. Chester was blowing hard and had raised a lather by the time Aaron pulled him to a halt beside the repeater tower.

Aaron jumped out of the saddle and held his phone in the air, as if it might come to life with just the strength of his will alone. The little bars that told him he had reception remained stubbornly blank.

"Come on, you piece of shit!" Aaron yelled at his phone.

He walked toward the metal construction, trying to remember exactly where he'd found reception before. Julie had said there was only one particular spot where the reception was good. His phone suddenly pinged with an incoming message.

Eureka!

Aaron scrolled until he found the app he was looking for and opened it, praying silently. *Please, please, please let it be working.* The app took ages to open, but finally a map appeared with a little blinking blue dot.

"Oh, thank God," Aaron said to Chester, who gave a quiet snort in reply.

Arron studied the map intently, trying to figure out where he was in relation to Julie. After a few moments, Aaron was pretty sure he found the stock camp because the billabong was marked as a blue expanse on the map. And Julie wasn't too far away, as the crow flies, perhaps only a few kilometers. Aaron didn't know what—if any—type of transport the stalker was using, but he was pretty sure the guy wouldn't have just walked into camp. His finger traced the faint lines of the various roads in and out of the area. Some of them would be so little used that they might not even be on the map. But the main one into camp was definitely there. He traced its trajectory with his eyes and saw another road turn off it, heading in the same direction as the dot. So, it looked like it was possible to get to the spot on the map by vehicle, but it was a round-about route, as the road meandered around hills and watercourses. It could take him an hour or more to get there by car. Whereas, if he went straight across country, he'd be there in no time at all.

The dot remained immobile, which meant the stalker had stopped for some reason. But why? Did he have a camp or some kind of shelter? Was he merely lost, and had stopped to find his bearings? Or had he discovered the anklet and torn it off her? There was one other alternative, but it was too terrible to even consider.

That blue dot didn't tell him whether she was still alive or not. But Aaron was a gambler, and he was going to gamble that she was still alive. He had no other option. Because if she were dead… He dared not let his mind go there. Squinting into the distance, he willed her to be okay with all of his heart. She was just over there, perhaps if he had the eyes of an eagle, he might even be able to see her. So close. Yet so far away.

He took a screenshot of the map and made a decision. Quickly, he dialed Jake's number and waited impatiently for him to answer, then started talking before Jake had a chance to speak. Jake had access to the same app Aaron did, and he'd soon pinpointed her location, as well.

"I'm going after her," Aaron said.

"Not a good idea on your own," Jake said calmly. "Let me contact Steve on his satellite phone, he'll have the guys back from the muster in less than an hour."

"I'm not waiting," Aaron replied impatiently. "But I do want you to call Steve, as well as Nash and anyone else who can help," Aaron said tightly. "See if you can get that chopper back from Comalga Station to do a sweep of the area, as well." It was a long shot. The chopper pilot who'd helped them with the muster for the first few days had left yesterday to fulfill another job over on an adjoining property. But the stations were so big out here, covering vast tracks of land, and the chopper could be anywhere. It might also depend on how much fuel the pilot had left after nearly a full day of mustering. If he was low, he'd have to refuel, which would add time and distance to a patrol of the area. Add to that it'd be dark in a few hours, and not too many pilots were stupid enough to fly in this country after dark, so they were probably stretching their luck.

"Will do," Jake replied efficiently. "But how am I going to stay in touch with you?" he asked quietly.

"On a wing and a prayer," Aaron replied and hung up.

He gathered Chester's reins and swung up into the saddle. "Sorry about this, mate." Aaron slapped the horse's neck. "But I'm going to need all of that strong heart and fast legs of yours." He dug his heels into Chester's sides and the horse leaped down the slope, in the opposite direction to the stock camp. "Hold on, Julie, I'm coming," he muttered under his breath.

Fifteen minutes later, Chester was blowing like a steam engine and his shoulders and whithers were lathered with foam. "You're doing great," Aaron encouraged the horse, but he knew he was asking a lot of his mount, they'd been riding at a punishing pace. But Chester was an Australian stock horse, with a heart as big as an elephant, and he'd probably keep going until he dropped.

It was time to check the map. They'd been riding in a northerly direction the whole time, and Aaron thought they might be getting close to where the blue dot resided. He reined the horse down to a walk and took his phone from his pocket. Lifting his head, he searched the horizon, looking for a specific landmark. A large outcropping of rock showed on the map. And there it was, almost dead ahead. Past that, a creek was marked, flowing toward a low set of hills on the skyline. The creek might be dry, but he should still be able to spot it through the scattered trees when he got near enough. He was getting close. Perhaps he should slow down, he didn't want to alert the guy to the fact he was coming.

Aaron urged Chester into a fast trot rather than a gallop, which was what his mind was screaming for him to do. If he had his way, Chester would sprout wings, and he'd fly over this terrain faster than a speeding bullet. In Aaron's mind, all he could think of was getting to Julie. It threatened to overtake all his logical thought and years of extensive training. He couldn't bear to think she might be hurt. A savageness he never knew existed was roaring to get out. To smash and to pound to and to hurt anyone or anything who got in his way. Kill them, if that's what it took. It was scary, that his emotions could be this fierce and completely untamed when it came to Julie. He didn't like to think what it all meant, but now was not the time to analyze his overpowering feelings. All he could do was try and rein them in enough so he could continue to use the rational part of his brain to help him find her.

They passed the mound of rocks to the left and Aaron had just turned to study them when Chester propped and reared suddenly, taking him off guard. He was thrown sideways, clinging onto the horse's neck like a crab, but then Chester bolted, bucking and weaving through the scrub and Aaron lost his fight to hang on, hitting the ground hard, trying to curl into a ball and roll, to break his fall.

"Fuck," he yelled. "Fuck, fuck, fuck." He lifted his head and watched the horse take off through the woodland. What the hell had got into that horse? Wincing, he gingerly got to his feet and began to take stock of any injuries. That's when he saw the snake, slithering off into a tussock, its brown body fat and loathsome.

"Oh." Julie's words came back to him. *"Chester's practically bomb proof, and really patient. He's only got one flaw; he hates snakes."*

Aaron straightened and then flinched as pain shot through his knee. And there was something wrong with his shoulder, as well. He leaned over to inspect his leg, finding a large tear in the fabric of his jeans and a trickle of blood running from a series of grazes and cuts on his knee and shin. Too bad. There was no time to play doctor on himself. As long as he was still standing and could keep moving, he only had one objective in mind. Just in case, he pulled his phone out of his pocket to check if by some miracle there might be reception out here. Nope, no signal. He began to jog in the direction of where he hoped the creek lay, grunting each time his wounded knee bent to take his weight. Chester was nowhere to be seen. The horse would hopefully turn up back at the stock camp, horses were smart like that. Aaron put the unfaithful steed out of his mind; he had no time to worry about a lost horse.

A sound had him lifting his head to stare at the floodplains in front, and he stopped to listen. A muffled bang echoed through the bush. Then another, and another. Shit. That was gunshots, coming from the direction he was headed. Sound travelled a long way in the country, and he had no idea how far away they were. Julie. He took off at a near run, fear driving him onwards.

Panting heavily, he wished he'd brought some water with him, his mouth was dry and he knew with all this sweating he'd be losing a lot of valuable moisture. Dehydration could kill you, but what was his alternative? He kept going. After ten minutes of running as fast as his damaged knee would let him through the outback scrubland, he thought he could make out a line of slightly larger trees than the surrounding scrubland. That could indicate the creek he was looking for.

Forcing himself to slow to a walk, Aaron wiped the sweat from his forehead and peered into the flat terrain ahead. It'd do no good to run headlong into a situation without scoping it out first. Especially if the stalker was shooting. For a fleeting second, he wished he had his own gun, or a weapon of some kind. Something glinted through the trees, a quick flash of sunlight off metal. Was that a car? Had he found them? Aaron took a few deep breaths to slow his heartbeat. *Think*. What to do next?

Movements stealthy now, he wound his way carefully and slowly toward the vehicle—he was sure that was what it was now, he could see the shape of a white four-wheel-drive half-hidden behind a large river gum. Aaron scanned the area for movement, but there was nothing. No sound either. Almost as if the place was deserted.

Quietly, he approached the vehicle. The driver's door was open, but there was no one inside. Aaron crept around the vehicle, checking in all the windows, but apart from some camping gear and food wrappers, it was empty. He checked the dashboard of the car, hoping it might have a UHF radio installed, so he could call in backup, but no such luck. In front of the car, on the other side of the large river gum, were some scattered tools. A large wood saw, some large nails, a cordless drill and other implements. What the hell…? He picked up a long-handled screwdriver. It wouldn't protect him against bullets, but it was something, at least.

A trail of footsteps led away from the car, and as Aaron followed them, he noticed marks that indicated something heavy had been dragged through the dust. His fist tightened at his side, but he continued to edge forward. Around twenty meters away, in a flat area away from the shade of the trees, was a pile of dead wood and something else scattered on the ground. As he approached, he could see that a scuffle had taken place, the ground was all churned up. Had Julie fought for her life here? The idea made his blood run cold.

Then he saw that what he first thought had been a pile of dead branches was actually a crudely fashioned crucifix, and he stopped dead. It was proof this was Julie's stalker.

But where was she? Why was the place deserted? Something had played out here that he couldn't understand. Turning on his heel, he spun around slowly, scanning the area for more clues. He noticed a pile of material a few feet away that he'd missed on his first quick inspection of the area. Stalking over to it, he picked up one of the dusty bits of fabric. It was a shirt.

Julie's shirt.

Quickly picking up the rest of the clothing, he saw it was her jeans, bra, and panties.

That fucking bastard.

Anger boiled up inside him, so hot and fast he thought it might destroy him. The inner demons inside him howled their anger and anguish, making Aaron want to scream into the outback, as well. But he dare not give himself away. Not yet.

Dropping the clothing, he scanned the ground around the cross, trying to decipher what'd happened here.

A few drops of blood lay in the dust beneath the cross. Who's blood was it? Had someone been shot? A set of bare footprints led away from the cross, toward a large clump of shrubby bushes, clear and precise in the red dust. Julie. Was that her? Running away? Escaping from this bastard. Here and there, the footprints were overlaid by larger boot prints. He must've chased her.

Breaking into a jog, Aaron followed the trail. Around the back of the bushes, the footprints were messed up again, and it took him a while to figure them out. Finally, he found more signs, the bare feet continued their way toward the line of trees and the dry creek bed. She was still running; still fighting for her life. Good girl.

Then he lost the trail for a second once he got beneath the shade of the trees towering over the watercourse. It was much rockier down here, the marks in the sand harder to decipher.

What was that? A shape farther up the tributary. Unmoving, like a pile of rags or... He ran as fast as his damaged leg would carry him.

It was a man, curled in the fetal position in the bottom of the ravine. It was the guest from Stormcloud, the man who'd called himself Chase. A gun—Aaron's handgun—lay a few feet away on the stony ground. Aaron leaned down and snatched it up before prodding the man with the screwdriver. Nothing. No movement, no sound.

Aaron Checked the ammo in his weapon. The clip was empty. Had this asshole fired at Julie as she tried to escape?

He knelt down awkwardly, gun held ready to strike him on the back of the head if the guy so much as twitched a muscle. With shaking fingers, Aaron felt for a pulse. After a few seconds, he decided the man was dead. Rolling him over, he noticed the pool of blood beneath the man's head. Examining the side of his cranium, Aaron found a large, round wound above his left temple. If he wasn't mistaken, it looked like he'd been hit with a hammer.

Aaron stood up with a grunt of disgust. If this guy wasn't already dead, Aaron knew he'd probably have killed him with his bare hands.

He studied the dead guy with barely disguised revulsion, but then something caught his eye. A glint of silver amongst the rocks near the man's hand. Aaron dropped the screwdriver and knelt to retrieve it. A thin chain with a single heart charm. It was the GPS anklet he'd given Julie, what seemed like an eternity ago now.

Shit, that wasn't good. He tucked the chain in his pocket.

Where the hell was she?

Aaron squinted into the flat landscape, willing Julie to appear before him, whole and safe and well. No such apparition appeared, however. Had Chase shot her, and she was lying somewhere, bleeding out, even as he stood here? The sun was getting low on the horizon, turning the ochre dirt a fiery red where the rays still touched the earth. He walked up the ravine, eyes searching the ground for signs of her. There. He spotted a random footprint heading up the side of the embankment. A little farther on, he found another half-print in the sand. It looked as if she were heading for the cover of the low hills. Should he follow her? Aaron was no tracker, he could very easily lose her trail and never find it again in the growing late afternoon.

If he waited, help would turn up soon, he was sure of it. Jake would've contacted Steve, and the muster crew would be here soon; probably within an hour or so. Within a few hours, the place would be swarming with people and cops.

But then it'd be dark, and Julie's trail would be harder to follow. What if she was hurt or injured? He couldn't wait that long. Julie was out there somewhere, naked and afraid, and he was going to find her.

CHAPTER TWENTY-TWO

Julie huddled, miserable and afraid, beneath the cover of a large jumble of boulders. She'd made it to the foothills of the escarpment rising from the flat plains below, but could go no farther. The soles of her feet were a bloody mess, cut to pieces from the limestone rocks, sharp sticks, and thorns as she'd fled through the grassy scrubland. Her skin was torn and scratched in a million and one places by the shrubs as she pushed her way through. And her shoulders and back were painfully sunburnt. So exhausted from her bid to escape, she'd lay down beside the rocks, heedless of the spiky grass, and curled into a ball. She could hardly believe her situation. Naked and lost in the Queensland outback, with a crazy man on her tail, who wanted to string her up on a crucifix for her supposed sins.

She was so thirsty, she could cry. But she wouldn't let the tears fall, as they'd be a waste of precious liquid, and she needed every drop. The sun was about to set, giving off a tremendous display of glowing pink clouds on the horizon. It'd be dark soon, then perhaps she'd be safe from Chase. Surely, he wouldn't be able to find her in the dark? But then again, neither would anyone else. Was Aaron out there looking for her? She hoped so. Because the alternative was that he was lying dead back at the stock camp, and that was unbearable.

Was Chase still following her? Or had she lost him as she'd sprinted up the creek bed? Gunshots had ricocheted off the trees as she'd darted this way and that, but she'd kept running, away from the noise and the unimaginable fear, until she could physically run no farther.

If only Aaron were here, she could snuggle into his big, strong body and feel safe and protected. She did the next best thing, surrounding herself with thoughts of him lying next to her as she drifted off into oblivion.

What seemed like mere moments later, a noise woke her from her dreams. What was that? But when she opened her eyes, it was pitch black, only the blanket of stars above to light her world.

"Julie. Are you there? Where are you?" a voice called faintly from the dark.

She sat up with a start.

"Aaron? Is that you?" she shouted. Was it true? Or was she dreaming? "I'm here. Over here." She tried to get to her feet, but they hurt too much, and she fell back onto the rough ground.

"Keep calling out, baby, so I can find you," she heard him say. "Where are you?"

"Here. I'm here," she called again, a sob of relief breaking from her throat. Was it true? Was she really going to be rescued?

The sound of breaking twigs and swishing grass broke through the night as boots crunched over the desert toward her. Then a brilliant beam of light pierced through the darkness, swinging around in a slow arc, and almost blinding her as the glare hit her face. She shielded her eyes and tried to stand again, filled with an overwhelming relief. He was here. She was saved.

Suddenly, strong arms wrapped around her waist, holding her off the ground. "I'm here, baby, I got you."

"Thank you," she sobbed into his chest. "I didn't know if you were..." The word *alive* didn't seem appropriate anymore. Because he was here in the flesh, solid and real.

"Sit down," he said, gently lowering her to the ground. She sat on the dry earth, then his arms left her for a second and she nearly called out to him like a child, but they were back as he wrapped his shirt around her, covering her nakedness, doing up the buttons for her one by one. Then he held her again, and it was the sweetest feeling in the world, to be in his arms once more. Settling his back against the largest boulder, he pulled her into his lap, so she was off the dirty ground, and she curled up like a kitten, wrapping her arms around his neck, and resting her forehead on his collarbone. Even now, in this precarious situation, even though she was battered and bruised, her body still reacted to his closeness. A surge of heat at his touch pulsed through her, and she would've kissed him if her lips weren't so parched. Instead, she let her fingers explore the warmth of his bare chest, to tangle in the soft curls and to run to the apex of his shoulder, feeling the heavy muscles there.

But even though all she wanted to do was sink into complete oblivion in his arms, reality kept crowding her brain. With a shudder, she lifted her head. There was so much to say. So much Aaron needed to know.

"Is anyone else with you?" She cast around in the dark, suddenly hoping her father or Dale would also miraculously appear out of the night.

"No, it's just me, Julie. But don't worry, I've—"

"But we're not safe," she wheezed between dry lips, interrupting him. "Chase is still out there. He was shooting at me," she added. Why was Aaron out here on his own? Where was everyone else? Maybe they should keep moving. What if

Chase was aiming his gun at them right at this moment?

"I know," he said, stroking her hair, gently tugging at the leaves and other debris stuck in there. "But it's okay, he's not coming after us. I guarantee you're safe."

"Really?" Her mind was struggling to keep up, her thoughts sluggish, like she was in a dream. "Are you sure?"

"I'm sure," he replied. "You're not going to die, Julie. Not on my watch, I promise you."

"Okay, if you say so," she said, happy to let that quandary go because she had a more immediate need. "Do you have any water?" she asked hopefully.

"No, I'm sorry." She heard the heaviness of self-reproach in his voice. "I should've grabbed a bottle, but I was so fixated on finding you… I'm sorry," he finished lamely.

"Oh." She licked her lips, but her tongue was so dry it was a fruitless effort. The euphoria of being rescued was fading fast as the reality of their situation finally hit her. They were lost and alone in the desert. "We could still die out here," she said weakly. "The desert is a harsh mistress. Without any water, if no one finds us soon… If nobody knows where we are." The last words came out as a soft wail. She knew she was being overdramatic, but she couldn't seem to help it. Her emotions were boiling up inside, the trauma of the past few hours threatening to drown her in her own fear.

"You're not going to die, Julie," he reiterated gently. "Someone will be here soon. I found your GPS anklet on the ground. You remember the one I gave you back at the lodge?" His voice was soft and low, his touch kind and compassionate as his fingers stroked her face, which brought her back from the brink of hysteria.

"Yes, I remember," she hiccuped through a sob. "But will it work out here?" She'd felt Chase pull the anklet off during one of her attempts to escape his clutches, but at the time, she hadn't thought a lot of it.

"Of course, it works. GPS trackers use satellites to get the coordinates. So as long as one of those bright little dots high in the sky is a satellite," he tipped his head back to stare at the stars above, "and I'm a hundred-percent-sure they are, then Jake will be able to find us. It might take them a few hours, but they'll be here soon. I promise."

Julie stared at Aaron, sketching his familiar profile against the starlight. "Okay," she said simply. If he said it was true, then she believed him.

"We just need to hunker down here, get comfortable and wait."

"Good." What better way to wait, than cocooned in Aaron's strong arms, his large biceps encircling her waist like he was never going to let her go.

There was so much she needed to tell him. So much she needed to know. She decided to start with the basics. "How did you find me?" she mumbled into his neck.

He gave a low laugh; the sound rumbling through his chest. "Chester helped me," he replied. "We both owe a lot to the bloody horse. Although we need to cure him of his phobia of snakes," he added, and she lifted her head to stare at him.

What *was* he going on about?

"I rode him to the top of the hill with the repeater station," he said by way of explanation. "I got your location on the GPS up there and decided it'd be quicker to ride cross-country than to take a car. Not sure if that was the right decision now," he added darkly. "Anyway, we were almost to Chase's camp, and the bloody horse saw a snake, reared, and I fell off."

She gave a low snigger, which was about all the levity she could muster, but let him carry on with his story.

"So, I walked the rest of the way and found the camp, right where the blue dot said you'd be. It took me a while to figure out what'd happened to you. But I finally worked out the puzzle and started to follow your footprints right up to this pile of rocks. Ta-dah!"

But he'd left out some vitally important points. Like where was Chase, and how did he know that the crazy stalker man wasn't still out there?

"How do you know Chase isn't following us?"

Aaron sucked in a breath. Why was he hesitating? Oh, God, had Aaron killed him? Flown into a viscous rage and killed him with his bare hands? Was that why he was hesitating?

"Is he dead?" she asked, voice small as she rasped the question out between parched lips.

"Yes. I found him lying in the dry creek bed, the empty gun by his side."

Her brain scrambled to untangle what he'd just said. "He was dead? How?" If Aaron hadn't killed him, then had he shot himself? Or... *Oh, shit*. It suddenly dawned on her. "I killed him?" she whispered, disbelief in every pore. She wasn't capable of such a crime. Was she? "But I only wanted to make him let me go. He's dead?" The concept was hard to grasp.

"Yes, Jules," Aaron said soothingly, running a hand down her back. "You'll never have to worry about that bastard again. It was self-defense. I'll attest to that, and so will the police, so you don't need to worry about any repercussions."

"He's dead?" she repeated, rolling the words around in her mouth, trying to decipher their meaning, almost failing to register his last words. Of course, it was self-defense, she wasn't worried about that part. "So, he's not coming after me ever again?" This was a good thing. It meant she was finally free.

"Like I said, you're safe now. You can go back to Stormcloud and live your life free and clear," he said.

"Oh." She should feel elated, but suddenly more tears

pricked at the back of her eyelids. "I'm free," she said, but the words released a torrent of unexpected tears. Because the full impact of that fact finally came to her. If Chase was dead, then there was no reason for Aaron to stay anymore. He'd pack up his belongings and head back to the city, back to his life and his job. And she'd be left alone once more. The thought made her tremble with the sudden loss. "But I don't want you to go," she wailed, lifting her head to the night sky, like a dingo howling at the moon. "I finally found you, after all this time, and now you're going to leave me." A small part of her brain understood that she was being overly dramatic, and a complete hypocrite, and perhaps he didn't want to hear this, but she couldn't help herself. She was wasting more of her precious liquid by crying again.

Aaron tensed slightly beneath her. "What? Sorry. You're not making a lot of sense, Jules."

"I don't want to have kids, but if I did ever have kids, it'd be with you," she wailed again, pushing away from his chest, so she could look him in the eyes.

"I don't understand?" he said, searching her face in the darkness as if it'd reveal the answer to all this irrational talk.

"I know I sound like a lunatic, but I can't help it." Large, fat drops ran down her cheeks, and her chest was heaving as she dragged in large gulps of air. Jeez, she was working herself up into a state, and she had no real idea why. Except that the thought of losing Aaron was like a knife to the heart. How did she explain this to him?

He was patting her back like she was a toddler who needed to be calmed.

Sucking in a few fortifying breaths, she tried to calm her racing heart. "When I first met you, back in Dalgety, I knew, even back then, that one day I was going to marry you, and have kids with you." She held up a hand to forestall his reaction. "I can't tell you why, but I had this certainty, this unadulterated feeling that it was going to be that way. That's all."

"You never told me that," he replied, not accusing, merely curious.

"Of course, I didn't. You would've thought I was bonkers." She swiped a hand across her face, and it came away all gritty as well as wet. She must look a sight, face covered in dirt, and now crying like a maniacal teenager. Lucky it was dark, and Aaron couldn't see her well. She kept talking, it helped her work through the concept in her head at the same time as she spoke the words. "It was something I felt in the marrow of my bones, but I couldn't express it at the time. And after you left, I put it down to stupid teenage fantasy. A dream that all girls have when they first fall in love." She smiled, and it hurt her cracked lips, but it was her first real smile since Chase had abducted her, and it felt good. "But in all the years afterwards, I could never find the right guy, never settle down. I always had some excuse as to why they weren't good enough. I never blamed you," she said quickly, in case he took it the wrong way, that wasn't what she intended, for him to feel culpable. Because, at the time, she wouldn't even allow herself to admit it. She'd been determined that she wouldn't let the loss of Aaron control her life. Determined to find her true soul mate, who must be out there somewhere. And she'd tried dating many men, three or four of which could well have been marriageable material, but she always ended up sabotaging it in some way. And her last relationship with Judd had been the most disastrous of all, with her ending up pregnant and then having the abortion. After that, her love life had lain in tatters on the floor, and she wasn't sure where to go from there.

Then, the second she'd laid eyes on Aaron in the hallway of Stormcloud lodge, her heart had known right there—even if it'd taken her stubborn mind a lot longer to catch up—that this was her chance at redemption; *their* chance at redemption. They were meant to be together. Their night spent making love in the swag had proved beyond a doubt that the chemistry was still there, stronger than ever. But was that enough? And more to the point, did he feel the same?

"So, what are you saying, Jules?" he asked gently.

"I don't really know," she confessed, laying her head back on his chest, suddenly feeling exhausted, completely wrung out, as if all emotion had finally drained from her. "All I know is that I don't want to lose you all over again." Had she done the wrong thing, acknowledging her feelings for him? This wasn't the right place or time to be pouring her heart out. To hell with it. She'd come this far. "I never stopped loving you, Aaron." Even though he'd ripped her heart out and stomped it into the ground, a small minuscule part— that'd remained hidden from even her own consciousness— had kept a tiny flame burning in the depths, ready to ignite, if she'd only let it.

She didn't raise her head from where she was nestled into his neck, didn't want to see what was going on in his face, because if he rejected her, it'd be unbearable.

There was a heartbeat of silence as Aaron considered her words, his hand stopped drawing soothing circles on her back. She flinched inwardly as she waited for him to let her down gently, tell her that he'd moved on, and there was no place in his life for her.

"I never stopped loving you, either, Jules."

"Really?" She lifted her head.

A spark of hope warmed her chest from the inside. In the past, Aaron hadn't been afraid to show his true feelings; he told her every day how much he loved her. Back then, she'd never doubted him, even for a second. So, if he was saying it now, then she believed it was the truth. An incomprehensible weight she'd been carrying inside her for so long suddenly loosened, lifted away, like a stain being washed from her heart. The first step along an uncertain path.

"Yes, really." His mouth sought hers in the dark, tender and gentle on her cracked lips. Then he drew back so he could look into her eyes, starlight reflecting in his own so she could just make out the different hues of each one. "You've always been the woman I measured all others by. I tried so hard to forget you, to work that little splinter of you out of my heart. And I even thought I'd succeeded for a while there..."

"But?" she asked.

"But the second you told me that you didn't need a bodyguard, was the second I knew I'd been fooling myself all these years."

"You did?"

"Yep. When you shot daggers at me with your beautiful blue eyes, I was transported back in time. I was a goner. I wanted to reach out and take your mouth and kiss sense into you right then and there."

She giggled. "Me too. Either that, or I wanted to slap you senseless. And *then* kiss you until you couldn't breathe."

They laughed gently together, and she stroked her hands down his cheek, the weeks' worth of stubble rough beneath her fingertips. She liked this unshaven, untamed version of Aaron, more than she thought she would.

"I'm not sure where this leaves us, though," he said, sobering slightly. "I'm assuming you don't want to quit the station?"

She shook her head. "Not really." Although she'd done it once, moved to the city to follow a career. Surely, she could do it again. For love, this time. Would she move to Brisbane to be with Aaron? Her heart was saying, yes, yes, yes. But her head sounded loud warning bells. She'd lose herself, her identity, if she moved back to the city. The one silver lining about this whole stalker thing was how much she'd found out about herself when she'd moved to Stormcloud. How much she was capable of. How much she loved working and living in the county. She was good at her job, enjoyed looking after the guests, and loved being this close with her family. It'd been a dream of hers all along.

"And my job is based in the city."

Which was also true. She wasn't sure if she could ask him to move to the station to be with her. Even though he'd slotted right back into station life, almost like he'd never left. That wasn't the path he'd chosen for himself any longer.

Aaron raised his shoulders in a shrug. "I guess it's complicated."

He was right. And at least he wasn't pulling any punches. Just because they'd revealed they loved each other, was love enough?

"Let's not talk about it anymore," she said, snuggling back into his warm chest. The night air was getting decidedly chilly. The days could be so hot in the desert, you could fry an egg on a flat rock, then the nights could get so cold you needed a jacket and a cozy bed to keep you warm.

He enfolded her in those deliciously strong biceps, holding her tight in his lap, resting his chin on the top of her head. As she saw it, she was doing him a favor as well. He'd given her the shirt off his back, the least she could do was offer her body warmth to keep his naked torso from freezing.

"I just want to be here, with you. Us alone together one more time."

"I can do that," he said huskily into her ear.

"Thank you. For coming to find me." She could never tell him enough how much it meant to her when she'd heard him call out her name. Because she'd never doubted that he'd come for her. "You rescued me," she said simply.

"No, you rescued yourself, angel." It was the nickname

he'd used for her twelve years ago. "You beat that bastard at his own game. You were strong and spirited and never gave up. You fought tooth and nail for your life. And I'm so proud of you, my angel."

Aaron once told her that she was the angel who was going to save him. But would they be able to solve their differences and rescue each other? That still remained to be seen.

CHAPTER TWENTY-THREE

Aaron woke with a start. He must've dozed off, although how he managed to do that sitting in this awkward position, propped up against a hard rock, with Julie nestled in his lap, was anyone's guess. He dared not move a muscle, not wanting to wake her, but he slowly scanned the nighttime plains laid out below them, wondering what'd roused him.

There, over to the left, a pinprick of light. It came steadily closer as he watched, sometimes veering off in another direction, but always coming back to point directly at their hiding spot. Sometimes the light disappeared for a few seconds, then reappeared, bouncing crazily off the low-lying shrubs. It wasn't until he was a-hundred-percent sure they were indeed headlights from a four-wheel-drive that he slowly shook Julie awake.

Rescue was on its way. Good old Jake must finally have told someone where they were.

Julie raised her head, groggy and almost incoherent for a few seconds, slow to respond to his voice. They were both suffering from dehydration and her poor body had taken a beating as she ran naked through the bush. She needed medical attention, and they both needed water. But he knew they'd made it. Together. She was safe, and that was all that mattered.

"Is it my dad?" she muttered through cracked lips.

"I don't know, Jules." It didn't really matter who was coming to collect them, but he understood that she was worried about how her father was going to take all this.

Lowering her gently to the ground, he got to his feet. Oh, Jesus, his knee hurt. It took him a few seconds before he could put any weight on it, after having been cramped in one position for so long.

While they'd been talking, Aaron had methodically catalogued all of Julie's injuries, to make sure none were life threatening. Her feet were in bad shape, but the rest were superficial scratches and bruising.

"Come here, angel." He bent down and picked her up. His sore shoulder protested at the weight, but he ignored the pain. There was no way she was in any fit state to walk out of here. So, he'd carry her, bum knee, wounded shoulder, and all. It was hard going, but he wasn't going to drop her, or fall over. Those two things were immutable.

He gathered her closer into his chest and she put her arms around his neck. "Let's get out of here," he said, as he picked his way down the rocky slope.

"Amen to that," she said huskily.

The headlights from the car picked them up the moment they emerged onto the flat plains below and kept them locked in their beam, as if dragging them towards rescue. Now he was closer, Aaron could see it was two vehicles, driving close together in tandem.

They must've looked a sight, walking out of the scrub in the middle of the night. Him limping, hatless and bare-chested. Her caked in dirt and blood, nude but for his shirt, which barely covered her backside. But they'd survived to tell the tale, that was the important thing.

He stopped as the vehicle drew close, blinded by the rays

of the headlights. The first car stopped with a jolt, raising a cloud of dust, the particles floating in the beams of light.

"Julie. Oh, thank God, you're okay." Steve jumped out of the vehicle and rushed to their side. Dale was right behind him. The second car was a police four-wheel-drive and Nash stepped out, his constable exiting the other side. But they stayed near their vehicle, allowing the family to have the reunion they deserved.

"Hi, Dad. I thought that might be you." Julie raised a smile and reached out to her father.

After a tender moment, where Steve kissed his daughter on the cheek and stroked her hair, he drew back and slapped Aaron heartily on the back. "I don't know how you did it, son. But I owe you a debt greater than words can convey for finding her. Thank you. Thank you." The normally stoic man had tears running down his cheeks and for a second, Aaron felt like he might be overtaken by the emotional reunion, as well. "When we found that guy back at the creek, dead, I thought the worst. I thought…" Steve's voice cracked, and he couldn't go on. Dale placed a hand on his stepfather's shoulder.

"It's okay, Dad. I'm alive. Aaron's alive. And we'll both be fine soon enough," Julie said.

"Do you need a hand?" Dale offered to take Julie from Aaron, but no way was he giving her up now. He shook his head and walked the last few steps around the side of the car. Dale opened the rear door and Aaron slid Julie gently onto the seat, with Steve hovering at his shoulder.

"Holy shit," Dale exclaimed. "I can't actually believe we found you. When your mate Jake—"

"Have you got water?" Aaron cut him off. Important things first. They'd spend the next few hours debriefing with everyone, but right now, he needed to take care of Julie.

"Oh, crap, of course." Dale raced off and was back in a few

seconds, handing them a bottle each. "Try and take it easy," he advised. "Otherwise, you might throw it all back up again."

Aaron slipped into the seat beside Julie, unscrewing her bottle and handing it to her, then taking her hand and laying it in his lap, as she gulped at the life-giving liquid. He didn't want to lose that contact with her. Not yet.

"Easy, Julie," he said, pushing the bottle away from her lips. "Like Dale said, little sips." She nodded her understanding, but her tongue came out to lick the few precious drops from her lips. He knew how she felt. He could drink a whole gallon of the stuff and it still wouldn't be enough. Showing more restraint than he felt, he opened his bottle and took a long swig, then lowered it and leant his head back against the seat. Julie lay her head on his shoulder just as her dad leaned in and covered her with an old blanket he must've found in the rear of the vehicle. He never said a word, but Aaron could see the rage at her abominable treatment by Chase boiling just below the surface. Then he took off his own plaid shirt and offered it to Aaron; he had a T-shirt on beneath the shirt, so Aaron took it gratefully. There was definitely a nip in the air. And he didn't really want to turn up at the campsite half-dressed.

Nash poked his head inside the car. "You two all right?" He queried. His concerned gaze rested on Julie the longest, but she'd closed her eyes and didn't respond, so Aaron answered for her.

"We will be, mate. You can tell Skylar she's safe now."

"I'll most certainly do that," Nash replied with a hint of satisfaction. But he soon sobered. "You do realize there'll be questions. Lots of them." Nash's blue eyes were serious, and Aaron knew he meant that until the police were one-hundred percent happy with his and Julie's account of what'd happened that night, then they may well be in some trouble.

There was still a dead body to be accounted for. Aaron's protective instincts spiked at Nash's implications, and he put a possessive arm around Julie's shoulder, pulling her into his side. He wanted to keep her from all that unpleasantness. But try as he might, she'd have to endure those questions on her own. As would he. He had no doubt they'd be believed in the end, and he just had to keep that foremost in his mind.

"I'll make sure they go easy on her," Nash said, as if reading his mind.

"I'd be grateful if you did," Aaron replied. He liked Nash. From the little he knew of him, he seemed like a good cop, and a good man; Julie spoke highly of him. Which was a good thing, if he was going to get to know this man, and the rest of the family, better.

Nash patted Aaron's shoulder. "It was a good outcome," he said, tilting his chin toward Julie. "And just remember you did the best job you could under the circumstances." He fixed his piercing gaze on Aaron, sending him an unspoken message. It seemed that Nash also understood the way self-condemnation worked.

Aaron guessed Nash had encountered the same thing during the time he and Skylar had been taken prisoner. It certainly damaged a man's pride when he was unable to protect the one he loved most in the world from getting hurt. And Nash was right on the button, because the shame and guilt were already starting to descend. All the ifs, buts, and maybes were circling his head like flies over a corpse. If only he'd recognized Chase as a threat back at the lodge, days ago. If only he'd been more alert when they'd first arrived back at camp at lunchtime. If only he hadn't allowed Julie to go on muster in the first place. The ways in which he'd screwed up were long and convoluted. Nash was probably right, he shouldn't dwell on all the ways he'd fucked up. Because if he did, it was all downhill from there. But it was so hard not to when his pride and self-worth were so intrinsically tied to his ability to protect his client. To protect Julie. Which he'd failed at.

"Just remember, regret is a wasted emotion," Nash added, then he turned and walked back to his vehicle, leaving Aaron pondering the deep meaning of his last words.

Dale jumped into the driver's seat and spoke into a sat phone that'd been resting on the front dash. "Hello, Jake, are you there? We've got them. I repeat, we've got them. Both are alive and not looking too bad, despite their ordeal," he reported.

Jake's disembodied voice echoed from the phone. "That's great news. You don't know how relieved I am to hear that. I've got some more calls to make, so I'll ring off now. But I want to talk to Aaron as soon as he's up to it."

"Thanks again, mate," Dale said. "We couldn't have done it without you." Aaron understood that with the lack of cell reception out here, Jake had probably directed them to where Julie's anklet was showing up on the map while talking to them over the satellite phone. That was a feat in itself, and showed a great level of ingenuity.

"You guys ready to head home?" Dale called over his shoulder, turning the ignition on.

"Most definitely," Aaron replied. Julie gave a small snore on his shoulder, and he smiled as he took another swig of water.

The sight that greeted them back at Chase's campsite was one of organized mayhem.

The place was lit by two bright-as-day spotlights strung up in large trees. Two more police four-wheel-drives were pulled up behind Chase's hire car. The area around the wooden cross and farther up the creek had already been cordoned off with police tape, ready for the homicide team to come in and inspect the site. Aaron knew from experience the team would have to come from Cairns, at the very least, if not Brisbane, so they could still be hours away. From this distance, Aaron couldn't make out Chase's body, but he was sure that at least one of the police officers would be standing guard, and they'd probably draped a blanket or something over him.

The whole motley crew from the muster were also there. The Scanlons had ridden their ATV's, but others, like Dave and Carrot, had unhitched their four-wheel-drive from the trailer and driven over.

Everyone converged on the car as Dale slowly drove up behind the gaggle of people.

"Is she okay?" Rosie was the first to reach the door and yank it open, Brian hot on her heels. "Please tell us she's okay." Rosie's face was a picture of alarm. "Because if she's not, I'm gonna kill that guy all over again."

"Yeah, well, get in line," Scanner growled from behind her, his large frame filling the open door. "We're all ready to do some damage."

Julie stirred and lifted her head from Aaron's shoulder.

The rest of the team crowded around, all firing questions at the top of their lungs. Even Lee, normally taciturn, was hovering at the back, a worried frown on his face. It was great that they all were so concerned. But they were all getting a little too close for Aaron's liking. Before he could push them away, however, Steve appeared at the back of the small crowd and said, "She's good, guys. We got her back in one piece, thanks to Aaron. Now, can you give them a little space, please?"

"Sure," said Scanner, ushering everyone else away from the door.

"Hi, everyone," Julie said from beside him. She leaned forward, so she could see past him out to all her friends gathered outside. "Did you all come to help find me?" she asked.

"Of course, we did," Scanner huffed. "That's what country people do. When there's a crisis, we all pull together. Right?"

There were calls of, "damn right", and "sure is", from behind him.

"Well, thank you," Julie replied, seemingly humbled by their ardent support.

* * *

Aaron stretched out on the bed carefully, stifling a yawn. Every bit of him hurt. Bruises from his tumble off Chester were appearing all over, and his knee had swollen to double its normal size. But it'd been worth it. As far as he was concerned, every bruise and scratch was a badge of honor, and he'd do it a hundred times over, if it meant Julie's safety was guaranteed.

Steve had told him that Chester had galloped back into camp just as they were returning from muster. At least Chester had returned unharmed, which lightened the load of guilt Aaron had been carrying around.

He turned his head to where Julie lay curled up, innocent as a small child, next to him. She'd begged him to stay with her, and he couldn't refuse, so he'd helped her into her bed and then stripped down to his boxer briefs and edged in beside her; but she was already asleep. It'd been a long night. Nash had driven them back to the station in Dimbulah, where they'd given their statements to Nash's superior, Senior Sergeant Robinson, and a forensics guy had collected samples from both of them. Then the local doctor had checked her all over and dressed Julie's feet, telling her to stay off them for the next few days, if possible. It turned out he'd twisted his knee, and it was badly bruised, but nothing time and rest wouldn't heal.

The sun was just rising over the floodplains when Dale drove them home to the lodge and Aaron had carried Julie inside, waving away Daniella and Skylar's concern, and they'd both crawled into bed, exhausted. Aaron craned his neck to catch sight of the small alarm clock Julie kept beside the bed. Gosh, it was three pm already. That'd explain the bright sunshine beating at the curtains to be let in. They'd slept most of the day away. There was still a lot to do today, he really should get up.

Details were still sketchy about Chase's movements in the previous few days, but Nash had filled them in from what they'd pieced together so far from the equipment, maps, and photos on a camera they'd found in the car. It seemed Chase had been watching the stock camp from the top of repeater hill, which Julie also confirmed to be true, from her stilted conversation with the stalker. When Aaron asked how Chase had found the stock camp, Nash relayed a conversation he'd had with Maddie Scanlon soon after he arrived at Chase's camp. As soon as she'd seen his body lying in the creek bed, she'd come straight to him to confess.

Nash relayed her words. "I recognize that man, he stopped me on the way back from the stables to talk the night before we left the lodge. He seemed really interested in the muster and how it all worked, and said he was sad that they weren't letting any guests attend this year. I thought he was harmless, and no one warned me not to say where we were going. So, I told him all about the permanent stock camp and how beautiful it was out there...and how to get there." Nash said she'd looked absolutely stricken at the thought this whole thing might've been her fault. Aaron kicked himself for their decision not to tell the rest of the muster crew what was going on. His choice to keep them in the dark might well have been the lynchpin that allowed Chase to find her. Maddie wasn't to blame.

There was also no sign of his wife, Maya, which left everyone with an ominous feeling. Julie said she thought Chase might've killed her, then she'd burst into tears. But until they found a body, Nash said they wouldn't give up hope, and a search team was out looking for her. They now knew the name Travis Mailmann was an alias he'd concocted to get in with the church group. The beard and outfit had all been fake, a way for him to hunt his intended victims in secret. And it seemed Maya had also fallen prey to his false charms. For all accounts it looked as if it were a rushed marriage, orchestrated by him to keep the young, gullible woman under his control.

It was now a police investigation, so Jake had handed over all the documents and info he had on the case to Nash. But there were still so many unanswered questions. He'd leave Julie to sleep peacefully on while he went and made some phone calls.

Julie mumbled something in her sleep, and one hand reached out, as if searching for something. Or someone. Gently, he took her hand and tucked it into his chest, and she immediately stopped fussing. Five more minutes wouldn't hurt. He shuffled around so he could look at her directly.

He traced the outline of her profile with his gaze. She was so beautiful. How had he never noticed that tiny freckle right in the corner of her eye before? And those long, luscious eyelashes, so chaste on her cheeks. Lips still dry and cracked from her ordeal yesterday, but he wanted to lean in and kiss them, anyway.

"I know you're staring at me," she mumbled, not opening her eyes. "You're starting to freak me out."

"Sorry," he replied. Not that he was sorry for staring at her. But he was sorry for so many other things. Sorry he hadn't been able to protect her like he should've. Sorry he'd allowed his father's legacy to fuck with his head. Sorry that he'd wasted twelve long years pretending he'd done the right thing by leaving her. But this wasn't the time for all that. This was the time to celebrate their win. To celebrate themselves.

He suddenly felt everything that'd happened between them smash into his senses. Not only over the past week, but right back to the beginning, when he'd seen Julie on her horse the very first day. The lust, the passion, the connection had been there from day one, and it was still there, even if the intermediate years had been filled with betrayal and rejection. He realized now that his struggles to come to terms with who he was and what he really felt about having a rapist as a father had less to do with his relationship with Julie than with his own dumb, immature, and self-centered need to avenge his shitty life. One thing was for sure, he was going to keep his promise to her this time, as long as that's what she wanted.

"Aren't I allowed to stare at the woman I love?" he asked teasingly.

Her eyes sprang open.

"What?" he asked at the obvious confusion on her face.

"I thought perhaps I dreamed that bit last night…when you said you loved me."

"No, we were both very much awake." He lifted a finger and stroked it down the side of her face. Tufts of caramel hair stood up at all angles, but he liked the disheveled look on her. Today, her eyes were the pastel, watercolor blue he loved so much, but they flashed with something brighter as she studied him. "And I meant what I said," he added, hoping like hell she wasn't suddenly going to renege on her declaration of love.

She snuggled closer into his bare chest, all soft and sleepy. "So did I." She lifted her chin so she could look him in the eye. "The whole of last night seems a little surreal right now, a bit disjointed, as if it happened to someone else."

He nodded in commiseration. Victims of violent crimes often reported feeling numb or disconnected from the crime. It was a mixture of shock, and the brain going into denial.

"But one thing remains crystal clear in my memory," she said, not breaking her stare. "The intensity of my feelings for you at that moment. It was like I'd been hiding behind a wall made from my own stubbornness, and when you uttered those words I've been waiting so long to hear, I could finally feel all the emotions clearly again." She bit her bottom lip. "I know that sounds a little silly, but…"

He lay a finger against her lips. "Not silly at all." He replaced his finger with his mouth, kissing her tenderly, careful of her cracked and split lips. His own lips were chapped and dry from their ordeal yesterday, but Julie didn't seem to mind, she even slipped her hand behind his neck and pulled him in for a deeper, more needy kiss. His cock was hard in a second. She was so perfect and desirable.

Nash had found her a spare pair of track pants when they'd got to the police station, so she wasn't walking around bare-assed all night. And when they'd arrived home, she'd slipped into a pair of sleep shorts, but left his shirt on, saying it made her feel safe. He had to admit that his shirt looked pretty damn hot on her right now, molding to her contours like it never did on him. Before he could stop them, his fingers were undoing the top button, feeling the brush of her velvety skin as he did so. She closed her eyes at his touch and gave a low moan of appreciation. His cock throbbed at the thought of her. The second and third buttons were undone before he finally came to his senses.

"We shouldn't do this," he said, pulling the edges of the shirt back together, and hiding the curves of her sweet body.

"Why the hell not?" she asked, skewering him with her indigo gaze.

"I don't want to hurt you." Her poor body was still battered and bruised, her feet swathed in yards of white bandages.

"I trust you," she said, and the simple words speared into

his heart. His hand slipped beneath the fabric and cupped her breast, possessive and needy. *Oh, so good.* He reminded himself to be gentle. His mouth found her neck, felt the pulse flutter beneath his lips as she tipped her head back to allow him better access. She pressed her body against his, urging him on. As slowly as the blood pounding through his veins allowed, he undid the rest of the buttons on the shirt, until it fell open to reveal Julie's flat stomach and lush breasts.

"Beautiful," he breathed. Quickly, he removed his boxers, never letting his gaze stray from her spectacular body.

"Not bad yourself," Julie rasped, her greedy hands flowing down his shoulders, over his pecs, finding each indent of his abs as they trailed downward. All he wanted was to be inside her.

Oh, shit. Reality dawned, dragging him out of his passion-fueled haze. "I don't have a condom," he said ruefully.

"I'm sure we can be careful, get creative," she answered with a purr.

"You're not worried about getting pregnant?" He levered up on his elbows to stare down at her. This was a change for the books.

"Don't get me wrong, I'm not aiming to get pregnant today," she replied. "But the thought no longer scares me as much as it used to."

Hm, interesting. It seemed that quite a few boundaries had been broken down last night.

He slipped his hand lower, down the front of her sleep shorts, caressed between her legs, loving how she gasped at his touch and her hips shifted toward him. As gently as he could, he slid her shorts off and rolled her over. Ignoring the pain in his knee, he hovered above her, staring down into her blue, blue eyes.

"Don't keep me waiting forever, Mr. Bodyguard," she said, lifting her hips to meet his and grinding herself against his erection.

With a groan, he let go of his last shred of self-control and plunged inside her. The feeling was even sweeter than it'd been the other night. This was next level, and he felt he might not last too long. She moved with him, nipping at his neck and his ear, then bringing his head down so she could kiss him, deep and big.

Their rhythm quickened, and she gave a low-pitched moan in the back of her throat. Oh. God. He was going to come. She was so sweet. So hot. So trusting. She was driving him to heights he'd never experienced with any other woman. Except her.

Her climax shook them both as she called out his name and her muscles clenched around him. He only just managed to withdraw in time, and they lay panting and spent on the bed, sheets swirled around their ankles.

Gently levering her to the side, he pulled her into his embrace, cradling her cheek on his bicep, his chin resting on the top of his head, as their breathing slowly calmed, and they lay in the afterglow.

He didn't want to get up, never wanted to leave this bed. If only they could stay cocooned in Julie's room for the rest of eternity. But that wasn't going to happen. He had a job to get back to in the city, commitments. Jake already had another client lined up for him, the job starting in the next few days, as soon as his knee healed. Could they juggle a relationship where he was in the city, and she was on the station, after only just finding each other again?

A long-distance relationship wasn't the answer, and they both knew it.

One thing was for sure. He was never going to just walk away from Julie Bradshaw again. It'd taken him twelve years to discover the meaning of true love, he wasn't about to give it up now.

But what was he going to do? How were they going to solve this dilemma? There was still so much he needed to sort out, including exactly what a relationship with Julie entailed.

CHAPTER TWENTY-FOUR

Julie fidgeted from one foot to the other and pulled her Akubra down over her eyes to block out the sun. It was bloody hot out here. Why the hell Steve was making her stand out next to the landing pad in this heat was beyond her. He might be ecstatic that their new helicopter and pilot were arriving—it'd been his dream for years now to have their very own chopper—but she really wasn't that impressed. Agreed, it'd be nice not to have to rely on the charter company as much and to be able to come and go with ease whenever they wanted. But Steve had told her this chopper was going to be primarily used for muster and other errands on the station. It was only a little two-seater Robinson R22, so most of their guests would still be ferried in from Cairns using the charter company. Steve had plans for a bigger helicopter too, but that was later down the track; there was no way Daniella was going to cough up the money for *two* choppers at the moment.

At least her feet had healed well. For about a week after her escape through the scrub, she could barely walk, and standing for half an hour like this would've been out of the question. But like the doctor had promised, her feet had healed, as had the multitude of other small injuries she'd endured. The physical part of her had been cured, but her mental state remained a little wobbly. It was still hard to reconcile the fact that she'd nearly died at the hands of her stalker. Images of Chase during her abduction came back to haunt her when she'd least expect it. The cruel twist of his mouth as he leaned over her while she was paralyzed might suddenly play over and over in her mind even as she sat down to eat dinner with her family. And she often woke drenched in sweat, panting and out of breath as she replayed her run down the creek bed while bullets whizzed over her head. Skylar had been a great help to Julie in those moments. Because she'd also suffered trauma at the hands of her kidnapper, she understood what Julie was going through, and it helped to have someone else to talk to. Skylar assured her the flashbacks and nightmares would fade with time, and Julie took comfort from that.

Skylar had also helped her talk through her confusing feelings of guilt over Maya's death. A search had uncovered her body in a shallow grave on the outskirts of Chase's campsite. With Chase dead, they'd never know the truth behind Maya's murder, but Nash guessed that she'd probably balked at going along with Chase's senseless plans any longer. Julie knew it was absurd to feel self-reproach over Maya's terrible demise, but nonetheless, she still wondered if there was some way she could've helped the gullible, young woman. She'd obviously been charmed by Chase, persuaded to help him in his sick endeavors, by feeding him confidential information from patient files. Love made you do crazy things, Julie knew that. But when Maya finally came to her senses and refused to go along with her husband, she'd paid the ultimate price.

Chase may well have conned Maya into leaking the details about women who attended family planning clinics for abortions, and then perhaps married her when she started to become suspicious of his motives. But it wasn't the first time Chase had been married. The police had discovered he'd been married before, and when they interviewed the ex-wife, it turned out she'd left him when she became pregnant, scared of his growing dark side—but not understanding the full extent of his perversion—so she'd got out while she could. Chase found out later that she'd aborted the pregnancy, not wanting to have any connection with him, and he'd erupted into an uncontrollable rage, beating her nearly senseless. The ex-wife had left town the next day, moving to Geelong to get away from him. It seemed Chase had transferred his rage onto other women who resembled his wife, who'd also had terminations, as a sick way to get revenge on his wife.

Julie shook her head, still hardly able to believe there were people in this world capable of such revolting and twisted atrocities.

Nash had conceded they might never know all the details of Chase's stalking, now he was dead. They still hadn't figured out how Chase found her at Stormcloud, even after going through all his paperwork and his computer the police had seized from his apartment. One small detail that'd been bugging Julie had been cleared up, however. After questioning everyone who worked or was associated with the lodge, Nash had finally tracked the leaking of Julie's phone number down to one of the contract cleaners who came out from town to help clean on most days. Maria had admitted that she'd been cleaning Chase and Maya's cabin, and Chase had stayed in the cabin as she refreshed the towels and scrubbed the bathroom, hovering around and asking her questions. Out of the blue, he'd said he had a complaint he wanted to make, and he needed to talk to Julie directly, as he'd met her a few times and knew she'd handle his grievance fairly. He said he didn't want to take his complaint to Daniella, as it was a delicate matter. The unsuspecting cleaner hadn't thought twice about giving Chase Julie's cell phone number. It seemed reasonable to her that Chase would prefer to talk to Julie, as Daniella could be a little...fierce, at times. Julie had smiled at that and had then gone and personally assured Maria that she wouldn't be losing her job. Chase was a manipulative, evil man, and it wasn't the other woman's fault she'd fallen for his ploy.

Skylar gave a loud sigh from her spot beside Julie, and then pointedly looked at her watch. Skylar was perpetually itching to get back to her kitchen, there was always something that needed tending. At least if Julie had to endure this, everyone else was being forced to witness the new chopper, as well. All the staff, and even some of the more interested guests, were down here. Alek, Bindi, and Sasha crowded behind her and Skylar, talking quietly amongst themselves. Dale and Wazza leaned nonchalantly in the shade by the big river gum down near the edge of the billabong, well away from the flat landing pad that was baking in the sun. Maybe she should go and join them; they had the right idea.

She was about to walk in their direction, when Steve said, "Here it comes." Barely able to contain his excitement, he was almost hopping from one foot to the other, like a kid in a candy store. A low buzzing sound reached Julie's ears, and she tipped her head back to scan the sky in the direction her father was pointing.

A white dot appeared on the horizon, flying high above the escarpment. It got quickly closer, morphing into the dragonfly shape of a small aircraft. Once it landed, she'd be able to get back to finishing putting in the order for next week's groceries for Skylar.

As she waited, her mind drifted to Aaron, as it always did these days. She was planning on flying down to Brisbane in a week or so to see him. Although, she hadn't mentioned the idea to him yet. She was so desperate to see him. They'd talked on the phone every single day of the six weeks since he'd returned to work. And he'd spent one gloriously short weekend with her at the lodge three weeks ago, before duty called him back to Brisbane. But… It wasn't enough. They both knew it.

Julie put her hand on her hat as the helicopter dropped toward them, averting her face as it descended, and the rotor kicked up dust and debris.

Steve hardly waited for the pilot to cut the engine, before he jogged onto the landing pad, ducking low to avoid the spinning blades. The door opened and Steve reached in to shake the pilot's hand.

"Great, can we go now?" Julie asked. Surely that was enough of a ceremony? She'd watched the damn thing land, and admired the new shiny, white fuselage. There wasn't much more to it. She turned to leave.

"Wait one minute longer," Daniella said, stepping in front of Julie. What now? Daniella took her by the shoulders and slowly spun her around to face the chopper. It was Skylar's gasp that made Julie look up as the pilot stepped out of the helicopter.

The figure dashed beneath the spinning blades and then stood to his full height beside her father. Those broad shoulder and big biceps, encased in a tight black T. One blue eye, one brown, regarded her with a hint of an apprehensive twinkle.

"Aaron?" The word left her lips more out of shock than any true comprehension. "What are you…?"

"Hi, Jules." Aaron beamed, the grin splitting his face from ear to ear, as if he could no longer contain his glee at the secret he'd been keeping. "It was your dad's idea to keep it a surprise," he added, as he registered the total confusion on her face. But Julie couldn't look at her father, she only had eyes for the man standing before her. The smile slowly faded from Aaron's face when she remained mute, unable to speak.

Vaguely, Julie registered Skylar's cry of delight from somewhere behind her, and Dale's whoop of glee from his spot by the tree.

It slowly dawned on her that Aaron had mentioned he had a helicopter pilot license, and he loved to fly in his spare time.

"Is this…?" Her gaze flicked to the gleaming new chopper on the pad. "Are you…?"

"Yes." Aaron came up and took her by the shoulders, so he could look directly into her face. "I'm the new Stormcloud chopper pilot. But only if you want me to be."

It took a second for his words to make sense. "You're not a bodyguard anymore?"

"Nope, I'm no longer a protection agent," he said with a wry twist to his mouth.

"You're going to work for Steve? For us?" Her mind was struggling to compute what was happening. Aaron was here? She hadn't seen him for weeks; hadn't expected to see him for another week and now he was here, invading her senses, bringing her body alive.

"Yes, as long as that's okay with you?"

"Oh, my God, you're here," she said as the truth finally sank in. She leapt into his arms, wrapping her legs around his waist and her arms around his neck, hugging him tight. "You're here," she said again, as the thunderbolt of shock finally morphed into joy. "I missed you." She gave him her best, biggest grin. To hell with it. She didn't care that her whole family was watching, she kissed him on the mouth, funneling all her rapture and passion into that kiss.

"I missed you, too," he said, when she eventually let his mouth go.

Everyone started clapping and Julie unhitched her legs

from around Aaron's waist and let her feet drop to the ground with an embarrassed smile.

"All right, all of you back to work, the fun's over now," Daniella clapped her hands, and everyone began to wend their way back toward the lodge. Dale and Wazza called out a welcome to Aaron as they meandered past, and Skylar swung by and gave him a quick peck on the cheek, before she turned and practically jogged up the slope.

Steve and Daniella were the last to leave, and her father thumped Aaron on the back. "Welcome to the team. Come and talk to me when you're finished here. I'll be up in the stables."

Julie grabbed her dad in a compulsive hug. "I'm not sure I agree with your methods, but thank you for making this happen," she whispered into his ear. "You're the best." She lifted her gaze and included her stepmother in her tribute, mouthing the words, *thank you*. Daniella waved away her gratitude, but the corners of her mouth lifted in a secret smile and Julie knew she was delighted that Aaron was here, too.

"I just want you to be happy, Julie. And I think he makes you happy," Steve said softly. "But if he ever makes you unhappy, you just let me know." Then he lifted his head and said loudly enough for everyone else to hear, "This was also a business decision. By all accounts, Aaron's a pretty good pilot." Steve released Julie and put his hat back on. "But he's still got a lot to learn before he's any good at bush mustering."

"Oh, I know that, sir," Aaron replied. "Toby's working over at Comalga Station for the next few months, and he's agreed to take me up with him, help me learn the ropes."

"That'll be a good start." Steve nodded his agreement, then in a surprising show of affection, took Daniella's hand as they headed up the hill toward the lodge, leaving her and Aaron alone beside the helicopter.

Julie moved into the circle of Aaron's arms, lifting her head to look up at him. "It's a dangerous job," she said, once her dad was out of earshot. "I saw on the ABC rural farm news the other day, that up to ten pilots die each year in crashes." That was a sobering thought, but when she'd watched the program, it hadn't occurred to her that those statistics might affect her directly one day. "They said it takes years of practice to become proficient." Not that she was trying to talk him out of it. More that she was trying to get her head around the whole concept of having a boyfriend who flew choppers for a living.

"Around fifteen-hundred hours of flying time, or so I've been told," Aaron said with a smirk, and she lowered her eyebrows in a worried frown. "Don't worry, I'll take it easy," he qualified. "Your dad realizes my limitations. Probably more than I do," he added quietly, which didn't help to ease her anxiety. "I've got nearly a whole year to improve my flying skills before next muster season starts," he told her. "Like I said to Steve, I'll go and train with some other top-notch pilots as well. They're still mustering in the Northern Territory and over in Western Australia. Toby said he'd help hook me up with some of his mates over there. It might mean I'm gone for a few weeks at a time, though."

"It sounds like you've got it all figured out." And he probably did. One thing she'd learned about Aaron while he'd been her bodyguard was that even though he took risks in his job, they were well mitigated to keep the danger as low as possible. He was always well-prepared, organized, and had a plan for everything. Well, almost everything. Except when she'd been kidnapped by a crazy stalker, then all protocol and rule books had gone out the window.

She tugged him toward the shade of the river gum Dale and Wazza had been standing under earlier. She could hardly believe he was real, that it was actually his muscular arm she had a grip on. Without waiting for him to come to a complete halt, she once again launched herself into his arms. He turned and backed up against the large tree trunk, sliding down the rough surface until his butt hit the ground so that she now straddled him as they sat in the dirt. She tugged her hat off her head and placed it on the ground. This time there was no crowd of people to witness the way she eagerly sought out his mouth, claiming his lips as her own. Oh, the sweetness of him, the scent of him, the feel of his strong body beneath her. They kissed like two teenagers, crazy for each other, as if they might devour each other whole, and she felt the time and the distance that had separated them over the past weeks begin to melt away. As if he'd never even left. As if he was never again going to leave. A growing pulse beat between her legs as her body readjusted to his, remembering his touch, wanting it more and more. She wanted him in her bed, needed to get him inside as quickly as possible. To cement this new relationship...or whatever it was. Their kiss slowed, becoming tender and poignant, until she finally drew back.

"Wow," she said. "Just, wow. I'm almost speechless."

"I guess it is a bit of a shock," he admitted, raising that scarred eyebrow in a cheeky hook.

"Yes, but a good one. I still can't quite believe it. I'm not sure of all the ramifications of you being here, though..."

Aaron's face suddenly turned serious. "You still haven't said if you're happy with all this. I knew I should've asked you first." His eyes took on a worried edge. "I shouldn't have let Steve and Dale talk me into it. This was a bad decision. I'm so sorry." Aaron scrubbed a hand across his brow, which was knotted in a worried frown. The scar bisected his eyebrow quivered as he stared down at her. It seemed like he was suddenly trying to talk himself out of his decision.

She sobered as well. "Yes, you should've asked me first. I mean, what if I don't want you here? What if I had other plans, and you've gone and ruined them?" It was a huge thing he'd done. A big move. She probably should be a little put out that he hadn't at least asked her what she wanted; that he'd taken her love for granted. She pouted and stared up at him.

* * *

Aaron stared into Julie's face, silently kicking himself that he hadn't asked this question first. Because if Julie didn't want him here...the thought was too much to bear. Steve had talked him into keeping his new job a secret from Julie; he thought it'd be a lovely surprise when Aaron arrived with the new helicopter. And in truth, the job offer from Steve and his unexpected acceptance had happened very quickly. It was less than a week ago that Aaron had made possibly the biggest choice of his life, to quit this job with Shield Solutions, uproot his whole life and move to far North Queensland. Jake hadn't been happy, but he also said he understood. From the very first time Aaron spoke about Julie to him over the phone, Jake had an inkling he might lose one of his best agents.

But Aaron knew now, he should've included Julie, allowed her a vote. Because this future entailed them both. He suddenly felt foolish and guilty for making such a rash decision without her, and he opened his mouth to say so, when she started laughing so hard, she nearly fell off his lap.

"The look on your face," she crowed. "I really had you going, didn't I?"

"What?"

"I'm kidding," she giggled. "I'm just messing with you. Of course, I'm happy you're here. I'm ecstatic." Her eyes sparkled with barely restrained humor.

"Shit, Jules, don't do that to me." He sucked in a deep breath.

"I'm sorry." She fixed him with a brilliant, blue-eyed grin, full of cheeky merriment and absolute love, so that his heart nearly exploded.

Fuck. He'd missed that smile. For twelve long years, he'd missed that smile. Now, it was his whole reason for being, all he wanted was to make her happy. Because if she was happy, he was happy. He found her lips, delving his tongue into her mouth, and she responded, tore the rest of the air from his lungs as her mouth consumed his. Hands roaming over her back, he clasped her hips as her core rocked against his cock, which strained for release from his jeans. She closed her eyes and moaned low in her throat, getting lost in their kiss. He was here to stay, forever. His muscles tightened at the idea of being able to touch Julie, hold her, whenever he wanted to. Actually, he wanted to drag her off to bed this very instant. But that thought brought up another minor problem that should perhaps be sorted out. He drew away until the back of his head hit the scratchy bark of the river gum. Slowly, she opened her eyes, wondering why he'd stopped.

"You know that means I'll be living on the station?" he said.

"Well, duh."

"And you're okay with that?" He needed to have her say it; needed to have this all out in the open, so they didn't start this fledgling relationship on the wrong foot. Steve had offered him a room in the staff quarters, for the short term, until they figured out how this was going to work, which Aaron had been grateful for.

"Yes. I am." She nodded slowly in agreement, as if finally catching the sincerity of his questions. "I'm more than happy for you to move in with me, but... What do you want to do?"

"I think that's a good start, but it might become a little suffocating, after a while. Don't you agree?" While Aaron knew he'd get along with Steve and the rest of Julie's family, they couldn't live in the lodge for the rest of their lives. They needed their own space and time to figure things out between them.

She wrinkled her cute little nose and nodded. "Yes. But what's your alternative?"

"Long term, I'd love for us to buy a property of our own together." He hoped he wasn't being too presumptuous, but when she flashed her teeth in a happy smile, he knew she wanted the same thing. The dream he'd had when he'd first met her had never truly died, it'd been blanketed with all his fears and self-loathing for a time, that's all. "But while we work toward that, we could rent a house in town together." He'd sorted through lots of different options in his head over the past week. None of them were perfect, but they could compromise, for a start.

"We could," she agreed. "But it's not ideal. The forty-five-minute commute each day would be a pain, especially if we've got an early start. There might be an alternative." She fixed him with her watercolor gaze, but bit her bottom lip as if suddenly unsure. "Nash bought a property down the road, about halfway between Dimbulah and here. He and Skylar live in the main house, but there are lots of other old buildings scattered around the property. Skylar mentioned to me the other day that there's an old barn that needs a lot of work, but it could be converted to a sort of one bedroom studio. It's secluded, around five hundred meters from the main house, hidden by a row of old pine trees the previous owner planted long ago."

"Sounds like you've been thinking about this, too," he said, tilting his head on one side.

"Maybe a little," she agreed with a cheeky flick of her caramel fringe. "So, what do you think? We'd pay Nash rent, of course. And it'd take a few months to get the place habitable, so we couldn't move in straight away."

"I think that might work." Aaron ran a hand up the nape of her neck, eliciting a shiver of delight. His fingers tangled in a fine necklace, and he stopped to tug it out from beneath the collar of her shirt. He stared at the small, diamond charm, his heartbeat erratic. "You kept it all this time?" he whispered as he rubbed the jewel between his fingertips.

"Of course, I did," she replied, her lips curving in a sensuous half-smile. "There were quite a few times it ended up in the garbage. But I always retrieved it, because I couldn't bring myself to get rid of the last thing that reminded me of you."

This was one more proof that Julie meant what she'd said, that she'd never really stopped loving him. "Thank you," he said, releasing the necklace and claiming her mouth once more. When he finally came up for air, his bulging erection reminded him of what he really wanted to do; get Julie to bed. And his mind went back to their living arrangements. "A couple of months is a long time, though. I'm not sure I can wait that long to have you all to myself; to move in with you."

"Really?" she asked, sitting back, her mouth screwed into a knot of concern. "Because I'm still finding this all a little hard to get my head around. I know we love each other, that part isn't in question," she added hurriedly. "But we're both a little...fucked up, to put it nicely." She smiled to lessen the sting of her words. "Can we really make this work?"

He studied her for uncounted seconds as a bird high up in the river gum warbled its midday song. He took her face in his hands. "I was scared before. Scared you might think I was a monster. Scared I might pass my terrible childhood on to my kids; that I'd be a terrible partner and a terrible father. But I'm not afraid of that side of myself anymore. And now I see you're stronger than I ever gave you credit for. I'm prepared to take the risk, if you are." He moved his hands down to her shoulders, suddenly tense as he watched different emotions cross her face.

"Love is complicated, but it's all about being vulnerable, and taking risks," she said at last. "I already told you that I'm no longer afraid of having kids, anymore. Not tomorrow, mind you." She held up a hand in a stopping motion. "But one day, definitely. And the whole reason I can even entertain that idea now, is because I'm with you."

Julie had told him that she'd started online appointments with someone—a professional in the field who helped women who'd lost a baby either through abortion or miscarriage—dealing with the shame and guilt she'd suffered after her termination. Aaron was so proud of her. During their long phone calls while he was in Brisbane, they'd talked over some of their many problems and flaws. Julie had finally revealed that a part of her not wanting to have children stemmed from her fear that her baby might suffer from the same disease which had caused her to abort her first pregnancy. But after talking to the counsellor, she found out the risk of having a second baby with Trisomy 18 was less than one percent. And she was at no greater risk than any other new mother of having something else wrong with her baby. Julie admitted that it'd probably take a lot more positive reinforcement before she was ready to try for a baby, but she was on the path to feeling one day happy to have a family of her own.

They'd both come such a long way. Maybe, in a twisted sort of way, the twelve years they'd spent apart had been necessary; had helped them grow and mature, so they were now capable of handling these strong emotions, and personal traumas which were sometimes terrifying. So they truly understood what it meant to love unconditionally.

"I would be honored to have a family with you, Ms Bradshaw," he said, deadly serious now. "We would make some beautiful babies together."

"Yes, we would." That mischievous smile was back, the

one that'd been burned into his soul, the one he missed so much when she wasn't around. The one where Julie was about to erupt with a funny joke, possibly at his expense. Or she might break into a spontaneous dance or do a magic trick. But he loved that positive, sunny, carefree side of her.

"By the way." He stilled for a second, catching her gaze and holding it. "I haven't forgotten that you never told me your nickname. You know, the one Dale used to call you when you were little."

Julie squealed in delight, then pouted suggestively at him. "I shall never tell," she declared. "My lips are sealed."

"Well, I have many ways of unsealing those lips, and I mean to try them all. I have all the time in the world to learn your secrets now." He ran his hands down her back and cupped her luscious ass in his palms, pulling her even closer. "I am inevitable," he said, wondering if she'd grasp this latest Avengers quote.

"Do your best, Thanos, but I am stronger than you know," she laughed, throwing her arms around his neck and holding him tight, giggling into his ear.

She was strong, and clever and sassy and stunning. They had a shared past, and now they'd have a shared future, as well. He couldn't wait to start their life together.

Want to know more about Stormcloud Station?
Get your FREE and EXCLUSIVE Prequel Novella
MISTY SKIES
Read Steve and Daniella's story.

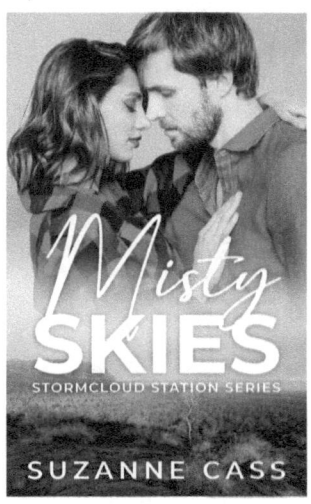

GO TO THIS LINK FOR YOUR FREE BOOK
https://dl.bookfunnel.com/xyuua14lyp

Stay in touch via my website
www.suzannecass.com

Facebook: www.facebook.com/suzannecassauthor/
Instagram: www.instagram.com/suzanne.cass/
Pintrest: www.pinterest.com.au/suzanne_cass/

If you liked Crystal Skies, you'll love;

Clear Skies

Fate and flooding rains brought them together. Secrets may tear them apart.

Starlit Skies

They're polar opposites, with only one thing in common… they survived the helicopter crash…but that's just the beginning.

Dawn Skies

When you love someone…you'll do anything to protect them.

Island Redemption
Glass Clouds
Chasing Bullets

Love in the Mountains Novella Series
Small Town Short Romance
Novellas can be read as stand-alone
Rain on a Tin Roof
Lost and Found
Rescue his Heart

Please Leave a Review

The greatest gift you could ever give an author is to leave a review. You will be helping other people to discover this book and making a difference to me as an Independently Published Author. If you liked this book and want other people to read it to, please leave a review.

About the Author

Suzanne Cass is an Australian author who writes rural romance and romantic suspense abounding with passion and danger.

Her debut novel, Island Redemption, won the Romance Writers of Australia Emerald Award in 2016. Suzanne was also a finalist in the 2019 Romance Writers of Australia RUBY award.

She had always had a fascination with the tough resilience of people who live in our amazing red-dirt outback country. When not writing about the characters that inhabit her head, Suzanne can be found roaming the Perth beaches with her border collie, or encouraging from the sidelines as her two sons play sport.

Stay in touch via my website
www.suzannecass.com

Acknowledgements

Crystal Skies is the third book in the Stormcloud Station Series, which is a spin-off from the Stargazer Ranch Series set in Montana USA. On the surface, this book is a rural romance at heart, with a whole lot of suspense thrown in to keep you on your toes. But I like to dive deep into my characters flaws and ambitions. One of the key themes this book tackles is the gritty, contentious topic of abortion and Julie has to struggle against her own guilt and prejudice to finally come to some sort of peace within herself. But she couldn't have done it without Aaron's steadfast support. Their story toward finding true love was a rocky road, full of second chances and self-doubt, but when two soulmates are meant to be together, their HEA is a foregone conclusion.

To my beta readers and my ARC team, who are essential to an Indie Author like me, I'm sending you all big (virtual) hugs across the globe. Big thanks to my editor, Tanya Saari for putting up with my total inability to learn where the comma's go. COVID 19 is still affecting us, even now, but isn't it great that all of these people can live scattered all over the world, but still belong to one big family, with one steadfast goal; producing and reading the next great book, connected through the internet and integral to each other's lives.

Gary needs a special mention, as do my two beautiful sons, who are now gorgeous young men. They continue to humor me when I lock myself away in my office for hours, days and weeks on end, when a deadline is looming. I'm also indebted to all the readers who have bought and enjoyed my books and who send me emails to let me know how much you enjoy them. Writing for you is what keeps my bum in the seat, wrangling my characters and the amazing Aussie outback setting into a story you will love. Thank you. Thank you. Thank you.